In the
room, Jess Brannigan held life and death in his hands...

The jurors were now seated. Carly studied the group again, blinking when her gaze collided with the dark eyes of the man on the aisle seat. She was still as she absorbed his harsh, unsmiling look. A little shiver darted down her spine. His hair was thick and as black as coal. High prominent cheekbones gave his face a raw, totally masculine look that would never be called handsome, but it was certainly arresting. Carly frowned as she studied the severe planes and angles, the full lower curve of his mouth, the chiseled symmetry of his chin.

Something about him seemed almost familiar...

MEN at WORK

1. HOODWINKED—
Diana Palmer
2. MACKENZIE'S LADY—
Dallas Schulze
3. AN IRRITATING MAN—
Lass Small
4. WINDSTORM—
Connie Bennett
5. HEAVEN SHARED—
Cathy Gillen Thacker
6. CONFIDENTIALLY YOURS—
Helen R. Myers
7. BODY AND SOUL—
Janice Kaiser
8. DESTINATIONS SOUTH—
Elizabeth Bevarly
9. DEFYING GRAVITY—
Rachel Lee
10. UNDERCOVER—
Jasmine Cresswell
11. GLASS HOUSES—
Anne Stuart
12. NIGHT OF THE HUNTER—
Jennifer Greene
13. A REBEL AT HEART—
Gina Wilkins
14. MISS LIZ'S PASSION—
Sherryl Woods
15. MAGIC AND MOONBEAMS—
Margot Dalton
16. HANDSOME DEVIL—
Joan Hohl
17. ANGEL VS. MACLEAN—
Cait London
18. HEALING SYMPATHY—
Gina Wilkins
19. SOUND OF SUMMER—
Annette Broadrick
20. THE FOREVER ROSE—
Curtiss Ann Matlock
21. KNIGHT SPARKS—
Mary Lynn Baxter
22. FIT TO BE TIED—
Joan Johnston
23. A SEASON FOR BUTTERFLIES—
Laurie Paige
24. CAPTIVE OF FATE—
Lindsay McKenna
25. UNDER THE COVERS—
Roseanne Williams
26. STARK LIGHTNING—
Elaine Barbieri
27. THE PRINCE & THE SHOWGIRL—
JoAnn Ross
28. MORE THAN FRIENDS—
Susan Mallery
29. WE GIVE THANKS—
Linda Randall Wisdom
30. COULD IT BE MAGIC—
Gina Wilkins
31. EXPIRATION DATE—
Aimée Thurlo
32. IT'S ONLY TEMPORARY—
Cathy Gillen Thacker
33. A CLASSIC ENCOUNTER—
Emilie Richards
34. THE MIGHTY QUINN—
Candace Schuler
35. SILVER NOOSE—
Patricia Gardner Evans
36. THE MIRACLE—
Muriel Jensen
37. A FRAGILE BEAUTY—
Lucy Gordon
38. FEAR FAMILIAR—
Caroline Burnes
39. SOMETHING WORTH KEEPING—
Kathleen Eagle
40. DILLON AFTER DARK—
Leandra Logan
41. THE HEART CLUB—
Margaret St. George
42. ONLY IN THE MOONLIGHT—
Vicki Lewis Thompson
43. TO DIE FOR—
M.J. Rodgers
44. THE COWBOY'S MISTRESS—
Cathy Gillen Thacker
45. ALL MY TOMORROWS—
Karen Young
46. PLAYING FOR TIME—
Barbara Bretton
47. THE PERFECT MATCH—
Ginna Gray
48. HOTSHOT—
Kathleen Korbel
49. VALENTINE'S KNIGHT—
Renee Roszel
50. STORMWALKER—
Bronwyn Williams

—MILLIONAIRE'S CLUB
—BOARDROOM BOYS
—MAGNIFICENT MEN
—TALL, DARK & SMART
—DOCTOR, DOCTOR
—MEN OF THE WEST
—MEN OF STEEL
—MEN IN UNIFORM

MEN at WORK

KAREN YOUNG

ALL MY TOMORROWS

Harlequin Books

TORONTO • NEW YORK • LONDON
AMSTERDAM • PARIS • SYDNEY • HAMBURG
STOCKHOLM • ATHENS • TOKYO • MILAN
MADRID • WARSAW • BUDAPEST • AUCKLAND

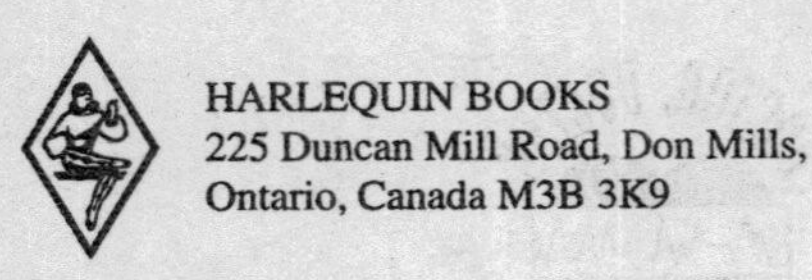
HARLEQUIN BOOKS
225 Duncan Mill Road, Don Mills,
Ontario, Canada M3B 3K9

ISBN 0-373-81057-1

ALL MY TOMORROWS

This edition published by arrangement with Harlequin Books S.A.

Printed in U.S.A.

Dear Reader,

Several years ago I actually served on a grand jury in Louisiana when I lived in New Orleans. Every Friday for eight months, twelve of us sat and weighed evidence against people accused of the most serious crimes. It was an interesting, enlightening and sobering experience. And I'm so grateful for having been given a chance to participate in America's justice system.

While the part of me who was a citizen listened to and weighed evidence, the writer in me was enthralled by what I heard and witnessed in the people who came before us. Many were children—abused and neglected young victims. I came away after that experience with material for several books. *All My Tomorrows* was the first.

I hope something in this story touches your heart. My own heart took a beating in that jury room, and I will never forget it.

All the best,

Karen Young

CHAPTER ONE

CARLY SULLIVAN STEPPED into her office and closed the door gently. *Just in time,* she decided, meeting the direct gaze of the tall youth, who was obviously on the point of walking out. She studied him discreetly. He was reed slim, but his shoulders, which were surprisingly broad, and his lean hips and long legs seemed to indicate that one day he would be a man to contend with. Mike Brannigan didn't look at all like the rest of the students at Padgett School. That had been Carly's thought the first time she'd seen him and now, six weeks later, her opinion was unchanged. It was going to take more than outfitting him in the standard white shirt and khaki chinos before Mike Brannigan would blend in.

His thick coal-black hair was too long, according to Padgett standards. He did sport a dark tan, which almost all the students did, thanks to the fierce New Orleans sun, but still Mike looked different from the vast majority of students she counseled. How in the world had his parents ever thought he'd fit in at an exclusive institution like Padgett? Carly found herself wondering suddenly. It was like sending a young savage to Sunday school. His dark flashing eyes and his wiry toughness made him look wild, untamed.

She lifted her tawny brows in a friendly salute. "Hello, Mike, have a seat." Waving a hand at a chair, she made her way around her desk, tossing her handbag onto the credenza as she passed it before unloading the stack of files she'd taken home the night before.

When she looked back at him, she discovered he was still standing, looking ahead impassively. He would stand as long as she did, Carly suspected, so she sank into her chair. After a second's hesitation, Mike did, too, easing down, only the tense set of his shoulders betraying any emotion. He was having a tough time. *Perfectly understandable,* Carly said to herself, opening his file. A private school in New Orleans had very little in common with his former high school in San Diego. With swift perception, she sensed that Mike wasn't going to be easy to help.

She met his look with a half smile, thinking how lucky she'd be to zero in on what was troubling the boy in the limited time she had. Although his records indicated that he was exceptionally gifted, it appeared he had never performed even close to his potential. Of course, he was still adjusting to New Orleans and a major move. That in itself could explain his apathy, but intuitively Carly knew there was more. He'd also had a bout with appendicitis that had ended in surgery. When had that occurred? She glanced at his file. Five weeks ago, just after he'd enrolled. Today he appeared strong and healthy. A sixteen-year-old recovered from an appendectomy with astonishing speed. She didn't think that was the answer.

"So, how do you like living in New Orleans after San Diego, Michael?"

"It's okay."

"People always say the humidity's the worst thing."

"Yeah, it's pretty hot."

Maybe he hadn't made any friends, Carly mused. Isolation and loneliness could imprison an adolescent more effectively than iron bars. She tapped the folder on her desk. "I see you live on Prytania. We have another student who lives in that neighborhood—Penny Lasseigne. Do you know Penny?''

''Not really.''

''But you've seen her around?''

''I guess.''

Great. It was going to be like pulling teeth. ''She's very friendly,'' Carly said, undaunted. ''I'll introduce you. After all, you're practically neighbors.''

''Practically.''

Carly didn't miss the hint of sarcasm. But at least it was emotion of some kind. ''By the way, Mike, there were no complications after your appendectomy, were there?''

''No, everything's fine.'' For the first time, his dark gaze shifted.

''Was that your first experience with surgery?''

''Yeah.''

''Pretty scary, hmm?''

''I did okay.''

She tapped the folder again and clicked her tongue. ''Of course. What's the matter with me? I forgot. You probably know more about hospitals than I do. Your father's a physician.''

Carly glanced up into eyes that were suddenly hard. She opened her mouth to say something, but his expression turned so forbidding that she thought better of it. Maybe his illness had been more serious than she'd realized. The Lord knew, sixteen-year-old males had more than their share of macho pride. Some kids simply wouldn't relax and be open, and unless she had read him wrongly, this boy was one of them. She cleared her throat briskly.

''Michael, I set up this meeting so that we could talk about your grades. I realize you've only been at Padgett six weeks and that you've been ill part of that time. Because of your ability, you were placed in accelerated classes.'' She sifted through some papers in his file. Michael remained upright in his chair and was carefully regarding her again.

"Chemistry," she said sympathetically, glancing down at her notes. "It's brought many a good man down, Mike. But not many with an IQ as high as yours. What seems to be the problem?"

"No problem," he said shortly. "I just don't like it."

"Oh." Carly appeared to give his statement careful thought. "Could you be a bit more specific?"

His eyes narrowed suspiciously. "Like, how?"

She sighed. "Like, do you need help, Michael? If you do, I'm here to assist you any way I can."

He swung his head to the window without replying.

"You know, maybe your father could give you a few pointers. Chemistry's probably a snap to a man in his field."

"You gotta be kidding."

"Not really. I'm perfectly serious. I assume that your father mastered high school chemistry," she said dryly, trying to coax him into a better humor. With a smile she added, "And what are fathers for, after all?"

"Beats the hell out of me," he said.

"I beg your pardon?"

"Nothing," he mumbled.

Carly frowned, not particularly interested in forcing an apology from the boy for swearing. She was more interested in getting a fix on what was wrong. Was it something to do with his father? It wouldn't be the first time Carly had run across high-powered workaholic parents who had no time for their children.

"You don't think your dad could find time to help you?"

Mike laughed shortly and thrust his long legs out in front of him. "Let's just say that since he hasn't had a whole lot of time for me in the past ten years, and I haven't heard from him since I've been in town, I don't think it's likely he'll find time to tutor me in chemistry,'' he said cynically.

''But what about when you were hospitalized?'' Would she never cease to be shocked in this job? Carly wondered.

''Maybe he forgot my name,'' he said, his words now openly sarcastic.

Carly resisted an urge to open the file and reread it. Even blessed with an excess of intuition and insight, it wasn't possible to uncover the father's neglect from the cold facts in front of her, which had told her only that Brannigan was a physician, and he did reside in New Orleans. The file didn't seem to contain much more about him. In case of emergency, they were to contact the mother, Lianne Landry. The parents were divorced. Ten years. The mother was married to Clifford Landry, vice-president of a company called ULT. Padgett was an expensive private school. Did the father pay? Maybe he thought meeting his financial obligations absolved him of any other involvement in his son's life. Carly studied the boy with troubled eyes. He was so beautiful. And so young and vulnerable. How could any father not feel intense love and pride for a son like Michael? And why did these situations always wring her heart?

''I'm sorry, Mike,'' she said softly, refusing to act as though a father's rejection was anything but tragic. ''But the fact remains that chemistry is still a problem. Whether you like it or not, you've got to pass it to graduate. I've got an idea.''

''Yeah?''

''Yeah. Penny Lasseigne.''

His dark eyes narrowed with suspicion. ''What's she got to do with anything?''

''She just possibly could be the answer to your problem.''

"Huh?"

Carly leaned forward, resting intertwined fingers on Mike's file. "Penny's a whiz in chemistry. She'd be a great tutor."

"Now, wait a minute, Ms Sullivan. I—"

"Don't thank me yet," Carly said, smiling brightly. She was determined not to give him a chance to voice the outrage she could see shimmering in his dark eyes. "Save it for the celebration we'll have when you get an A in chemistry."

SWEARING SILENTLY, Mike closed the door of Carly Sullivan's office. Tutored. *Tutored!* He had never needed help in any subject before, and he still didn't. He could handle chemistry. Ten minutes a day to review the lesson, and it'd be a snap.

He veered abruptly from the turn that would have taken him to the cafeteria, and headed instead for his locker. Suddenly he had no appetite. His body craved the satisfaction of a good hard run, not food.

Suggesting that his father might help him with his chemistry had been a big joke. Mike couldn't see Dr. Jess Brannigan bothering to involve himself in his son's life. He sure hadn't bothered before.

All the old feelings Mike had thought he'd buried long ago suddenly twisted in his gut. It wasn't chemistry or the prospect of requiring a tutor that bothered him. It was being reminded again of his father and just how insignificant he was to him. But it was juvenile to waste even a minute wishing life was different. Life was no TV situation comedy in which things always turned out nicely. Real life was hard and cruel. Only a jerk wasted time fantasizing.

He slammed a palm against a locker and headed for his own.

AN HOUR LATER, making her way to the lounge for a cup of coffee, Carly was still smiling over Mike's expression as he'd stamped out of her office. He'd been too polite to express himself, but she'd had no difficulty imagining his thoughts. He wasn't going to be easy to help, but there was something so appealing about him that she knew she wouldn't give up—not yet. Actually her plan had a twofold purpose. Not only could Mike use the tutoring, but he'd make a friend at the same time. Ten to one he wouldn't be able to resist Penny Lasseigne.

It would be good for Penny, too. She was still grieving for her father, who had been shot and killed less than a year earlier in a mugging incident in the French Quarter. Since then, Penny, who had been vivacious and outgoing, had become quiet and withdrawn. Reaching out to befriend Mike just might help take her out of herself, Carly thought, turning the corner. Yes, bringing Mike and Penny together could work....

The lounge was empty. Glancing at her watch, Carly decided she had enough time for a quick coffee break before she had to leave for the courthouse. She'd received a subpoena several weeks before regarding possible selection for the Orleans Parish grand jury. It could mean that all her Fridays for the next six months or so would be occupied with deciding the destiny of some of New Orleans's numerous criminals, but while everyone had groaned and expressed sympathy when she'd mentioned it, Carly was looking forward to the chance to become directly involved in the justice system.

After helping herself to coffee, she ripped the corner off a tiny pink envelope and carefully tapped a bit of artificial sweetener into her cup.

"Sixteen grains." Rachel Lasseigne's soft drawl came from directly behind her. "I haven't figured out why you even bother."

Startled, Carly whipped around, sending her golden hair swirling. She barely managed to keep from sloshing the hot coffee everywhere. "Oops! Hi, Rachel." Her quick glance took in the tall and elegant form of Penny's mother and her own best friend. "Doesn't anything look bad on you, Rachel?" she grumbled. "I looked like a bag lady in that outfit when I tried it on at Macy's." Carly grabbed a plastic stick and stirred her coffee briefly. "And I use only a little sweetener because I would be two sizes bigger in two weeks if I used real sugar."

"A gross exaggeration, as usual," Rachel said, stepping up to the coffeepot. Plunking down a man-size mug, she filled it to the brim and dumped two heaping teaspoons of sugar into it. Leaning against the table, she eyed Carly's five-foot-two-inch frame. "Do you know how desperately I used to long to be petite? At fourteen, I towered over everyone in the eighth grade—even Mr. Sims, the principal."

Carly laughed, shaking her head. "What a crock, Rachel."

"It's true. I hid in my room for a whole year, only coming out at mealtimes."

"I suppose that explains why you're so shy and insecure."

Hands on her hips, Rachel pretended outrage. "This coming from a former cheerleader, homecoming queen and all-around campus beauty! It was great-looking petite blondes such as yourself who gave me my complex, I'll have you know."

Still smiling, Carly rolled her eyes, knowing she'd never get the last word. She and Rachel had been fast friends since the day she had begun working at Padgett School, three years earlier. Nearly every other teacher on the staff conformed exactly to the expected image at Padgett, one of New Orleans's most exclusive private schools. Rachel, on the other hand, had a slightly wicked sense of humor and a streak of plain old unadulterated horse sense that Carly found refreshing.

"So..." Rachel eyed Carly over the top of her mug, and Carly knew immediately what was coming. "Tell me how it went with Peter Mason last night."

"Just as you predicted," Carly told her matter-of-factly. "I discovered I'm not particularly interested in anthropology or the pitfalls in a two-party political system."

"No kidding."

Carly glanced at Rachel and shrugged ruefully. "I know, I know. You told me so."

"He's so stuffy that instead of showering every morning like a real man, he has to be dusted off."

"Rachel—"

Rachel put up a hand. "Okay, okay. At least I understand why you went out with him, otherwise I might be genuinely concerned for your judgment, not to mention your eyesight."

"Peter is articulate and intelligent and *nice*," Carly argued stubbornly. "Those are qualities that all men don't have, as I well know."

"He's a wimp."

"You forget I was married to a 'real man,' and we both know how that ended."

Carly paused and stared into her coffee as the inevitable ache came upon her. The memory was like a sore tooth, shooting pain through her unexpectedly whenever she thought of her marriage. To her surprise she realized the pain had dulled since the last time. Could it be that she was finally moving beyond the emotional trauma of Buck Sullivan's rejection of her and their divorce? After all, it had been three years.

"Your ex-husband wasn't a real man, honey," Rachel said softly. "Being a football coach and working in a world of athletic types doesn't necessarily make a man truly masculine. Buck was an inarticulate, emotionally impotent jock. And he would still have been that even if he had been a pharmacist or a musician."

Carly grimaced and set her cup down. "I know that, Rachel. I have a degree in psychology, remember? I just prefer to avoid certain types."

"Just so long as you don't judge all men too hastily." Rachel finished off her coffee and walked over to the small sink to rinse out her mug.

"Not to worry," Carly said, still savoring the discovery that her failed marriage didn't appear to hold the pain for her that it once had. "I think I just made a major breakthrough."

Rachel turned and gave her an inquiring look. "How so?"

She flashed her friend a quick smile and began gathering up her purse and a few case files. "Tell you later, Rach. I need to get out of here. It's almost quarter to ten. Are we still on for tonight?"

"Quarter to...? I realize it's Friday, but nobody told me we were quitting early."

"You're not, just me. My grand jury summons, remember? Today's the day I have to appear," she said, adding, "The chances of my being selected are pretty slim. They summon over two hundred people and only pick twelve."

"You sound as though you'd like to be one of the chosen."

"I think I would."

"Whatever for?" Rachel demanded, tossing a paper towel into the trash and falling into step beside Carly. "Don't bother to answer. It's your Earth Mother complex. I can see you now, rending your heart over every case. You'll probably vote against indicting anybody." Her tone was slightly brittle. It had been ten months since Phillip

Lasseigne had been killed. She had more than just cause to want to see justice done.

"I hope I won't be that stupid, Rachel."

Rachel laughed shortly. "I know, Carly. We both know I'm not exactly an unbiased person on this subject, am I?"

"Hey, what would I want with an unbiased friend, anyway?" Carly squeezed the other woman's arm affectionately.

"Did I tell you Kyle followed up on that tip they got about Phillip's killer, and it just led to another dead end?"

"Oh, too bad, Rachel."

Rachel's mouth twisted. "Makes you wonder about the justice system."

"But surely as long as there are people like Kyle Stratton in the police department, justice will prevail." Carly's tone was full of admiration. "Kyle's something else, the way he's focused on finding the killer."

"I know," Rachel said. "He's like a German shepherd and just as single-minded."

Detective Kyle Stratton had been Phillip's best friend. He and his date had been with Rachel and Phillip that fateful night. Kyle had been nearly as devastated by Phillip's death as Rachel. The foursome had separated at the door of the restaurant they'd eaten dinner at, because their cars were in opposite directions. At the shot, Kyle had rushed over, his gun drawn, but the killer had disappeared. Phillip had died in Kyle's arms. Since then, Kyle had assumed responsibility for Phillip's wife and daughter. He was always around and was a friend to Rachel as well as a surrogate father to Penny—out of guilt and a cop's overprotective tendencies, Rachel had told Carly. Rachel had given up trying to convince him that he wasn't responsible for her. Personally, Carly wasn't so sure the man stayed so close to Rachel out of duty. There was a certain something in Kyle Stratton's eyes when he looked at Rachel. And it sure wasn't guilt.

"I need to get going," Rachel said, picking up her pace. "If you get selected, try to toughen up. Forget trying to come up with every possible reason why a person would be forced into a life of crime, Carly."

"You forget I won't be the only person deciding the fate of the accused. There'll be eleven other 'good men and true.'"

A gleam appeared in Rachel's eyes. "Hey, you could very well be right about that," she said slowly. "This may turn out to be a good thing, after all. Wouldn't it be a hoot if one of those 'good men' turned out to be just that—a real man?"

"Rachel—"

Rachel laughed. "I'll keep my fingers crossed."

"I appreciate that," Carly said flatly, slowing as they approached the intersection of the hall. "So, what about tonight?"

"It's Friday, isn't it?"

"At long last, and I'm ready for my weekly pizza fix. Oh!" Carly snapped her fingers suddenly. "I've lined up another tutoring assignment for Penny. I'll give her the details tonight—that is, if she's going to be home."

Rachel nodded. "As far as I know, she hasn't got anything else planned."

"Will Kyle be there?"

Rachel made a face. "He's out of town again. Baton Rouge, I think. Some kind of FBI training course."

"Uh-huh." Carly wagged a finger. "You miss him."

"How can you miss a German shepherd?" Rachel retorted, and was off before Carly could reply.

Smiling, she watched Rachel stroll away. *Lucky Rachel,* she thought wistfully. Phillip, and now Kyle Stratton. But her determination to find the right man for Carly was sometimes a pain. Yes, Carly thought, she needed to erase the memory of Buck Sullivan, as Rachel had pointed out more than once. The right man would go a long way toward rebuilding her confidence in herself as a woman. But she wasn't counting on it. The next time she got involved with a man—*if* there ever was a next time—she was going to give it long and serious thought. One thing was certain, she told herself resolutely, turning and walking in the opposite direction from Rachel: she wouldn't be easily dazzled again. Those strong, domineering, mostly silent types might seem appealing, but she'd learned the hard way that they were hell to live with. Never again, she vowed. Shaking her head, she glanced down at her watch. With a startled sound, she dashed off in the direction of her office.

By the time Carly climbed into her car to leave for the courthouse, she was running late. Easing out of her parking spot, she glanced toward the practice field in the rear of the school. One lone youth was covering the quarter-mile track in rhythmic ground-eating strides.

Mike Brannigan ran with the grace and natural ease of a born athlete, she noted as she watched him burst ahead with another spurt of speed, as though he were attempting to overtake an imagined opponent. The boy had a lot of potential. He just needed a little help reaching it. Pairing him with Penny had been a good idea, she told herself as she merged with the traffic on St. Charles Avenue. A smile tugged at her mouth. Naturally she was a little biased on the subject of Penny, but how could she not adore Rachel's daughter? The teenager had her mother's sharp intelligence and was just as quick with her tongue. She would be a wonderful friend for Mike.

Carly's smile faded as she recalled the bitterness in the boy's tone when he mentioned his father. What kind of man chose a profession like medicine, then turned his back on his own son? Wasn't caring for people an essential element of a medical career? How could he not care for his own son?

Shaking her head, Carly slowed her car as she approached the courthouse. It never failed to amaze her how casually some people looked upon their responsibilities to their children. While she— Pain, swift and deep, cut through her. She might have overcome the pain of her failed marriage, but another loss was still as sharp and hurtful as ever.

She had lost her child. Her tiny son had survived only a few hours after birth. Divorce was a painful ordeal, but nothing, *nothing* in her life could ever touch the total black despair she had had to endure after losing her son. The pain could still pierce to the center of her heart. Nothing would ever heal it. Inhaling deeply, she headed for the courthouse parking lot, and turned her thoughts determinedly to the present.

Moments later she was inside the huge building. She took a second to figure out where she was going, then headed for the elevators. When she slipped into the courtroom, she stood against the door feeling embarrassed and conspicuous. Dismayed, she realized that the proceedings were under way. Oh, Lord, it looked as if they had already started calling the jurors. A few were already seated in the jury box. Quickly, she looked around for a seat, but nothing was immediately accessible. Edging along the dark panelled walls, she leaned against a massive column and hoped she wasn't as exposed as she felt.

"Arthur Raymond Milhouse."

Carly's gaze swept over the assembled crowd. Mr. Milhouse was short, overweight and about fifty. He had bright blue eyes that seemed to be permanently crinkled, ready to laugh. He moved surprisingly quickly down the aisle to the jury box.

"Joseph James West." A much taller man, with a shock

of red hair, stood up with a resigned look on his face. Apparently everyone wasn't as pleased at the prospect of serving as she would be, Carly thought, hiding a smile.

As the bailiff continued calling out names, Carly studied the men and women who were already seated. Besides West and Milhouse, there was one white-haired old lady, with a sweet expression on her lined face, and two other women, one in her mid-twenties, Carly guessed, with beautiful skin the color of café au lait. The other appeared middle-aged, but it could have been her clothes and hairdo that gave that impression. *A schoolteacher,* Carly mused. The sixth-grade math teacher at Padgett could have been her twin.

Ten jurors were now seated—three women and seven men. Carly swallowed a disappointed sigh. It didn't look as though she would be chosen. She studied the group of jurors again, blinking when her gaze collided with the dark eyes of the man on the aisle seat. She was still as she absorbed his harsh unsmiling look. A little shiver darted down Carly's spine. Rachel's teasing leaped into her mind. *What would she say if she could see this guy!* Carly thought. His hair was thick and as black as coal. High prominent cheekbones gave his face a raw, totally masculine look that would never be called handsome, but it was certainly arresting, Carly decided. She frowned as she studied the severe planes and angles, the full lower curve of his mouth, the chiseled symmetry of his chin.... Something about him seemed almost familiar.

"Carly Kent Sullivan."

Carly started with surprise. Forcing herself to look away, she started down the aisle toward the bailiff, who was politely holding open the gate to the jury box, and the fleeting moment of familiarity was forgotten. She went through the small space, walked up two steps, then sank into a chair and turned her face toward the judge, who was launching into the charge to the grand jurors.

CHAPTER TWO

JESS BRANNIGAN LEANED back in his chair, crossed his long legs at the ankles and surveyed his fellow grand jurors. John Hebert, an assistant D.A., who was apparently to be mentor and guide for the duration, was winding down after having given the jurors an idea of what to expect. When the judge had finished his piece, Hebert had herded them en masse from the courtroom up two floors to the chambers designated for grand jury sessions. While he had spoken, they had listened raptly, seated around a U-shaped dais. Now they were looking slightly uncomfortable in the manner of people who were total strangers. *What we need is an open bar,* Jess thought with a quirk of his sensual mouth.

"There'll be no official business today," Hebert told them when he was done. He was a slightly built man and spoke with a soft Creole drawl. "Why don't y'all go around and introduce yourselves, get acquainted." He glanced around at the group. "Some of you may already know each other, but even so, I guarantee you'll be amazed at how much better you'll come to know your fellow jurors. We'll be dealing with some of society's worst offenders. Whether you plan it or not, your reactions will reveal your prejudices, your moral standards and how much tolerance and compassion you have, if any." He smiled slightly. "It's been my experience after dealing with grand juries for more than five years, folks, that people don't have too many secrets from one another after their tour of duty is done.''

After a beat or two of total silence, someone laughed—a little self-consciously. Hebert's eyes were amused behind his horn-rims. ''Wait and see,'' he predicted. ''Meanwhile, relax and enjoy. Serving on the grand jury is sort of like falling in love. It's a telling experience—not something you want to repeat too often. Now, for those of you who haven't found them yet, the vending machines are in the alcove next to the secretary's office.''

A slightly sardonic smile lingered on Jess's mouth as he studied the group and watched the easy way the jurors fell in with Hebert's suggestion. Soon he followed suit and went in search of the machines. Cradling a cup of dark rich coffee in his hands, he sought out the woman with the sun-streaked hair who had arrived late, looking as though she expected the judge to dress her down on the spot. He examined her discreetly, his eyes lingering on her softly rounded breasts and shapely bottom.

She was not a beauty. Her nose was not quite classic enough, and her mouth was a little too wide, he decided, noting the hint of sensuality in her full lower lip. Her hair was thick and vibrant, a tawny shade of blond.

He watched as she put up a hand and tucked an errant wisp behind one ear. Although her hair was confined at her temples by clips of some kind, it still managed to look unruly. He imagined plunging his hands in it and popping the clips open, freeing her mane. Wild and untamed, it would delight a man. She glanced up at that instant and met his gaze head-on. Her eyes were thickly lashed and tipped up slightly at the outside corners. He drew in a swift breath. No, there'd been no danger of the judge reprimanding her.

He watched her move away from the old lady and approach two men—Milhouse, he thought and... Who was the other one? West? In seconds both were hanging on to every word she said. She was totally at ease. Small talk seemed as natural to her as suturing a bloody wound was to him. He wondered what she did for a living.

He shifted his weight and shook his head. What the hell was he doing? He hadn't been this intrigued by a woman in... He couldn't remember when, but it had been a long time. Too long. She probably had cotton candy beneath that tawny mane. Or worse yet, she could be obsessive about her career and too aggressive. He waited until she disengaged herself from the two besotted males, then set his cup down on the desk and walked toward her.

Apparently Hebert had the same idea. She greeted the D.A. and smiled. Her voice was slightly husky, pitched low for a woman. To Jess it was sexy as hell.

"Mr. Hebert, I've been waiting for a chance to ask you some questions," she said, flicking Jess an impersonal smile as he drew up to them. "Have you got a minute?"

"More, if necessary," Hebert replied affably, as susceptible to her as the next man. "And please, call me John."

She nodded, flashing a dimple. "John. And I'm Carly." She smiled at Jess again, and he replied with a sardonic lift of one black brow. Damned if he'd give her his name until she gave him her attention.

"What was it you wanted to know?"

"You find all this pretty routine, I imagine, but I can hardly wait until next Friday." She talked with her hands, Jess observed, as well as her body. As she moved he caught the scent of her perfume. It was something subtle, but flowery and feminine. He liked it.

"Anybody who reads the *Times Picayune* knows New Orleans has its share of crime," she said. "I was wondering about how many cases on an average we can expect each week."

Hebert transferred his weight to one leg and crossed his arms over his chest. ''Well, that just depends. We can have as many as six or eight cases, but the average is about four.''

''Every Friday!'' she exclaimed.

''Except when it falls on a holiday,'' he declared.

She shook her head, looking dismayed. ''I'm shocked. Especially since the cases won't exactly be the kind of stuff you can discuss at a dinner party.''

Hebert's expression turned serious. ''Actually, the cases aren't the kind of stuff you can discuss, period. Remember, you took an oath of confidentiality. You don't want to be responsible for violating the rights of an individual.''

''No matter how rotten his crime may be,'' Jess put in dryly.

Carly looked directly at him. ''His alleged crime, don't you mean?''

''I don't think the D.A.'s office is likely to bring us any half-baked cases, Ms Sullivan,'' Jess said cynically. ''The vast majority of the defendants we deal with will be guilty as sin.''

''Our whole justice system is based on the premise that a person is presumed innocent until he's proven guilty,'' she reminded him stiffly. ''Or have you chosen to ignore that?''

His dark eyes held hers. ''If I'm tempted, apparently I can depend on you to bring me in line.''

Her eyes were an enchanting shade that defied description, he decided. Like a cat's. And right this minute he guessed she wanted to spit at him like a little cat. What a delight it would be to stroke her into a better humor.

''John,'' she said, turning firmly away, ''do you often have jurors who demonstrate a blatant disregard for the rights of criminals?''

Hebert seemed torn between amusement and discretion.

"It happens, Carly. In the opinion of some folks, the pendulum has swung a little too far to the left. There's no denying it isn't quite as safe to walk the streets as it used to be. Fortunately, juries tend to have people with varying political philosophies." He gave Jess a thoughtful look. "What's your speciality, Doc?"

"Trauma," Jess said briefly.

Nodding with understanding, Hebert eyed him, his head to one side. "Crescent City, isn't it?"

"Yeah."

"I thought I recognized you. You head up emergency, I believe."

Jess breathed in deeply. Carly was looking at him as though he'd crawled out from under a rock. Why the hell had he needled her like that? If she wanted to see the scum who would come before the jurors as poor pitiful misfits who'd never had half a chance, it was her privilege. A couple of hours in Crescent's emergency room watching his team try to staunch the blood of an innocent victim would give her another perspective on the lowlifes she was so ready to defend.

"I imagine you get a few gunshots in the course of a shift at Crescent City," Hebert was saying.

"A few."

"Not to mention knifings."

Jess's features became harsh. He didn't like talking about his work. It was bad enough living it.

"Abused wives...kids..." Hebert looked at Carly. "It would tend to give a man an attitude problem, Carly, wouldn't you think?"

"Actually, you're probably right," Carly said, giving Jess a faint smile when he glanced quickly at her. He almost laughed as it dawned on him that she was extending to him the same tolerance she displayed for criminals.

"You're gonna feel right at home," Hebert observed.

"Looks like it," Jess murmured, his eyes still on Carly's. Someone hailed Hebert from across the room, but Jess barely noticed when the other man moved away. "So, what do you do, Ms Sullivan? Wait, let me guess.... A degree in English...no, psychology. That bleeding heart comes from a liberal arts major—no pun intended—right?"

She laughed and the sound went through Jess with the heady effect of a belt of sweet potent Southern Comfort. Did he really care that he was redeemed somewhat in her estimation?

"I'm a high school guidance counselor," she told him, pretending to sound dignified. "What?" she demanded when he nodded slowly.

"That explains it."

"Explains what?"

"Your crazy urge to be lenient with murderers," he said. "Anybody would be crazed if they had to deal with teenagers every day."

"That's absolutely untrue. I love my job and I love the kids I work with. It's true they're intense and difficult and insecure and brash, but they're also fiercely loyal and have the most incredible sense of justice." She gave him a knowing look. "In fact, you could take lessons from some of my kids, if you don't mind my saying so."

"I think I'll just leave it to you to keep me in line, justicewise," Jess said with a hint of indulgence in his tone.

"Haven't you ever noticed how quick children are to sense injustice no matter how adults try to rationalize it?" Carly asked.

He shook his head. "I can't say I have."

Instantly Carly sensed the change in him. For a few minutes, the harshness on his face had disappeared, making her feel as if she were on the point of discovering something. She searched his face now, but his expression was severe, warning off anything that even hinted at familiarity. And his eyes! Fierce was the only way to describe the look in his eyes. Unnerved, she wondered what in the world she'd said.

"I take it, then, that you aren't a parent," she said.

"Then you take it wrong."

"Oh." He did have children? Her eyes went to his left hand. He wore no ring, but that could mean nothing these days.

"I may not be up on the habits of teenagers, Ms Sullivan, but I am a parent, of sorts. I have a son."

"Call me Carly," she murmured. Her eyes slipped quickly over his face, noting the ruddy skin and the wide mouth that didn't quite match the forboding cast of his other features. She considered the clean square line of his chin. Not many men had such an uncompromising... Somewhere in her mind, memory stirred. That fleeting sense of familiarity she'd felt when she had first seen his face was back again.

She tilted her head and looked at him intently. "Do I know you? Have we met?" But even as she asked it, Carly didn't think it was possible. This wasn't the kind of man who was easily forgotten. If she'd ever met him, she would have remembered him, she was certain. "I arrived late and didn't catch your name, Dr....?"

"Brannigan, Jess Brannigan."

Brannigan. In less than a heartbeat, Carly realized why he seemed familiar. Was this Mike Brannigan's father? Brannigan wasn't a common name in New Orleans, and that coal-black hair and those intense dark eyes were absolutely unique. With renewed interest, she looked for more similarities. He looked hard and trim under his button-down shirt and casual sport coat. He wore comfortable cotton slacks, no tie. Every other male juror was wearing a suit; this was a man who wouldn't be influenced one iota by what anyone else did. He had to be Mike's father.

"You said you have a son," she prompted, her eyes on his profile as he stared across the room looking remote. "Does he live here in New Orleans?"

"Yes."

She cleared her throat. "Brannigan's not a very common name. One of my students is a sixteen-year-old boy named Michael Brannigan."

His gaze swung back to her abruptly. "What?"

"Mike Brannigan," she repeated. "He's a transfer student from California. Six weeks ago."

Jess swore softly. "What high school?"

"Padgett."

A muscle flexed in his jaw. "That's on St. Charles, isn't it?"

"Yes. Is Mike your son?"

"Yes."

The man did not even know where his son went to school! Carly was not a judgmental person, but still clear in her mind from that morning was the vulnerable look on Mike Brannigan's young face and the bitterness in his voice as he'd spoken to her of his father's indifference. She had been unable to imagine a man capable of ignoring the existence of his own son for ten years. Even now, for some crazy inexplicable reason, she found herself hoping Brannigan would come up with some good reason for having neglected Mike.

"Surely you know the location of your son's school?"

"How is he doing?" he asked, ignoring her question.

"Not very well," Carly retorted, feeling her objectivity slipping. She took a breath and, almost unconsciously, slipped into her professional role. "Look, we can talk about this in my office, if you're really interested, Dr. Brannigan."

"What do you mean, not very well?"

She made an impatient sound. "Just what I said, Dr. Brannigan, not very well."

"What seems to be the problem?"

Carly hesitated, sensing the intensity behind the question. For a man who practically ignored his son for ten years, his interest struck her as odd.

"These things are emotional sometimes, other times... Well, some kids are just naturally rebellious."

"Is he rebellious?"

"You tell me," she challenged him.

Looking away from her, he pressed his palm against the back of his neck and held it there for a moment. "I wish I could," he muttered, but in so low a tone she couldn't be certain.

"Yes, well, doesn't your interest come a little late, Dr. Brannigan?" In spite of herself, a sarcastic note crept in. It was unprofessional, but she was finding it damned difficult to be objective with this man.

"Mike's grades have slipped seriously. As I'm sure you know, his test scores are in the gifted range, but he consistently underachieves."

For a second she thought she saw a flash of uncomplicated fatherly pride. "Gifted," he repeated, nodding. "But he underachieves, you say."

"You must know he does," she said impatiently.

He looked at her. "Why do you think that is?"

"Why do I think that is!" she repeated in an astonished tone.

"Yes, why?"

She stared at him. "You mean aside from the fact that he's sixteen, friendless, and has just been transplanted from one culture to an entirely different one—"

He put up a hand to stop her. "Yes, aside from all that. Do you think he has an emotional problem?"

She drew in a deep breath and looked him in the eye. ''The real miracle here, Dr. Brannigan,'' she said, making no effort to mask her rapidly disappearing patience, ''is that Mike is as well-adjusted as he seems to be. What with making a major move clear across the country, suffering renewed rejection by his father, falling ill and having surgery...''

Shock flared in the opaque darkness of his eyes. He stared blindly at Carly.

''Dr. Brannigan—''

Abruptly, he looked away, locating the door. Muttering an apology he turned on his heel and left her. Carly watched him sidestep a couple of people who spoke to him, but she could have sworn he didn't even hear them. His eyes straight ahead, his mouth grim, he shouldered his way through the group to the exit and disappeared.

''SO, HOW WAS the grand jury?'' Rachel asked, pushing a wedge of pizza toward Carly, then folding her own piece and biting off nearly half of it at once. ''Oh Lord, this is wonderful! Do you think anything this good could possibly have nutritional value?''

Carly licked sauce from the corner of her mouth and reached for the last piece. ''Mmm, nutritional value, no. A trillion calories, yes.''

Friday night pizza with Rachel was a regular event. Somehow Friday, the last day of the workweek, just wasn't a night to spend alone.

''Well?'' Rachel prompted.

''You won't believe it, Rachel.''

Rachel's eyebrows lifted. ''What?''

''One of the jurors is Mike Brannigan's father.''

Rachel frowned. ''Our Mike Brannigan? The boy Penny's going to tutor?''

"Yes. He's a doctor—he heads up the emergency room at Crescent City Hospital."

Rachel made a face. "I'll bet he sees some sights."

Carly nodded, recalling Brannigan's harsh features and his open cynicism.

"The boy's a carbon copy of his dad," she said. "Both are dark and intense, totally—"

"Masculine?"

"I was going to say totally introverted and uncommunicative."

Rachel's tongue darted out to capture a string of mozzarella cheese. She nodded. "Ah, we're talking strong silent types here."

"For the father you can add insensitive, cynical and neglectful."

Rachel lowered her pizza. "That bad, huh?"

Carly tossed a crust into the empty box. "What would you call it when a man virtually ignores the existence of his son for ten years? When I mentioned to Mike that his dad might be able to help him with his chemistry, I could have cried at the reaction I got. It was awful, Rachel. Although he tried to cover it up with something flip and sarcastic, the bitterness and hurt were there. Other parents manage somehow when divorce separates them from their children. Brannigan could have visited, even though the boy lived in California. He could have had Mike here for the summer."

She stood up suddenly, pacing the length of the kitchen. "That's not all, Rachel. You remember Mike had that bout with appendicitis and wound up having surgery? Brannigan didn't even show up at the hospital." She stopped and stuck out her wineglass accusingly. "But you're right, that's not neglect, it's inhuman! Animals have more concern for their offspring than that."

Rachel refilled both their glasses and leaned back in her

chair. "Are you sure you have all the facts here, Carly? Maybe he was denied custody or something. You only have the boy's side of the story. Lord knows teenagers don't always stick to the truth."

"He didn't even know Mike was at Padgett, Rachel!"

"You talked to him about Mike? Today, at the courthouse?"

"He asked a dozen questions." She picked up the wine and took a hefty taste.

"About what?"

"About Mike. Who do you think?"

"Hmm." Rachel studied the etched pattern on her wineglass. "Is that how you discovered how disinterested he was in his son?"

"I hate it when you do this, Rachel," Carly said, setting her wineglass down firmly. "You can sit there and play devil's advocate if you want to, but I'm not making all this up. Nothing can change the fact that Brannigan has ignored his son for years. Mike's the victim in all this."

Rachel sighed and shook her head. "Carly, Carly, lighten up, will you? I'm not being insensitive to the hurt and pain of a sixteen-year-old, but we haven't heard from all the people involved here."

Carly sank back into her chair. "I know. All day at school, I hear the kids' problems and hang-ups, and I know there are at least two sides to every story." She stared broodingly into the pale gold wine. "It's just that this boy is so beautiful and intelligent. It kills me to see him hurting. And most of the kids' complaints *are* valid. Half the time the parents simply aren't interested enough to help them."

Leaning forward, Rachel stared into Carly's face. "Stop me if I'm on the wrong track here, but I find your reaction to Brannigan very interesting. In the three years you've been at Padgett, Carly, you've dealt with dozens of parents a lot worse than this guy sounds, but I don't recall you getting this steamed over a single one." She fixed Carly with a narrow-eyed look. "Tell me again what he looks like."

Carly gave an impatient swipe of her hand. "I told you, he's dark and sort of—"

"Tall?"

"Well, yes. And he's..."

"Sexy."

Carly's anger surged again. "It's nothing like that, Rachel!" She turned her face to a window that overlooked a courtyard. "I know this man's type, Rachel. Whether you're ready to believe it or not, he's a rigid and cynical—" she held up a hand to stop Rachel from interrupting "—so-and-so. And I've had enough experience with the type to recognize one when I see one."

IT WAS LATE when Carly got home. Usually a night with Rachel left her in a good mood. But tonight... She turned on a light in her small living room, dropped her purse onto a chair and headed for her bedroom, where she stripped off her jeans and shirt, feeling unsettled. Rachel was right. Her reaction to the Brannigans, father and son, had been entirely too personal. She saw a lot of mistreated kids, and sometimes she did get involved—more than someone prudent and practical would. Usually she saw no harm in it. After all, she had no husband and no children of her own. Her parents were retired and living in Florida. She had no sisters or brothers. But Carly did have her kids. She enjoyed them as individuals. They trailed in and out of her office every day, confused, emotionally deprived, hungry for love. They poured out their hearts and she listened, genuinely interested. She had a lot of love to give.

Sighing, Carly put a hand to the small of her back and idly kneaded it. She would have to make an exception with

Mike Brannigan, she acknowledged reluctantly. It would be unwise to get too close to him. Any in-depth dealings with the son would invariably bring her into contact with the father. Although Jess Brannigan couldn't be more wrong for her, she was attracted to him. Rachel had picked up on it instantly. Before she had known who he was or anything about him, she had felt something stir deep inside her, something that had lain dormant for a long time. It had almost been like coming alive again. Sadly, it wasn't the first time she'd been attracted to a man who was all wrong for her.

Carly considered herself to be an expert in recognizing the emotionally impotent males of the world. Three years with Buck Sullivan had seen to that. Thank God she no longer had to cope with the sheer frustration of living with a man who was incapable of sharing his thoughts and feelings but was all too ready to point out her faults.

She slipped off her peach-colored teddy. Just before tossing it into the laundry hamper, she ran her fingers over the soft sleek satin. She loved beautiful lingerie, both the look and the sensuous feel of it. She indulged her femininity in countless ways—in the soft pastel decor of her house, the dainty patterns of her linen and china, and especially in the decoration of her bedroom. She'd refinished the white bentwood rocker herself and searched high and low for the lush down coverlet that lay on her white enamel and brass bed. One look and there was no doubt that this was a woman's domain. Rachel teased Carly about it; she would have been shocked to know the insecurities her friend felt as a woman.

Six years ago Carly would have laughed at the idea that her spirit could be crushed by a man. As an adolescent she'd had more than her share of confidence and self-esteem. She was attractive, an honors student and a cheerleader in high school. Her steady boyfriend was the captain of the football team. When she went off to college, there was little change. She managed a nice balance between her studies and her social life, so that by the time she was a senior, she felt confident that she was ready to take on the challenges of the real world. That year she met Barclay "Buck" Sullivan.

Buck was the new assistant football coach and an overnight sensation on campus. He was big and blond and handsome, the quintessential hero-athlete. He'd been drafted by the pros as a quarterback but had been permanently injured in his fourth season. His arrival at the university was hailed with a flurry of newspaper and television publicity. Carly had been as star struck as everyone else. When she was singled out by Buck, she was thrilled and delighted. In six months, they were married.

Even to this day, she didn't know why Buck had wanted to get married. He was a terrible husband. He spent five nights out of seven with his male cronies. He made no secret of the fact that he preferred the undemanding company of his buddies to the more sophisticated friendships that Carly longed for. She tried to interest him in sharing time with her at something—anything—but he simply ignored her.

Even sex was a disappointment. She had come to her marriage fairly inexperienced, so she wasn't certain that her expectations in bed were reasonable. Making love, she decided after about six months of marriage, was nothing like the passionate experiences written about in romance novels. Her attempts to talk about the problem enraged Buck and only produced scathing criticisms of her own love making skills.

When she'd gotten pregnant, Buck had reacted with mixed emotions. On the one hand, he seemed happy about the proof of his masculinity. On the other, Carly sensed his deep fear of the responsibilities and demands a baby represented. But she deliberately closed her mind to his reaction, hoping the baby would somehow change everything. She could see now that she'd bottled up her emotions out of desperation and fixed her expectations on the baby.

After her baby died, she existed in a state of despair and loss for several weeks. Then one night when Buck felt she'd "moped around," as he put it, long enough, he decided it was time to resume their physical relationship. Until that night he hadn't touched her or offered the comfort and sympathy she had expected to share with him over their loss. Devastated, she'd been unable to respond, and he'd rolled away in disgust. "It's like having sex with a zombie," he'd snarled. "In bed or out of it, you're a miserable failure, Carly. Do you realize that?"

The words were seared into her soul. But as painful as they were, they served one good purpose—they were exactly what she had needed to push her into filing for a divorce. Her marriage had been a dreadful mistake. Buck had trampled her pride and disdained her passion. Today, no matter how hard she tried, she still thought of his cruel words sometimes. The legacy he had left her was a bitter one. She still wondered if her femininity wasn't fatally flawed in some way.

Carly walked into the shower, turned it on and lifted her face to the warm spray, wishing that she could wash away all the hang-ups she still carried from her marriage. Being a professional counselor had helped her understand herself, but it hadn't helped her heal herself. Carly gasped as water soaked her hair and cascaded over her body. She had been so happy and confident six years ago on her wedding day. The person she'd been then was gone forever. She was wiser now. Her emotional nature demanded too much of a man, she'd come to realize. Besides, she doubted if there actually existed a man capable of the total sharing of heart and mind that she longed for. Jess Brannigan definitely wasn't such a man.

CHAPTER THREE

JESS HAD PROBABLY DRIVEN past Padgett School on St. Charles Avenue hundreds of times, but he'd never particularly noticed it. Today he pulled to the side of the street and stopped. Monday morning traffic crawled by—nothing else was possible in the congested rush hour. He got out of his car and stood a minute with a hand on the door. Squinting against the glare of the October sun, he looked through the wrought iron fence that protected the grounds. The brick building was covered with ivy and was very old. Through the windows he could see a few students milling around, a teacher lecturing and a woman at a desk. Generally, it looked the way he'd expected it to. The best New Orleans had to offer. His mouth thinned. Tuition was steep at Padgett, although it probably fell far short of the astronomical amount he sent Lianne every month, Jess thought cynically.

He shifted his long frame and slammed the car door. One hand went to the knot of his plain dark blue tie, then fell to his side. It had been a hell of a weekend. He felt like a soldier who'd been in a prolonged battle. He stopped short before plowing the fingers of one hand through his black hair. He needed to make a good impression today, but he wasn't counting on anything. He didn't even know for sure what he was doing here. He only knew he wanted some kind of contact with Mike, and school seemed a good place to start since he seemed to have killed his chances of any sort of welcome where his son lived.

He'd been a fool to storm over there Friday half-cocked. He winced at the recollection. But, Lord in heaven, he'd been shocked speechless to discover Mike had had surgery and Lianne hadn't even called him. For the tenth time, he wondered if it was truly his own fault. Should he have pushed harder when they had first gotten back to New Orleans? But, damn it, he'd wanted to make a fresh start now that Mike was close at hand again. He'd known that if he pushed too soon, Lianne would make it so tough to get to the boy that it would be all-out war again, just as it had been when they'd first divorced. It hadn't mattered a damn then that he had joint custody. She'd married Landry and moved to California the week their divorce was final.

If he had pushed then, would he have had a relationship with his son now? he wondered. Or would it have been a case of history repeating itself? His own parents had divorced when he was six, and he'd been the weapon each had used against the other throughout most of his childhood. He'd been tugged at and disputed over until he'd finally learned to shut his own emotions off. He'd sworn he would never subject a child of his to that kind of bewildering pain. The divorce had been Lianne's idea. He didn't blame her for having been unhappy married to a struggling medical student, but he sure as hell blamed her for poisoning Mike's mind against him. At the time he'd honestly believed the only way to maintain any kind of peace was to keep a low profile in Mike's life. He knew now that he'd played right into her hands.

Legally, he'd have no problem seeing Mike. Jess dragged his fingers through his hair, forgetting the need for making a good impression. Unfortunately, Mike wasn't a six-year-old. Jess's instincts told him that forcing Lianne's hand would provoke a negative reaction in Mike. He was sixteen and old enough to know the court could dictate rights—but it couldn't force him to like or respect his father. Which was exactly what Jess wanted from Mike: affection—love, even—and respect. He was going to work out a way to win Mike back, but it wouldn't come via an order of the court, by God.

Had he taken the easy way out? Suddenly he remembered the censure in Carly Sullivan's eyes, and he was swept with a fierce sense of injustice, as though her opinion mattered. He was still puzzled over his reaction to Carly. It had been a long time since any woman had captured his interest for more than a passing moment. Even caught up as he was in coping with Lianne's vindictiveness and trying to find a way to break through Mike's hostility, the thought of Carly had hovered just at the edge of his mind all weekend.

He glanced up at the school's closed doors. Did his attraction to Carly have anything to do with his decision to start here? Could the rift between him and Mike be fixed? Was it too late? Was Padgett the place to start? Suddenly he felt an urgency unlike anything he'd felt in years. He was being handed a golden opportunity now that his son was back in New Orleans. He had a right to get to know his son. He had a right to try to win Mike's respect and love. He was determined to settle for nothing else. Quickly, with impatient strides, he pushed through the gate and climbed the stone steps that led to the huge oak doors of the school.

Inside the doors Jess hesitated, feeling nostalgic momentarily. Did all schools smell the same? What was it? Kids and chalk—books? If a stern-faced nun appeared and rapped him on the knuckles, he would have sworn he'd stepped into a time warp. He blinked to adjust his eyes to the inadequate lighting. About halfway down the hall, he spotted an open bay manned by a couple of students and headed for it. A young girl with dark hair and vivid blue eyes looked up and smiled at him.

"Can I help you?"

Jess's gaze went beyond her to the half-glassed walls of the principal's office. The door was closed, but he could see a woman behind a desk. Amused, he noted the salt-and-pepper hair, impressive bosoms and, yes, the stern face. She wasn't a nun, but she had the same look. Padgett and his old school did indeed have a couple of things in common.

A smile edged his mouth as he turned at a small sound down the hall. He looked up just as Carly Sullivan appeared at her office door. He felt a wave of pleasure as he met her startled eyes. Maybe his decision had been influenced by his attraction for this woman, but he couldn't think of a single reason why it could be a problem. Lord, she was lovely! For a second, Mike and his purpose for being at Padgett was lost. She was in a pink running suit and was slightly sweaty. She'd attempted to subdue her hair by pulling it up into a high ponytail, but a few tendrils had escaped at her temples and on her neck. Her damp disheveled look was more appealing than anything he could have fantasized.

"Dr. Brannigan?"

He shook himself out of his reverie and walked toward her, extending his hand. This was hardly the time to imagine the delights of Carly Sullivan. "Good morning, Carly."

For a second, Carly hesitated. What in the world was he doing here? she asked herself. The last person in the world she'd expected to see this morning was Jess Brannigan. Mechanically she put out her hand and felt her cool palm become enveloped in the excessive warmth of his. A totally unexpected emotion streaked through her. Her heart actually skipped a beat or two.

She was suddenly aware of how grubby she looked. She'd been called out of her gym class before she'd had time to shower and change. She was hot and sticky and now, ill at ease.

He looked good. His suit fit his lean body as though it had been tailor-made for him—which it probably had been, Carly reminded herself. His ice-blue shirt contrasted sharply with his dark skin and made him seem even more compellingly masculine. Seeing him again she realized that he was younger than she'd thought. *He must have been very young when Mike was born,* she mused.

She realized that she was staring and that he still had her hand. She gave it a gentle tug. He relinquished it reluctantly. Clutching a file folder against her breasts, she gave him her coolest, most professional look. "Is there something we can do for you, Dr. Brannigan? Are you here to see Miss Gates? Do you have an appointment?"

"Miss Gates?"

"The principal."

"Uh...no." He stopped and drew in a deep breath. "Actually, I came to see you, Carly. I know you're probably busy, but I hope you can give me a few minutes."

Carly glanced over at the two teenagers, who were watching the little scene wide-eyed. "Come into my office, please. Gina," she said to the dark-haired girl, "if Kristy McGee shows up, tell her I'll call her out of gym class after lunch, okay?"

"Yes, Ms Sullivan."

Carly stepped back, inclining her head toward the open door of her office. "Come in, Dr. Brannigan."

"But Terry Faust is on the line, Ms Sullivan," Gina said suddenly. "She's holding."

Carly hesitated, looking undecided. Brannigan was already in her office, cautiously lowering himself into an undersize molded-plastic chair. Terry Faust was a fourteen-year-old with serious problems at home, but it would be hard to concentrate on that with Brannigan listening and following her every move with that dark intent gaze.

"She sounded real upset, Ms Sullivan."

Carly sighed. "Okay, I'll take it in my office, Gina."

She headed directly for her desk after pulling the door closed behind her. She regretted it instantly, feeling crowded. She spent most of the waking hours of her day in this office closed up with dozens of people, students and adults alike. How was it that Brannigan seemed to fill it up totally?

"Excuse me a moment," she murmured, reaching for the phone. She studied him in a sidelong glance, taking in the casual male confidence he exuded even in the rickety chair. His long legs were bent. One ankle rested on the other knee. Both arms were folded across his broad chest. She might feel self-conscious carrying on business as usual in front of him, but he appeared totally at ease watching her do it.

"Hello, Terry? This is Carly Sullivan. How are you?"

His dark eyes watchful, Jess listened as the polite inquiry in Carly's voice sharpened to something else. "Where are you now, Terry?" she asked, pulling a white pad in front of her and swiftly writing down an address. "No, honey, don't do that. The worst thing you can do is run away." Another pause. "You have friends here, Terry. You don't know anybody in Houston. Let me try to talk to your mother before you—"

Carly's eyes flew to Jess's, but he suspected she didn't even see him. "Look, Terry, why don't you go over to your older sister's place and stay a few days?...It doesn't matter whether she's on your side or your mother's, Terry. She would still take you in rather than see you on the streets of Houston!" Carly tossed her pen down and leaned back in her chair suddenly. "Okay, then how about my place?...No, of course not, Terry. I just don't want you doing something that will change your whole life until you've thought it all out and considered all the angles."

Carly straightened, nodding. "I know.... I understand. You know where the key is." Her tone dropped. "Don't do anything until we talk, okay, Terry? Promise?...Right, I'll see you then."

Carly replaced the receiver and looked up into Jess's intent eyes. "Sorry about that, Dr. Brannigan. Now, what can I do for you?"

"Do you make it a regular thing to tell everybody where you keep the key to your house?" he asked, feeling oddly concerned for her safety.

"No, there are a lot of people who don't know where I keep my key, Dr. Brannigan."

"This child...Terry. Is she someone special? Or are you running a one-woman way station for teens?"

Carly felt a surge of irritation. What did this man expect her to do with a desperate fourteen-year-old girl who hadn't exchanged a civil word with her mother in more than a year? Let her take to the streets of Houston? Maybe he could turn his back on kids like Terry, but she never would. Never could.

"You're here about Mike, I assume," she said, pointedly ending the discussion he'd begun.

He stood up and Carly followed his movements as he paced. For an odd moment, she imagined what his hair would feel like in her fingers...dark silk? She frowned. What was the matter with her this morning? Here she was for the second time drifting off into a fantasy starring Jess Brannigan. Rachel's remarks and a restless Friday night must have gotten to her. Where was her common sense? After five minutes with him in the grand jury, she'd recognized a streak of cynicism in him a mile wide. Then, on the heels of that, she'd discovered what a miserable father he was. Two minutes ago he'd criticized the way she'd handled Terry. How could she find him sexually appealing after all that?

"...but I knew that it would cause a lot of questions," he was saying. "That's why I came to you."

Carly blinked and tried to pick up the thread of the conversation. "Um, you want to see your son's records? Is that what you—"

"Not just his records, Carly. I want to see Mike himself."

She stared at him. "Well, of course, Dr. Brannigan. But why here at Padgett?"

When he started to say something, she held up her hand. "I already know from Mike that you haven't seen him since he's been back in New Orleans, Dr. Brannigan."

He stopped pacing and faced her across the desk. "Carly, could we get back to first names? I know I haven't made a good impression on you as fathers go. My reaction Friday in the grand jury room must have seemed odd. Actually I'm not as bad as the situation makes me look." He smiled. "How about it? Will you drop the Dr. Brannigan...please?"

Carly murmured something and nodded. As she feared, this interview wasn't shaping up like the usual parent-counselor conferences she handled so well. Of course, Jess Brannigan wasn't exactly a run-of-the-mill father figure, either.

"I kept a low profile in Mike's life while he was in California, Carly, but I had a good reason. Or at least, I thought I had a good reason."

"I understand." But she didn't, and she wondered if she ever would. How could he bear to stay out of Mike's life for ten whole years?

His smile was bleak. "No, you don't, but maybe someday we can talk about it."

Carly looked up, startled. Revealing anything about his

flawed relationship with his son was the last thing in the world she expected from Jess Brannigan. She frowned, searching his harsh features. Could Rachel have been right? Had Carly leaped to a wrong conclusion about Jess based on appearances and scraps of misinformation?

"I saw Mike this weekend," he told her quietly. "It was Friday night, after I left the grand jury. And by the way, I apologize for rushing off like that. I was upset."

She nodded thoughtfully. "You seemed upset. Was it something I said?"

"I didn't know about Mike being in the hospital until you mentioned it."

"Oh."

"Yes—oh." He drew a weary breath and went back to his chair. "Look, Carly, I'm not particularly interested in his records so much as in what's been going on in his life, and as you know, that doesn't show on records." He gave her a compelling look. "So, do you think you can help me?"

Carly leaned back, feeling a return of her natural confidence now that he was appealing to her as a counselor. She didn't have to hold back as long as she was in her professional role with this man. She folded her hands together on the top of her desk and smiled. "I can answer some questions, of course, but don't you think Mike would be the best person to tell you about himself?"

"I don't think he feels particularly inclined to talk to me about himself or about anything, for that matter," Jess said dryly.

"It can't be as bad as all that," Carly said, feeling an odd urge to comfort him.

"Oh, yeah?" He laughed, but it had a hollow sound.

"Have you tried talking to him at all?"

He nodded. "Friday night, but I sensed that he felt awkward around his mother. I asked him to take a ride with me, but he refused.''

Carly had the strangest urge to reach for his hand. Instead, she linked her fingers together tightly and reminded herself that she wasn't going to get personally involved in this case. ''His reaction is understandable, don't you think? He may feel that any concessions he makes to you, now that you've finally decided to acknowledge him—'' she held up a hand when his eyes flashed warningly ''—would be disloyal to his mother.''

''It's possible,'' Jess conceded slowly.

''You need to spend some time with him. Get to know him, let him get to know you.''

''Tell me about it.'' Jess shifted in the chair, turning slightly to gaze out the window. ''The trick is, how do I manage that without making him feel as though he's betraying his mother?''

She was surprised. She hadn't expected Brannigan to show much insight regarding the problem Mike might have at home if he went along with his father's efforts to rebuild their relationship.

''I've got an idea,'' she said, glancing at her watch. ''It's almost lunchtime. Why don't I call Mike in and you can treat him to a Big Mac? McDonald's is only a few blocks away. The two of you can walk it in ten minutes easy.''

Jess looked wary. ''You think he'll agree to go? I don't want to force him into anything.''

Carly pretended a look of astonishment. ''Force him? A sixteen-year-old male getting a chance to leave the school grounds in the middle of the day? With the added incentive of a couple of Big Macs thrown in? Are you serious?''

He laughed. ''Okay, I get the picture.'' His harsh features softened as he held her gaze. ''I owe you one for this, Carly.''

"No problem." She smiled with professional poise. "It's my job." Turning to the credenza behind her desk, she quickly riffled through the card file that contained student schedules. "Now, let's just see where Mike is right this minute."

Jess was still for a second, wrestling with mixed emotions. On the one hand he felt he'd hit a gold mine in Carly Sullivan. She was a compassionate caring woman. Her manner with the teenager, Terry, had proved that. He was counting on that same compassion to ease the tension between him and Mike. He wondered if she would be that cooperative when it came to dealings between them that had nothing to do with her role as counselor to his son. She was wary of him for some reason, Jess knew. He didn't quite like the idea that she was helping him because it was her job. It followed that she wouldn't be willing to give him the time of day if it weren't for Mike.

He leaned back in the frail plastic chair, watched her flip up a card in the *B*s and decided he was going to need a lot of her attention.

Carly turned back to her desk, studying the three-by-five-inch card in her hand. "He's on the track team, and they're just winding up a practice session." She looked up and smiled. "Prepare yourself. He's going to be hungry."

"I think I can handle it."

She nodded. "Right. I'll call him."

He got to his feet when she stood up. The office was so tiny she was almost forced to brush against him to get to the door. He inhaled, enjoying the delicate flowery perfume she used. He was used to women who wore more exotic scents that had very little effect on him. For a second he thought about that, then shrugged it away. She headed for the open bay and disappeared behind it. Seconds later, he heard Mike's name amplified on the public address system.

"He's on his way." Carly swept past him again and sunk quickly back into her chair.

"I didn't realize he was on the track team," Jess said, sitting down. "What is his event?"

"The hurdles, and he's on the relay team. He runs like the wind!"

Jess felt a surge of fatherly pride. "How long has he been involved in track?"

Carly glanced at Mike's file. "Several years, according to his records from San Diego. He was drafted for our team about ten minutes after his tuition was paid. Actually—" she smiled into his eyes "—Mike *is* our track team."

Hungry for any information concerning Mike, Jess listened to Carly's enthusiastic predictions for the spring track meet. But his pleasure quickly became concern when she said, "As an athlete, Mike's a natural, you must surely know that. However, we have a rule here that a student must maintain a C average to participate. He's having trouble with chemistry."

Jess's gaze sharpened. "Chemistry? I thought you said he was gifted."

"I did. He is. But he's not applying himself, for some reason. I suggested—"

"I wonder if he would let me help him."

Carly leaned back suddenly. "Dr. Brannigan—"

"Jess," he reminded her.

Carly inclined her head. "Jess. I suggested that myself, which is when I discovered the rather unusual situation that exists between you and Mike. If I were you, I think I'd just let things stand as they are, at least for now. Penny Lasseigne, an honor student in Mike's class, is going to tutor him. It'll be an opportunity for him to make a friend, and if I know Penny, she will have him involved in the thick of things at Padgett before too long."

Jess sat without moving, his dark eyes fastened on

Carly. "You're certain that—" He broke off as Mike stepped through the open door of the office.

"Ms Sullivan, you wanted to—"

Jess came to his feet slowly. "Hello, Mike."

"Mike—" Carly quickly broke into the moment of silence that stretched a little too long as father and son warily eyed each other. "I was just telling your dad how you plan to ace the competition when track season begins."

Mike sent a quick look to Jess's face, his expression guarded, then turned deliberately back to Carly. "Was there something you wanted to see me about, Ms Sullivan?"

Carly sighed. She dealt with prickly supersensitive teenagers and their equally trying parents every day. At best it tested her patience. These two were probably so much alike that it would take a miracle to even get a dialogue going between them. Before she could think of a way to get them talking to each other, Jess said, "I'm looking forward to the track meets, Mike, but I'm afraid you'll have to clue me in on the finer points. I'm more up on football than track."

Mike fixed Jess with a dark look. "Sure you can work it into your schedule?"

Jess gave a little laugh. "I'm sure, Mike."

Carly jumped up, glancing at her watch. "Heavens! It's lunchtime already, and I've got a couple of things that just won't wait." She glanced down at herself, wrinkling her nose. "Like a shower, for starters. Mike, your next class is at one-fifteen, right?"

Mike responded with a wary look. Carly smiled brightly, then looked at Jess, lifting her eyebrows expectantly.

Jess cleared his throat. "Didn't I see the golden arches a couple of blocks from here?" Mike remained silent, but Jess had come too far to be put off by anything other than a flat no.

He looked directly at his son. "How about a couple of Big Macs with jumbo fries?"

The moment was fraught with a million things unsaid. Eyes dark and guarded, both Brannigan males faced off, waiting. *A real Mexican standoff,* Carly thought, holding her breath.

"What d'you say, Mike?" Jess's tone was quiet, compelling. His mouth had a wry tilt, but Carly could see the tense way he held himself. *Please, Mike, please say yes,* she prayed.

Mike nodded once curtly and turned on his heel. He was out of the office in a heartbeat. Jess started after him, but stopped at the door to look back at Carly. He wanted to say something—or at least he seemed to be searching for words—but after a second, he simply shook his head with a muttered "Thanks," and left.

Feeling almost as wrung out as Jess had looked, Carly sank into her chair. The scene between father and son had been emotional. She dealt with that kind of thing fairly often. The difference was that she didn't usually feel...emotional herself. She bent her head and wearily kneaded the bridge of her nose. Her instincts had been right on target as far as the Brannigan men were concerned. Mike was entirely too lovable, and now that she'd glimpsed the vulnerability and hidden pain in Jess, he was entirely too dangerous.

Her head snapped up as Rachel appeared in the door of her office. "I think I'm beginning to get a fix on what's going on here," Rachel announced, her eyes on Brannigan and his son making their way down the hall.

"Not now, Rachel."

Still craning her neck in the opposite direction, Rachel almost fell over the chair Jess had just vacated. "Oops!" She fixed the chair and sat down in it. "Let me get this straight, honey-bun. The gorgeous man who just left this office looking a lot like an ordinary harassed parent is the same one you pegged cynical and unfeeling. Right?''

Carly stood up and reached for her purse. ''If you want to have lunch with me, it has to be in the gym. I need a shower.''

''You did have him pegged accurately otherwise, though. I'll give you that.''

Carly glanced at her friend suspiciously, but refused to rise to the bait.

''He's definitely tall, dark and sexy.'' Chuckling, Rachel got up and hastily followed as Carly turned on her heel and marched out of her office at a telling pace.

''Seriously, Carly, I think you're in trouble at long last.''

At the big double doors, Carly pushed hard. ''I'm not in trouble, Rachel. Just because I happened to mention Brannigan Friday night is no reason to make anything out of his being in my office today. I have no control over who comes into my office.''

Rachel's eyebrows rose eloquently.

''I mean it, Rachel. I'll admit I was a little hasty when I first met him, but now I don't know what to think. He claims he wants to get to know Mike.''

With her long legs, Rachel kept pace easily. ''Does he know it's against the rules for a student to leave the school at lunchtime?''

''I suggested it,'' Carly said, busily searching in her purse for the keys to her gym locker. ''It seemed like a good idea, since he'd obviously made an effort to be with Mike.''

''Hmm.'' Rachel looked at her over the open locker door. ''This is the way you don't get involved?''

Carly sighed and began untying a shoe. ''I don't know, Rachel. Apparently the boy's mother isn't cooperating, although I don't have any details. Brannigan isn't exactly a man to reveal personal details. Maybe she has good reason not to encourage anything between him and Mike. After all, she ought to know her ex-husband better than anyone."

"Why do I get the feeling you don't really buy that?"

Carly wrenched off the shoe and tossed it into the locker. "No kidding, Rachel, I don't know what to think. He seemed so...so sincere. When he asked Mike to go with him for lunch, I was almost ready to try and persuade the boy myself if he refused." She laughed shortly. "When he said he'd go, I almost hugged him."

"Which one?" Rachel asked dryly.

Carly shook her head, knowing she wasn't making any sense after all the things she'd said to Rachel Friday night. But after hearing Jess talk about his lost relationship with his son and then seeing the two of them together, Carly didn't know what she thought anymore.

Rachel leaned back and surveyed the graffiti on the wall as Carly disappeared into a shower. "Yup, it's like I said, Carly, my girl. I think you're in trouble at last."

CHAPTER FOUR

THE FIRST THING Carly noticed when she got home that night was that her spare house key was still in its place under a loose brick in the sidewalk. She climbed the steps to the porch, tried the door and found it locked. Her brows came together in a frown as she unlocked it and went inside, carelessly dropping her bag onto a chair and depositing a stack of Padgett files on a long narrow library table.

"Terry?"

As she started down the hall toward the kitchen, she glanced up the stairs. But even as she called, she knew the house was empty.

At the door of the kitchen, she sighed and stepped out of her shoes, idly reaching for a foot and kneading her pinched toes. She would have to call Terry's home. If she wasn't there, only God knew where she might be. She sighed, not looking forward to tackling another teenager's problems tonight. She was still feeling edgy from her encounter with the Brannigans. In spite of her efforts, she hadn't quite been able to put them out of her mind.

Sighing again, she peeled off her panty hose and tugged at the tail of her blouse, freeing it from the waistband of her skirt. She rolled her head slowly first to one side, then the other, relaxing some of the tension. Her eyes thoughtful, she moved to the kitchen window and stood looking out into the night. Unfortunately she didn't have the kind of job that could be neatly tucked out of sight and forgotten upon leaving her office. Terry Faust was somewhere out there feeling desperate and alone, just desperate enough to do something dangerous. She tensed at the distant wail of an ambulance and felt the skin along her arms prickle. Abruptly she turned on one bare foot and headed back to the hall for the stack of files. Terry's phone number would be there. If not, she could try a couple of Terry's friends. She pulled out a file with a bright blue tab, hoping she wouldn't wind up the evening with a call to the runaway hot line in Houston.

She opened the file and was flipping through it when her doorbell rang. Startled, she looked up. Through the oval glass, she could make out the converging silhouettes of two people. One was definitely a man, tall and broad shouldered. The other...she couldn't be certain. Cautiously, the file still in her hand, she moved to the door and turned on the porch light.

Her lips parted soundlessly. There was no mistaking the features cast in harsh relief by the overhead light. Through the polished lead glass, Jess Brannigan's eyes gazed directly into Carly's. As she stood transfixed, he shifted impatiently. ''Well, how about it? Can we come in?''

His voice seemed to release her limbs, and Carly hastily dropped the folder. For some reason, her fingers were especially clumsy with the safety chain, but finally she managed it and opened the door.

''Jess!'' Her eyes seemed permanently linked with his so that at first she was only vaguely aware of her name spoken in a broken whisper from the young girl beside him.

''Terry!'' Carly took in the tear-streaked face and the white bandage around the girl's forehead before her eyes flew back to Jess. ''What's going on here? What's happened?''

Terry's voice caught on a fresh sob. "I didn't mean to cause all this trouble, Ms Sullivan."

Jess's arm around the girl's shoulders tightened as he met another questioning look from Carly. "If you'll just let us in, I'll be happy to explain," he said with sardonic patience.

Carly found herself stepping back and watching Jess usher his disheveled charge over the threshold and into the house. "Come in and sit down, Terry." Her eyes went to Jess in concern. "Or should she lie down? What in the world happened?"

Now that they were inside, Carly could see that Terry was pale and shaken. Her eyes had a shocked look, and her expression as she met Carly's was filled with misery.

"Yes, she should lie down," Jess said, still supporting the tearful teenager. "She's just about used up, aren't you, Terry? But you'll feel a hundred percent better after you sleep off that shot." Over her head, she looked at Carly. "Were you going to put her upstairs?"

Carly blinked. "Oh, yes. I've got a spare bedroom. It's the one up front." She motioned Jess ahead of her, making a little sound of concern as Terry swayed with fatigue and medication. Without missing a beat, he swung the young girl into his arms and headed up the stairs.

Carly followed close behind, snapping on the light at the top of the landing. A million questions jostled for position in her mind as Jess paused at the bed and waited for her to pull the spread down. He was the last person in the world she expected to see with Terry Faust. Even though he was a doctor, intuitively she knew he was not a man who made a habit of befriending troubled teenagers. In fact, she suspected he rarely involved himself in the affairs of anyone, but especially teenagers. That impression wasn't pulled out of thin air, she told herself as she plumped up a pillow vigorously. If he had any interest in befriending teenagers, why didn't he start with his own sixteen-year-old?

She watched him gently deposit Terry on the side of the bed. When he looked up and caught her eye, his expression was enough to still the questions trembling on her tongue. "I'll just wait downstairs while you settle Terry in," he told Carly, who nodded mutely.

Ten minutes later, Carly had helped the distressed teenager into an oversize T-shirt and tucked her in for the night. At the top of the landing, she looked down to see Jess gazing around her house with undisguised interest. As Carly slowly descended the stairs, she followed his gaze and wondered what he was thinking. Anyone could see the place belonged to a woman. From any angle it was a soft, inviting, utterly feminine domain, in peach and gray tones. The floor was oak and bare except for an off-white shag rug in front of the white brick fireplace in the living room.

She was almost all the way down before she remembered her bare feet and the loose tails of her oversize top. She hesitated, then shrugged. Her questions couldn't wait.

At the bottom step, she rushed into speech. "What happened, Jess? Terry seems dazed. Her forehead... How badly is she hurt?"

He reached for her, and with his hand on her arm, he urged her toward the kitchen. "Since you practically run a way station," he said, "could I beg a cup of coffee while I give you all the details? I've had a long day."

"Of course," she murmured, feeling a little tingle where he touched her. She motioned him to a stool and turned to start the coffee. "Please, have a seat."

Jess sat half on, half off the stool, and his eyes followed her as she poured water into the coffee maker. She accomplished the task with practiced ease, utterly unmindful of her bare feet, he noted, amused. When she was done, she wiped a few loose grounds and a little puddle off the counter, then turned to him. "Did she take any drugs to-night?"

"Only the one I gave her for nausea."

"Nausea? Why was she sick? What about that bandage on her head? And how did you get involved?"

He patted the stool beside him. "Come over here and sit while the coffee brews." He waited until she was perched on the stool, her toes curled around the bottom rung, then he said, "First of all, she's okay, Carly. She was nauseous because she'd been drinking."

Carly sighed, not surprised.

"She upchucked everything," he said, smiling. "Which is probably a good thing. Maybe she'll remember the price for getting drunk."

"I knew it. I was afraid she was going to get into trouble if—" She looked into his eyes. "But that still doesn't explain how you come in."

"I was on duty when they brought her in with an older boy," he explained. "He was driving. Apparently he lost control and rammed a pole on the Esplanade median. Terry's forehead was cut by a piece of flying glass. Fortunately, she wasn't concussive. The boy did get a pretty good bump, so we had to admit him overnight."

Carly pressed the fingers of one hand over her mouth. This wasn't the first time one of her kids had met with disaster after too much beer or worse. Still, it never failed to unnerve her. "She has stitches, I suppose."

"Six."

Carly shook her head helplessly. "I guess it's no surprise. She was so upset today, feeling as though there was no one to turn to—" She gave a startled "Oh!" then said, "Her mother, I'll have to call—"

"There's no need," Jess said, pushing away from the stool and reaching for the coffeepot. Using the two cups Carly had ready, he filled both and handed one to her, nudging the sugar bowl toward her with a raised brow. Carly was hardly even aware of how easily he'd assumed the role of host.

"Her mother couldn't be reached," he said, sitting down again, "so we called her older sister. Terry insisted on coming here instead of going to either one of them, and since I knew you were expecting her, I volunteered to drive her over. The sister agreed."

"Thank you. I'm glad you happened to be there and that you remembered."

For the first time since she'd opened the door, she smiled at him, and Jess felt an unexpected rush of pleasure. Inwardly he admitted that his behavior tonight was totally out of character. He wasn't in the habit of rescuing runaway teens. He wasn't in the habit of rescuing anybody. His philosophy of noninvolvement was all-encompassing. He still hadn't stopped to analyze why he'd acted as he had. It had been risky and highly unprofessional of him to remove her from the hospital when he'd been the attending physician in the emergency room. But when he'd discovered her name and that she was a student at Padgett, he'd known immediately that she was the girl Carly had been expecting.

He glanced up to find Carly studying him over the rim of her coffee cup. Maybe it was fate. After all, the girl had practically landed on his doorstep. And having Carly's near green eyes looking at him that way without the censuring criticism he'd seen in them the first time he had met her was worth a little extra effort. Hell, he might as well be honest: he'd *seized* the opportunity to bring Terry to Carly. He *wanted* Carly to feel indebted to him.

"What is it?" he asked, reading the question in her eyes.

"I'm just wondering how many other times you have

personally rescued a runaway teenager,'' she said with a knowing lift of one delicate brow.

He shrugged and tasted the coffee. ''Not many.''

''How many?''

Jess put the cup down and stared into her eyes. ''Let's just say this was a special occasion. I knew from the phone conversation this morning that relations between Terry and her family were strained. I figured you would be the best one to help her.''

She nodded slowly, still watching him.

He crossed one knee over the other, idly toying with the coffee cup. ''Now if you can just figure out a way to smooth relations between Mike and me, I'll know for sure that you're an honest-to-God miracle worker.''

Sympathetically, she said, ''Things didn't go too well at lunch today?''

''No.''

Carly sighed. No details. Just no. Father and son were remarkably alike, whether they'd spent much time together or not. Neither wasted words. She studied his face—as much as she could see of it behind his cup—but his expression told her nothing. She swallowed her impatience. As with Mike, getting this man to talk was going to be like pulling teeth. Still, she was intrigued. He had to have come to her for a reason. Apparently he wanted her to dig it out of him.

''So what happened with Mike?''

''Nothing,'' he said shortly. ''That's just it.''

''You mean you two didn't get into a meaningful dialogue over fries and Big Macs?'' she said with just the tiniest bit of sarcasm. The man was totally self-contained, so much so that Carly wondered whether he could ever find the words to express himself, even if he wanted to.

He looked at her. ''We didn't get into any kind of dialogue. Every word he said I had to pry out of him.''

Carly laughed, but Jess wasn't in a mood to appreciate life's ironies.

He shrugged. "It makes me wonder if it's a lost cause."

Carly tucked a bare foot under her. "Wait a minute. Has it occurred to you that you're being a bit unrealistic? You admit you've seen very little of Mike in the past few years and haven't talked to him on a one-to-one basis since he was a little kid. You wouldn't expect very much in the way of intimacy from a friend you'd just been reunited with after all that time, would you?"

Without waiting for a reply, she went on. "Mike has a lot of tangled emotions to sort out before the two of you can begin to act like an ordinary father and son, Jess. He needs time to get to know you before he can feel at ease with you."

"I feel like a stranger to my own son, Carly."

"It must seem that way," she agreed, "but it's hardly surprising considering he's lived the past ten years of his life in California, and you've been here."

"I should have spent more time with him when he was a little kid," Jess said bleakly. "But I thought..."

Carly held her breath, waiting. Tonight Jess didn't sound like a man who'd callously sidestepped his responsibilities as a father. Intuitively she knew the regret and pain in his voice was genuine, and, true to her nature, she responded to his need. She wanted to understand what had happened to alienate this man from the son he obviously loved. He might consider her questions out of line, but she didn't think he would. If he hadn't wanted to talk about his difficulties with Mike, then surely he wouldn't have brought them up.

"Until Mike moved back here, how long had it been since you'd seen him?" she asked.

"Not so often in the past three years," he said, glancing into her eyes when she nodded knowingly. He laughed shortly. "Yeah, I know I hardly sound like a model father, but I swear to God, it seemed the best way. A few weekends here and there was about all I could manage without causing a major confrontation. Lianne—"

"Is that his mother, your ex-wife?"

"Yeah, we—" He stopped, then clamped a hand around the tight muscles in his neck. "Look, you probably don't want to hear this. Hell, all you do every day is listen to the problems of kids and their screwed-up parents."

She smiled. "Usually the parents describe it the other way around," she said, explaining when he looked blank, "Usually it's the kids who are screwed up, according to their bewildered parents."

"Well, this time you may have stumbled onto a double problem," he said darkly. "Screwed up parent and kid."

"Usually both are," she assured him, "only neither wants to admit it."

They exchanged a long look, then both smiled slightly. Carly watched as Jess toyed with the now empty coffee cup. His hands were well shaped, with long fingers and immaculate nails. He stroked the cup absently, and Carly remembered the feel of his fingers around her arm as he'd ushered her into the kitchen. How would it feel to be stroked all over by those sensitive hands? she wondered.

"Would you like a drink?" she asked quickly, before her thoughts got completely out of hand. "It's a little late for more coffee."

He pushed his coffee cup firmly aside. "God, yes," he said instantly.

She slid off the stool and opened a cabinet door. "Let's see...Scotch, bourbon, white wine... I don't keep much on hand, just the basics."

"Scotch," he said, watching when she stretched to reach the bottle, her baggy top hiking up. She must be one of those women who got comfortable the moment she came through her door, he thought. She looked beat, and well she might, coping with teenagers all day. With her shirt out and no panty hose on, she looked soft and slightly blurred at the edges. And sexy. She looked very sexy. He felt desire stirring, heavy and deep, inside him.

He felt himself relaxing, letting the frantic pace of his workday slip to the back of his mind. That hardly ever happened. Lately he was finding it more and more difficult to remove himself from the violence and sheer waste of human life he dealt with at the hospital every day. How long had it been since he'd actually relaxed in the company of a woman? Absently he took the drink she offered, tilting the glass toward her before taking a healthy belt.

"Let's go sit somewhere more comfortable," she suggested, motioning him toward the living room with the wineglass she'd just filled for herself.

Jess came off the stool with an easy movement, glad to follow her to the invitingly feminine room he'd glimpsed earlier. Evidence of her passion for collectibles was everywhere. There were carved seabirds on the mantel, a bisque magnolia and some interesting paperweights on a glass table and twin cloisonné bowls on the coffee table. Glancing wistfully at the luxurious shag rug and the floor pillows in front of the fireplace, he settled on the sofa and wondered about her other passions. There would be time later to explore the secrets of Carly Sullivan, he decided, looking forward to the prospect.

"So, you and Mike have a lot to catch up on," Carly said, tucking both feet under her at the opposite end of the sofa.

He leaned back, studying her. "Are you sure you want to hear all this? It's not a particularly happy story."

"Maybe it can have a happy ending."

A happy ending. If he could have a place in Mike's life, that would be a happy ending. More than Carly could ever know, Jess wanted that. He stared at her and felt the lessons of a lifetime lock the words inside. He could hardly say something like that. Hell, already tonight he'd found himself saying things to this woman that made him sound like a stranger to himself.

"Were you very young when Mike was born?" Carly asked.

Jess took a deep breath and balanced his Scotch on one knee. "Lianne and I got married when we were in college." He stared into his drink then briefly at Carly. "But we made it through, which was something, I suppose. Then came medical school and my residency—longer and longer hours, stress. You've heard it all before. Lianne decided divorce was the answer."

Carly felt a pang of sympathy. No matter what the circumstances, she understood the pain of divorce.

"Mike was six years old. We had joint custody, but she got married again right away and moved to California."

The first hint of bitterness crept into his voice, and Carly wondered whether Lianne had found her second husband before or after walking away from Jess.

"I tried to hold it all together—being a long-distance father and working toward a speciality in trauma. It required a lot of hours in emergency. You see a lot of—" He broke off before giving her a clear picture of what he saw a lot of in emergency, but Carly had a good idea.

"I got to where I hated that flight to California."

"It is a long way from here," Carly murmured.

He nodded and drank some more Scotch, but Carly sensed that he was only half-aware of her. He seemed fixed on some inner picture, intent on seeing it clearly. "It wasn't only that. I didn't want to see Mike victimized by Lianne and me. My folks were divorced when I was very young. There was a lot of tugging back and forth."

"Many divorced parents manage to share their children,'' Carly said, sensing something besides the obvious problems of distance and the demands of Jess's job.

''How can I say this without sounding like a sore loser?'' Jess demanded. He turned to face her, one knee bent on the sofa. Carly could see the tension in him as his fingers closed around his ankle. ''I don't claim to be a psychologist, but it didn't take much insight to figure out what was going on. Lianne wanted to be married to a doctor, and when things didn't turn out as she planned, she felt cheated. My residency meant we had little time together and less money. The baby made a lot of demands, too. I think reality was far different from her expectations, and she blamed me. Whether she realized it or not, she communicated her resentment to Mike.''

''So rather than see Mike hurt the way you were by your own parents, you decided to let her have him,'' Carly guessed.

He seemed to consider that, frowning. ''It wasn't so much that I 'let her have him.' It just seemed best to keep a low profile.'' He laughed with open bitterness. ''I didn't count on being shut out totally, but that's what happened. Mike thinks I stopped loving him.''

''Children do tend to see things in black-and-white.''

''Yeah.'' The look he gave her was bleak. ''And how can you explain these things to a kid?''

Carly returned his gaze, turning over in her mind all the reasons she had already deemed it unwise to get involved in the problems of the Brannigan men. But as she stared into Jess's dark eyes and saw the genuine distress he felt over his son, she knew she would have a hard time keeping to her plan. What was it about these two that got to her so easily? First, she'd been tempted to console Mike when he'd pretended he hadn't been hurt by his father's rejection, and now here she was ready to console Jess—another victim.

"If it's any comfort," she heard herself saying, "kids are fairly perceptive if given enough time. Mike is hardly a toddler anymore. He's sixteen and will soon be mature enough to see life from the perspective of others. Instead of just seeing you as his parents, he'll see you and Lianne as individuals. When that happens, hopefully the lines of communication will open. Then he'll have some understanding of why you acted the way you did."

He stared at her. "You think so?"

Carly met his look, and something in his expression sent a little shiver down her spine. Suddenly she rose from the sofa. It was getting late; it was time to end this. "I've seen it happen before. I can't see any reason why you and Mike should be any different."

She didn't want to know any more about Jess Brannigan's past, didn't want any more insight into the reasons why he and his son were strangers. Such knowledge was dangerous; it enhanced his appeal when she was already too aware of him as a man. Almost irritably she looked down at him sprawled on her couch in his snug jeans. His casual black pullover was oversize and worn, but she could still see evidence of hard muscle and a sleek middle. Against the soft pastel sofa, he looked like a dark jungle predator in a rare moment of...vulnerability? Ridiculous! Predators were never vulnerable, were they?

Jess stood up, feeling slightly embarrassed. He didn't know what Carly's secret was, but without realizing it, he'd spent the evening basking in the warmth of her smile and spilling his guts. For a moment he felt an amused kinship with her other troubled adolescents. She was almost too good at what she did.

"I take it the way station and counseling service is shutting down for the night," he guessed with a half smile.

"I'm afraid so," she said, taking his empty glass and setting it down beside her own. "But I owe you one for

Terry, and I wish you luck with Mike. He's a wonderful boy, a son to be proud of."

They were at the door. Carly opened it with a purposeful air and stood aside slightly, waiting for him to come around her. He took only one step, stopped and looked down into her face. "Thank you for the drink," he said.

Her eyes wide, she froze as his hands went to the clip that confined her hair at the crown of her head. He snapped it open, and her thick hair fell free in an untamed mass. She made a move with one hand to catch it, but he stopped her.

"No, don't. Please. I wanted to see it down. It's beautiful," he said huskily. Using both hands, he sank his fingers into its softness.

Instantly Carly's heart started to pound, and her breath caught in her throat. He was so close that she could feel the heat of him, could smell his strangely intoxicating after-shave. Without her shoes, she was suddenly aware of the height and breadth of him and her own vulnerability.

"Jess—"

"And thank you for listening." He bent, almost touching her lips. His hands fixed her face just so.

"Oh, it was...I didn't..." The ability to express a coherent thought was lost while every nerve cell in her body strained in anticipation of the taste of Jess Brannigan. All other senses seemed heightened. The night was alive with smells and sounds. She breathed in the fragrance of jasmine and Jess's Scotch-scented breath, felt the press of the door frame against her hips, heard the sudden clang of the iron gate next door. And then footsteps.

Jess made a short profane sound and stepped back. For a moment or two, Carly couldn't move for the swift keen feeling of disappointment. They watched a couple stroll down the sidewalk, laughing and talking. A car door opened and closed. The man glanced over at Carly and Jess, waved casually, then got into the car and drove off.

Then Jess, too, was gone.

CHAPTER FIVE

DURING THE NEXT FEW DAYS, Carly alternated between thinking she might have misjudged Jess Brannigan and fearing that he was everything she'd originally thought. The former idea seemed to be winning out. There was his unexpected rescue of Terry to consider, as well as Carly's new knowledge of his divorce and his dilemma over Mike. Now that she knew firsthand how he and Mike had come to be so far apart, she was filled with compassion. For both. Nevertheless, she still felt cautious about getting any closer to either one of them. No matter how hard she tried to shrug it off, that last couple of minutes at her door stuck in her mind. She'd wanted to experience Jess's kiss, even though he was the kind of man she had carefully avoided since her divorce.

Friday finally came and with it, the first session of the grand jury. If she'd been thinking she had misjudged him, the very first case quickly disabused her of the notion.

She arrived a few minutes early and took her seat behind the dais, as instructed, telling herself the heightened anticipation that had been with her since the moment she had woken up that morning was due entirely to being on the grand jury. Never mind the flutter in her midsection when she looked up into the dark eyes of Jess who was virilely attractive in a forest-green polo shirt and seated directly across the dais from her.

Rich dark colors enhanced his dusky coloring, Carly decided. Glancing around, she saw that she wasn't the only woman who'd noticed. Michelle Bordelon, one of the three other women jurors, wore an expression of indisguised approval in her huge liquid brown eyes. Even Mrs. Cohn, who wasn't a day under seventy, wasn't immune.

"My, he's certainly a good-looking rogue, isn't he?" the old lady commented, craning her white head slightly to look past John Hebert, who was handing out copies of the docket to each juror. Elizabeth Cohn might have been seventy-odd years old and her bones brittle to the point of creaking slightly when she stood after a "spell of sitting," as she put it, but her mind was as alert as ever.

"Who, Mrs. Cohn?" Carly asked, her eyes on the docket she had just been given.

"Why, Brannigan, of course," the old lady retorted. "I've looked them all over, and he's the pick of the lot, take my word for it, darlin'."

Mrs. Cohn had married and buried four husbands, she'd informed an amazed Carly that first day, which probably accounted for her habit of eyeing all men as potential mates. Carly was saved from having to reply when Hebert rapped sharply on the surface in front of him and, satisfied that he had the attention of the jurors, announced that Dr. Jess Brannigan was to be jury foreman for the duration of their term. The appointment had been made by the judge, they were told, and aside from a few looks and shrugs, the choice seemed to provoke no objections. Hebert nodded briskly, then began to outline the facts in the first case.

"Okay, gang," he said, his gaze roving over the twelve faces turned to him expectantly, "this first one may turn out to be a trial by fire." He held up an apologetic hand at the good-natured groans. "Sorry 'bout that. We have here a charge of first-degree murder against Martha Jean Owens. On September 25, Martha Jean went into the bedroom, where her husband, James Earl Owens, lay reading on their bed. She pointed his own gun at him and shot him.''

Hebert paused while the jurors absorbed the facts, then continued. ''In the statement she gave to the investigating officer, she claimed she could no longer cope with his abuse.'' He looked around at the jurors. ''Any questions?''

''That's it? That's all?'' said Joe West.

''Except for what Martha Jean might have to say for herself, yeah, that's it,'' Hebert said.

''Is she going to testify?'' Michelle asked in her husky voice. ''I didn't think we could question the person charged.''

''In this instance, Martha Jean asked to be heard personally,'' Hebert replied. ''Her lawyer, who was appointed by the court, incidentally, will be stationed outside should she desire to consult him, but you're free to ask her anything. She knows her rights and understands them.''

The jurors were silent while Hebert went to the door and summoned Martha Jean Owens. Carly sat still, shocked by John Hebert's brief recitation of the facts. When the woman entered and sat down in the chair, Carly took in the pale skin and dull look in her eyes, and felt a swift rush of compassion. This woman didn't look like a murderer. She looked more like a victim.

To put her at ease, John asked her a few casual questions. How old was she? Thirty-one. Carly sucked in a little breath. The woman looked fifty. How long had she and James been married? Fourteen years. Did she have children? Two: a boy of thirteen and a girl of twelve. Where did she live? In the lake district. Address? She gave it, looking at her hands. Her fingers, Carly noticed, were twisted together tightly.

''Tell us in your own words,'' John requested gently, ''exactly what happened the afternoon of September 25.''

The woman's gaze remained on her hands a few seconds, then she raised her head. Carly noticed again how tired and strained the woman appeared. Her expression was almost blank. She glanced at a juror or two, but Carly had a feeling she wasn't really seeing anyone. "I'm sorry I shot James," she said in a barely audible tone, "but I swear I didn't see any other way."

John gently requested that she speak up.

Her mouth trembled, but she nodded. "That day started like every other day, with James badgering and criticizing. He's a diabetic, and I gave him his needle, as usual. It was my day to go to the library, so I got on my bicycle and went. On the way back, I witnessed an accident at the intersection, and the police detained me. That caused me to be forty-three minutes late."

"Forth-three minutes," John repeated with a puzzled look. "Were you on some kind of schedule?"

"I guess you could say that. You see, James let me go to the library twice a month. He figured out exactly how long it would take me to ride there, choose four books and then ride home." Unaware of the incredulity on the faces of the jurors, she mopped her eyes with a tissue. "Because of the accident, I was late and he ranted and raved about it, accusing me of all kinds of things. Everything was always in front of the children, too."

"Go on, Mrs. Owens."

"Jacob—he's my son—went outside and was working on the lawn mower. He came to the door and asked me to help him for a second, to hold something in place while he tightened it. The man who lives next door came over and was talking to us, you know, just passing the time of day like neighbors do. My husband yelled at me to come inside. He called me a filthy name in front of our neighbor and my son." Her hands stilled in her lap, her gaze focused inwardly as though viewing a scene inside her head, preparing to relate it for the benefit of the jurors.

"I came inside and stood there while he cursed me and accused me of unspeakable shameful things. I know my little girl heard him, because I could hear her crying in her room. Then James said he was going to take a nap, so he went into the bedroom and closed the door. I went to the kitchen and got his gun out of the drawer, then I sat down in the living room and thought for a while." She raised her head and stared directly into John Hebert's eyes. "My children were already scarred for life. They had no friends, and they weren't allowed to socialize because no one was good enough for us, according to James. I was a prisoner in my own home." She shrugged fatalistically, dropping her gaze to her hands again, her head bowed. "This was just one instance—there were a thousand other similar ones. None of us was ever going to be happy as long as James was alive."

"And then?" John prompted, his voice quiet.

"I checked to see that the gun was loaded," she said softly. "Then I stood up and walked to the bedroom door. It was closed. I stood there a long time—I don't know how long. Then I opened it and pointed the gun at James lying there. He looked up, surprised to see the gun. Then he sat up and put his hand out. 'Don't be a fool,' he said. 'You're too stupid to get away with it, anyway.'" She drew an unsteady breath. "That was when I shot him."

A tiny shocked silence fell over to the jurors, who were trying to fathom the desperation that could drive a person to commit such a drastic and ultimately self-destructive act.

Hebert looked at them. "Does anyone have a question for Mrs. Owens?"

Joe West cleared his throat. "Uh, Mrs. Owens, exactly how did your husband abuse you?"

Carly felt a spurt of indignation. How indeed! Constant

criticism and demeaning of the woman's self-esteem might not be physical abuse, but it was just as cruel.

"He was a tyrant, sir. He ruled our home as a dictator. No one was allowed any opinion unless it coincided with his."

"But did he ever beat you, physically hurt you in any way?"

Her eyes fell to her hands in her lap. "It does hurt to have your pride and self-respect trampled every waking moment and your children bullied."

"Did you ever consider counseling, Mrs. Owens?" Carly asked.

"He would never have allowed it," she said hollowly. "Once I brought one of those self-help books home from the library—one about women and assertiveness. It enraged him. He took it back to the library himself."

"You said you gave him his insulin, as usual," Carly said. "Did you always administer his needles?"

"Yes, he refused to do it," the woman said.

"If you wanted him dead," Jess said, "you could have given him an overdose of insulin, or given him a placebo and induced shock. No one would have been the wiser, and you would have been free."

She sat mute.

"Why didn't you do that?" he asked.

"It just wouldn't have been right."

"I SAY IT'S MURDER, plain and simple."

"But the woman suffered almost fifteen years of cruelty at this man's hands," Carly argued, weary of Joe West's unsympathetic attitude. After hearing all of Mrs. Owens's testimony and that of two other character witnesses, the jury was in closed session to decide whether or not to indict.

"Maybe not plain and simple," Jess put in mildly, "but murder all the same."

Carly threw him an indignant look. "Do you think this woman should be locked up after all she's been through?"

"I wouldn't like to see it," Jess retorted, "but you can't just go around shooting people who provoke you."

"He's right," Joe West said flatly.

Carly tapped her pen against the legal pad each juror had been issued to make notes on. The personalities of the jurors were already shaping up. Jess Brannigan was a pragmatic man who saw things in black-and-white terms, as did most of the other men on the jury. The women seemed more willing to consider extenuating circumstances. Recalling Martha Jean Owens's defeated demeanor, Carly couldn't believe that incarceration was the right answer. What would be the point? The woman was not a danger to society.

Forty minutes later there was no unanimous verdict, to the obvious disgust of Joe West and Colonel George Buckley, a retired U.S. Marine. Jess, as jury foreman, marked his legal form accordingly.

The group was still debating the case at lunch in a closed dining room at a restaurant within walking distance from the courthouse. Two other cases had been heard and quickly acted upon by the jury. One concerned a fatal stabbing in a bar, the other, a vehicular homicide by a drunk driver. Although Carly thought she'd been prepared for grim details, she found her appetite for lunch almost nonexistent.

To make matters worse, she and Jess were seated side by side, a circumstance Jess had maneuvered somehow. There wasn't much elbowroom, and Carly was keenly aware of the occasional brush of his arm against hers and the scent of after-shave drifting her way when he moved.

And he moved frequently, first reaching across her for cream for his coffee, then for sugar.

"This may be the longest six months of your life, if you're going to take every case personally," Jess said to her when the waiter appeared with their trout amandine.

"How can you hear a woman like Martha Jean Owens and not be touched?" Carly demanded. "She's not a criminal. She was so browbeaten by her husband that she couldn't see any alternative."

"I agree," Jess said, picking up his knife and fork. "But our purpose isn't to psychoanalyze her, Carly. It's to apply the law."

"I don't believe the law was intended to punish people like Mrs. Owens. There's such a thing as compassion."

"Tell it to the poor sap she emptied that thirty-eight into," Jess said dryly.

"He deserved it!"

"Irrelevant."

Carly was suddenly aware of the silence at the table as the jurors listened with unabashed interest. She swallowed hard and attacked the trout. It was stupid to get into an argument with someone whose philosophy of life simply wasn't compatible with her own. She certainly didn't condone a woman shooting her husband, but she could identify with the woman's despair. Words could hurt just as much as a bullet to the heart.

"You're a miserable failure in bed and out of it." Carly clenched her fingers on her glass as she recalled the painful words, then she quickly drank. The ice water didn't chill her half as much as the old memory....

"Colonel Buckley," Mrs. Cohn spoke up when the silence threatened to stretch out too long. "I understand that you live in a house in the Quarter that has a fascinating history. A refuge for Southern sympathizers during the Civil War, wasn't it?"

The colonel cleared his throat and began to expound on the colorful background of his house. Carly heard none of it. Instead, she kept her eyes on her plate—even though she was only pushing her food around, wondering if Jess Brannigan was going to trigger memories better left behind. If so, the next six months would be no picnic.

"My ears are burning."

Carly froze as Jess's warm breath touched the sensitive nerves in her ear and sent a sharp tremor all the way through her. The words were a mere whisper, meant only for her. She looked around warily, but everyone seemed engrossed in the story of the colonel's house.

"Why don't we just agree to disagree, Dr. Brannigan," she said.

He appeared to think that over. "I wouldn't want to be too hasty. There are some things we might get together on."

"I can't imagine what they could be!" She glanced up and met the look in his eye. Immediately she felt her face heat up.

"Not that," he drawled, his dark eyes gleaming. "Although the idea certainly has appeal."

"Dr. Brannigan—"

He touched her arm. "Jess. Eat your lunch, Carly. At the rate your heart bleeds, you're going to need lots of nourishment to face the rest of today's docket."

The waiter appeared just then with a variety of rich desserts, which they both refused. Jess stood up, and with his hand under her elbow, Carly found herself on her feet with him. He said something to John Hebert, and then, piloting Carly in front of him, they went through the main dining room and out a pair of French doors into a shady courtyard.

"Just what do you think you're doing?" Carly demanded as soon as they were alone.

"I wanted a few minutes alone with you, and it didn't look as if I was going to get an opportunity. And by the time we're finished today, you'll be tired and ready to go home."

"A few minutes for what? And for your information, I'm used to being asked when someone wants to talk to me. In the future, please try to remember that. I don't like being railroaded in front of other people."

"And do we have a future, Carly?" His gaze caught and held hers. "I apologize for my lack of finesse, but it probably saved five minutes of debate." His eyebrow arched. "You seem determined to argue with everything I say today."

She sighed. "Get to the point, Jess," she said. "What is this all about?"

He glanced at an ornate iron bench. "Can we sit a minute?"

Without a word, she walked over and sat down.

After dropping down beside her, Jess seemed at a loss for words. He shifted so that he was in the corner of the bench facing her. "I saw Mike again Monday night."

As usual when the subject was Mike, she sensed a difference in him, a hesitancy almost, that contrasted oddly with his personality as she'd come to know it. In every phase of his life, she suspected he had more than his share of self-confidence. He was a physician and a good one. He was a natural leader. He'd easily won the jurors' confidence and had effortlessly taken charge that morning. Aside from his professional expertise and his charisma, she suspected that he could also have any woman he chose.

And yet, when the subject was Mike...

"He really admires you, you know."

"What?"

"Mike. To him you're 'pretty special.'" Jess flashed her

a grin that was reminiscent of his son's. "That's a direct quote."

She dismissed the compliment with a wave of her hand. "It isn't too difficult to win the approval of teenagers. They're so used to being tolerated or maligned or simply ignored, that when someone is willing to listen, or even go so far as to consider their opinion, they often overreact." She smiled at him. "I remember when I was just discovering boys. All the teen magazines suggested that the best way to get a boy to like you was to listen to him, engage him in conversation about things he was interested in. It's not very original, but it still works. I do it every day."

"I don't believe it's an act with you," Jess said. "I think you sincerely like the kids you work with, and they sense it and respond."

She shrugged, her fingers idly tracing the lacy pattern of the iron bench. "What does this have to do with anything, Jess?"

Jess reminded himself that what he wanted from Carly Sullivan was help in winning his son back. Though he found her far more desirable than anyone he'd met in a long time—and very different from the sophisticated, sexually experienced type he was used to—she was definitely skittish and wary around him. He sensed something fragile about her, something wary in the way she responded, almost as though she was aware of him as a man but was determined to deny it. He would take it one step at a time. Mike was the first priority here.

Finding the look of her distracting, he rose from the bench and took a few steps. "I can't think of any way to lead up to this," he said, turning and capturing her gaze. "I need a favor, Carly. A big favor."

Carly leaned back, her eyes wary. "What kind of favor?"

"It has to do with Mike."

"What about him?"

Jess drew in a deep breath. "Mike and I have grown so far apart that I sometimes think only a miracle could fix everything." He looked at her. "I need you to help me, Carly. Mike knows you and likes you. I can tell that he's taken with Penny, and he'll be spending a lot of time at her house. You're right next door."

"You seem to have gleaned a lot of information on Monday night," Carly said dryly.

"I pumped it for all it was worth," Jess admitted.

Carly was vaguely aware of the sounds that intruded around them: the crash of a dish in the kitchen, an angry exchange in the service alley behind them, the distant wail of a riverboat.

"So what do you say, Carly? Will you help me?"

Carly rose from the bench, not looking at him. With every shred of intuition and all the caution in her soul, she knew she ought to make up some excuse and flatly refuse to be a part of any scheme that allowed for such intimacy with Jess Brannigan. Everything about him marked him as someone she should steer clear of. His personal life was a mess. Not only had his marriage failed, but he was so emotionally inept that he was alienated from his own son.

Unfortunately, she seemed to be drawn to Jess in spite of everything. Already he had touched a deeply buried part of her. Somehow he had breached defenses that had remained firm and tight for more than three years, closed to the many other men she'd met. And without ever even putting a hand on her, she thought wryly. Or did that near kiss at her door count? If ever he did kiss her, how would it feel? she wondered.

"What do you want me to do?" she asked, looking at him over her shoulder. She could see his relief, and something more. "I mean, exactly what is it you're asking?"

"Nothing major," he reassured her quickly, "so you don't have to look like that. I haven't even thought it out myself." He started pacing back and forth in front of her. "I guess being in close proximity to Mike as much as I can be is probably the best way to go."

"Exactly how do I figure in this?" Carly asked, still skeptical. Somehow reassurance coming from Jess didn't ease her mind.

He shrugged, still pacing. "Like I said, I don't have any particular strategy worked out. Just don't slam the door in my face if I happen to drop by your house."

"Well..."

"Frequently."

"Oh, Jess...."

He stopped in front of her. "Basically you don't have any objection to helping me out with Mike, do you?"

"Not really, I guess." Through the French doors, she could see the other jurors rising, getting ready to leave.

He caught her hand as she rose and guided her over the uneven patio. "I'll be over about seven-thirty tonight," he said.

Her eyes flew up to his. "What!"

"Tonight, seven-thirty," he repeated patiently.

Things were moving too quickly. She'd been exposed to only a fraction of this man's charm, she suspected, but it was enough to throw up warning signals in her wary soul. She must be crazy!

"Or is that too early? We'll go somewhere for dinner. How about Occhipinti's in Metairie?"

"Wait a minute. Has it occurred to you I might already have a date?" She watched as his dark brows came together. For heaven's sake, did he think he could just move in on her life lock, stock and barrel, with her hardly noticing?

"Do you?"

She pulled at her hand, still captured in his. ''As it happens, I do,'' she said.

Clearly disappointed, he released her hand.

''I have a standing pizza date on Fridays,'' Carly heard herself explaining, ''with Rachel Lasseigne.''

His gaze narrowed. ''Penny's mother?''

''Penny's mother.''

''I suppose it's a closed club,'' he ventured, but looked hopeful anyway.

Shaking her head, Carly sighed, feeling a smile begin. ''My place, around seven.'' She'd definitely been right about the power of his charm. Unleashed, it could be lethal.

''I'll bring the pizza,'' he volunteered.

''There's no need—''

He waved her to silence. ''I insist.''

He bent to open the door for her. ''See you tonight,'' he said, his mouth actually brushing her ear. That, she told herself, was the reason for the shiver that streaked down her spine.

CHAPTER SIX

CARLY HAD ALL the hours from midafternoon until evening to consider the pitfalls of getting involved with Jess Brannigan. She had promised him her help in mending his fences with Mike. That was it, pure and simple—or so she kept telling herself. But upon rethinking her impulsive offer, she found herself getting more and more nervous. This nagging sense of impending...something, was ridiculous.

Easy to say, she decided, hurriedly pulling on jeans and a dusty peach top, with one eye on the clock. It was silly to feel so threatened by the situation. Jess's interest in her stemmed from his determination to win back his son. It was nothing personal. She was simply a means to an end, a way to bridge the gap between him and Mike.

She should at least feel comfortable about her ability to help him do that, she thought, frowning into her mirrored reflection. She was a professional counselor, after all. But doubts had been nagging at her all day. What did she truly know of the secrets of a successful relationship? Oh, she knew all the right words, the right moves according to the textbooks, but all the communication skills in the universe hadn't provided the right answers when she'd needed them to deal with her own crumbling marriage. She'd failed abysmally there. Who was she to show Jess how to make it work with Mike?

But was that all it was? She'd never before gotten into anything quite as provocative as this with a parent. Maybe the problem was simply Jess, she admitted with sneaky honesty. He'd already breached the careful line she always drew between the personal and the professional.

She sighed, both hands poised to fix a clip in her hair. She was certain about one thing—she didn't want to provoke anything except professional interest and respect from Jess. That was the extent of her appeal as far as men like him were concerned, anyway. She had the practical experience to back up her belief, thanks to Buck Sullivan and three years of misery. She'd learned her lesson well.

The doorbell rang and, tossing the clip on the top of her dresser, she gave up the effort to style her untamed mane. "The heck with it. What you see is what you get," she muttered, unaware of the sensual appeal of her hair left in soft wild disarray.

It was Rachel, not Jess, at the door. "We're in for some nasty weather," her friend said, stepping inside and shedding her jacket. A rumble of thunder could be heard in the distance. "We should order right away before the downpour begins, otherwise the streets might flood and who knows how long it will be before we eat. I'm starved!"

"We don't have to order," Carly informed her, resigned to the inevitable questions. "I, uh…someone else is coming."

Halted in the act of hanging up her jacket, Rachel eyed Carly curiously over her shoulder. "Great, someone's treating us? Who?"

Before Carly could reply, the bell sounded again and Rachel, who was closest, pulled the door open.

"Carly forgot to tell me we had dates," Rachel quipped, stepping aside and motioning Jess, who was bearing two giant-size pizzas, inside. On his heels, another broad-shouldered, dark-haired man entered the small foyer. It was Kyle Stratton. To Carly, the sight of two large wholly masculine men invading her feminine domain was slightly unnerving.

"Hello, Jess," she said, hoping her smile didn't betray her edginess.

"Carly." His voice was deep and vibrant, his mouth tilted in a half smile.

Tearing her gaze from his, she quickly turned to his companion. "Hi, Kyle." She smiled warmly and with easy familiarity into Kyle's gray eyes.

"I ran into Kyle getting out of his car at the curb," Jess explained. "He assured me he has a standing invitation to Friday night pizza."

"I usually have to spring for it when I crash this club," Kyle said in his soft drawl.

"I thought you were in Baton Rouge!" Rachel exclaimed to Kyle, obviously pleased. She reached for their jackets.

"I was. I got in about an hour ago."

Carly divided a look between Jess and Kyle. "Do you two know each other?"

"Wait, let me guess," Rachel said. "It's professional, right? Kyle is in homicide and Jess is a trauma surgeon. How could they not know each other in this town?" she tacked on dryly.

"You guessed it," Kyle said, smiling with the warmth he always displayed to Rachel. "I'm impressed."

"It was elementary," Rachel returned with a smug look, grinning.

Aware of Jess standing silently at her side, still holding the pizzas, Carly suddenly came to life. "Rachel, you haven't actually been introduced. Jess, meet my friend Rachel Lasseigne. Rachel, Jess Brannigan, Mike's father."

Rachel put out her hand. "Hello, Jess. Even if I hadn't seen you and Mike together in the hall on Monday, I would have guessed who you were. Your son bears a remarkable resemblance to you."

Balancing the pizza, Jess took her hand and smiled into

her eyes. "I understand Mike has had an immediate change of heart regarding chemistry, thanks to your daughter."

"Speaking of Penny, where is she tonight?" Carly asked, reminding herself of Jess's real reason for being there. She knew the kids were probably together. Chances were they'd drop in before too long, and Jess wouldn't have wasted a whole evening.

Rachel laughed. "Would you believe studying?" Her dark brows rose at three skeptical looks. "I'm only repeating what I was told, folks. They're at the Superdome watching a demonstration of a new source of energy invented by some guy in Mississippi." She gave Jess a straight look. "It was Mike's idea."

"Yeah."

"Right."

Both men spoke at the same time, and everyone laughed.

"It's true," Carly said, feeling compelled to defend the kids. "I saw it on the morning news. Maybe it's more physics than chemistry, but they could be doing a lot worse."

"Yeah."

"Right."

Rachel laughed again as everyone watched color wash over Carly's face. "Okay, you two, stop teasing! You might make Carly mad, and she's like a tiger when it comes to defending the kids."

"I can't wait to get a personal demonstration." Jess's low tone at her ear stroked over her senses like a caress. She was beginning to think breathing into her ears was one of his favorite things.

"Hey," Kyle rubbed his hands together briskly and motioned toward the boxes Jess held. "I'm ready to attack that pizza. I just hope you ladies didn't forget the beer again."

"Oh, Kyle, I did forget it," Carly said, still slightly breathless from Jess's seductive taunt. Why was she so susceptible to the most casual come-on from him? "I've got wine but not much else, I'm afraid. Jess finished the Scotch Monday night." The words were out before she realized how they sounded.

Groaning inwardly, she saw Kyle and Rachel turn identical speculative looks on Jess. She glanced over for his reaction and felt like pinching him. Above the two pizza boxes, he was giving her a look that could only have been called provocative.

Rachel, eyeing the glint in Carly's eye, quickly spoke up. "There's a six-pack in my refrigerator. It'll just take a second to run and pick it up." She glanced at Kyle. "Want to come with me?"

He reached for their jackets. "What do you think, woman? It's dark outside. You just try to go out there alone—even if you are just next door."

"ARE THEY LOVERS?"

Carly raised startled eyes to Jess as the door closed behind Rachel and Kyle. "No! Not that it's any of your business."

He backed up with mock haste. "Uh-oh, does the best friend come under the protection of the little tigress, too?"

"That is not funny," Carly said with chilly annoyance. "Rachel doesn't need me to defend her. Or Kyle. They're two of the nicest people I've ever known."

Still holding the two pizza boxes, Jess subjected her to a narrow-eyed study. "What is it with you, Carly?"

"What does that mean?"

"This is the twentieth century. The fact that your friends may be having an affair isn't going to change the way I think of them one way or the other. Kyle Stratton is already a man I respect and admire, and Rachel seems like a nice woman.'' He shrugged. ''I know it's none of my business whether they sleep together. But they seem close, almost like a married couple. So I just wondered.''

''They seem close because they are,'' she said, feeling stung but not quite certain why. Did he see her as a prude? ''Kyle was Phillip's best friend,'' she explained. ''All three—Rachel, Phillip and Kyle—went to high school together right here in this neighborhood.''

''Phillip?''

''Phillip Lasseigne, Rachel's husband. He was killed about ten months ago by a thief in the French Quarter.''

Jess swore softly. ''My God, that's rough.''

''Yes.''

''You say Kyle was there?''

''Not exactly. At least he wasn't an eyewitness. They'd had dinner together but had come in separate cars. Kyle and his date were getting into theirs a block or so away.''

''Was the killer ever found?''

She shook her head. ''Never. Not even a hint of a lead surfaced. Naturally Kyle was obsessed with finding him, but there just wasn't anything to go on except Rachel's efforts to pick the guy out of the mug books, which turned up nothing. Since then, Kyle has been there for Rachel and Penny. So I guess you could say that they are close.''

One dark brow lifted knowingly. ''That explains the vibes I got in that round of introductions.''

''Oh?''

''A man always recognizes another's territorial signals,'' Jess said dryly. Shifting suddenly, he said, ''Am I going to stand here all night with these two pizzas?''

She made a startled noise and gestured to the living room. ''I'm sorry! Put them down on the table in front of the sofa, and I'll get glasses and napkins. Just make yourself at home. I'll only be a minute."

He put the cartons down where she directed and immediately followed her to the kitchen, watching as she bent to open a cabinet. "He's a little overprotective."

She straightened. "What?"

He lifted one shoulder. "Stratton. He wouldn't let her run across the yard alone in the dark."

Carly raked him over with a look. "Rachel witnessed her husband's murder on a dark rainy night, Jess. For months she wouldn't venture outside at night at all. She's only now beginning to conquer that fear."

He was immediately apologetic. "I guess I'm so used to the graphic results of street violence that I sometimes lose sight of the problems of the other victims. It's no excuse."

"It's probably a method of self-protection," Carly said, slipping easily into professional jargon. After all, that was what he wanted from her, wasn't it? She slammed a drawer shut. Fine. Then why didn't she confine herself to that role? the voice of reason mocked. She wasn't certain how he managed to provoke her so easily. "In a job like yours, the burnout rate must be high." She opened and closed a couple of cabinets with less force, looking for a serving tray.

Jess grunted without commenting and took the tray from her, not particularly pleased to have her applying psychology to him. It was okay as far as Mike was concerned, but that wasn't what he wanted from Carly. He shoved the tray onto the countertop, aware that he wasn't certain exactly what he did want from Carly Sullivan, beyond the obvious, naturally. He'd known from day one that he wanted to take her to bed. But there was something about her that made him hesitate to launch a straightforward attempt to seduce her—aside from the fact that he didn't want to complicate matters before this thing with Mike was resolved. She seemed...vulnerable, somehow. There was an air of innocence about her that was damn near as effective in deterring him as virginity would have been.

Chiding himself for being tempted by the outward appearance of a woman, and knowing from bitter experience how little appearance had to do with reality, Jess leaned against the counter and watched Carly organize things on the tray. She'd been irritated with him only seconds before, but there was little evidence of anger now. He liked watching her, studying the quick, utterly feminine way she moved around her kitchen. *She should be doing these little chores every night for her own family,* he thought. Was that why she had so much time for the kids? What did she get out of it? he wondered. Teenagers could be a hell of a headache. What motivated her? Frustrated maternal needs?

"Where's your houseguest?" he asked abruptly.

Carly was stretched on tiptoe reaching for wineglasses on top of the refrigerator. She turned to look at him over her shoulder. "You mean Terry?"

"You haven't taken anyone else in, have you?"

She bounced a little, trying to reach the glasses. "Oh!" Her heart leaped a little as Jess's hands clasped her waist, and he gently moved her aside. Breathless and flustered, she took the glasses from him without meeting his eyes. She was going to have to stop acting like a teenager every time the man touched her!

"You look great in those jeans, did you know that?"

He looked great in his, too. The thought came unbidden, along with the flurry in her stomach. He was wearing a trim-fitting sport shirt and faded jeans that looked as though he'd been melted down and poured into them. How could she find him so attractive when he was so wrong for her? she thought ruefully. God, was it really true that opposites did attract? And was she so stupid as to fall right into a trap that had nearly destroyed her once before? She took a grip on her runaway senses. "She's...uh, Terry's sister picked her up after school. They're deciding what Terry's going to do."

He was standing close, very close, looking down at her with a half smile on his attractive mouth, and he didn't look at all interested in her houseguest. He looked interested in *her*. The thought was enough to panic Carly. Feeling hemmed in, she looked toward the small basket of napkins on the counter, prepared to retreat to the living room, but he stayed her by putting out his arm.

He was going to kiss her. And just like that other time at her door, she felt a spiral of anticipation mixed with fear of her own reaction. She was not equipped for a casual fling in the big leagues, and with all the intuitive power in her soul, she knew Jess Brannigan was big-league material. He was trouble with a capital *T*.

"Wait a minute." She put out a hand, and when it connected with his chest, she snatched it away. "This is not what I agreed to, Jess. You're only here because Mike will probably show up with Penny. I think we should keep that in mind."

"Hush, Carly."

Without taking a step, he moved so that for a second or two, she felt the heat of him pressed firmly against her. They fit together perfectly, she thought frantically. Why did that have to be so?

He bent and nuzzled the sensitive spot right under her ear, and more wild sensation streaked through her. She closed her eyes as warm firm lips touched the side of her neck. Delicious chills broke out all over her. Unconsciously her head fell to the side and back slightly.

"Do you like that?"

He knew she did. Sheer unadulterated sensuality radiated from him in waves. Carly took it in and felt it shimmy through her.

The front door suddenly opened, and with it came the sound of Rachel and Kyle laughing. Carly's eyes flew open, and the world righted itself.

"Damn it to hell!" Jess complained. "This place really is too crowded. Every time we—"

"Hey, in the kitchen!"

Carly pushed hard against him.

Reluctantly, he stepped aside. He hadn't intended to come on to Carly. But there was something about her that made it hard to keep his distance. Suddenly concerned, he darted her a quick look. Color was high on her cheeks. He eyed the unsteady line of her mouth, and a surge of protectiveness caught him by surprise. But he had no time to stop and analyze it, as Rachel stuck her head around the door.

"Two more hungry mouths to feed, Carly. These two just happened to appear on your doorstep looking very hungry and only slightly wet."

Over Rachel's shoulder, Carly could see Penny and Mike. Luck was with Jess, it seemed. His time wouldn't be wasted tonight, after all. Carly shoved the tray into his hands and ushered everybody out of the kitchen.

"I THINK MIKE'S warming up a little, don't you?"

Jess was standing at the open door, watching Carly's four guests disappear in a wild dash in the direction of the house next door. Mike's laugh and Penny's lilting voice blended with the deeper tones of Rachel and Kyle as they leaped and dodged puddles in the dark.

When Carly didn't answer, Jess looked at her quickly. "Well, isn't he?"

"He seems to be, yes," she said.

He closed the door and turned to face her. "But we still have a long way to go, you're thinking?"

Carly shrugged, unwilling to strike a depressing note. "Well, it took a long time for him to grow apart from you. Your relationship is not likely to change overnight." But it would change, and probably sooner than Jess expected, if she was any judge of human nature. The more she saw of Jess, the more convinced she became of the depth of his feelings for Mike. And Mike would respond to that. Although tonight he'd been wary and aloof at first, he'd soon thawed out.

Carly really couldn't see the boy managing to hold a grudge against his dad for any length of time now that they were back in contact. Jess was just too...what? *Charming* wasn't the right word, she had realized tonight. He exuded an air of innate confidence and male magnetism that was more compelling than charm, or so it seemed to Carly. She'd seen it in the grand jury sessions and again tonight. Even Kyle, who was one of the strongest, most confident men Carly knew, wasn't immune. Despite his strengths, however, Jess was very private and self-contained. That might be a major stumbling block to winning Mike. Intuitively Carly knew that Jess would find it difficult to open himself to anyone. Even Mike.

"Tonight turned out better than I dared to hope," Jess said. "At least my instincts were right about something. I owe you, Carly."

She took a deep breath. "It's nothing. You would have managed with or without me. Your own instincts would have guided you, Jess. You need to have more faith in yourself as a father."

"You wouldn't say that if you could be there when it's just Mike and me. He's as touchy as a bear and suspicious of everything."

She smiled slightly. "Well, you'll have another chance tonight when you drive him home."

"He's spending the weekend with me, did I tell you?"

Carly's eyes widened in pleasure. "No, that's wonderful. How'd that happen?"

"Lianne and her husband are going to Las Vegas and generously consented to allow me to baby-sit."

"How did Mike react?"

"He was wary as hell," Jess said. "He refused to go to my place across the lake in Covington, and I didn't push it. I'm just glad to have him for the couple of days. I'll save Covington for another time."

"It won't be long," she assured him, heading for the living room. "Wait and see. Come on, you may as well wait for him in here. Have another beer. I think there's some left."

He refused the beer but followed her to the living room. Instead of sitting on the sofa, he dropped to the floor and stretched out on the thick rug, pulling a pillow under his head. He looked big and dangerous sprawled on the deep lush pile. To Carly, his dark skin looked too good against the stark white rug. All it would take was a zebra stripe, she found herself thinking, to complete the fantasy of a relaxed replete jungle animal in her living room.

Smiling, he leaned on one elbow and watched her. "Well, what'll we do while we wait for my son to say good-night to his tutor?" he asked mock-innocently.

"Get out the Trivial Pursuit?" she retorted.

He smiled slowly into her eyes. "You want to play games?"

"Our audience is gone, Jess," she reminded him dryly. "Behave yourself."

He shook his head and laughed outright. "Ah, Carly, you haven't played the singles scene, so you don't know your lines. You're not supposed to suggest Trivial Pursuit.

You're supposed to drop down here on this rug beside me and let Mother Nature take it from there.''

''Ah, Jess.'' She dropped down onto the sofa, instead, and shot him a telling look. ''You wish.''

She was determined not to give him the satisfaction of knowing how he made her feel, although only a blind man could have failed to notice the times she'd betrayed herself. All evening she'd been aware of Jess's dark gaze, a speculative—or was it predatory?—gleam lurking half-masked, for her eyes only. She had felt the vibrations and had known they'd come from Jess. Something unfinished quivered between them. Mentally she braced herself, determined not to get caught up in something she couldn't control.

Still smiling, he got up and sat down on the sofa beside her. ''You don't have to look like that. I'm just teasing you.''

''Look like what?''

''I'm not sure. I'm still trying to figure it out—figure *you* out.'' He looked at her. ''You want the truth?''

Her nod was slow in coming.

''You're a divorced woman. You've been married and exposed to...the usual hassling.'' He paused at her blank expression. ''Being divorced and beautiful—the whole singles scene,'' he explained.

The compliment, tossed off so casually, caught her off guard. Did he think she was beautiful?

He leaned back on the sofa and studied her intently. ''In spite of all that, I get this feeling that, experiencewise, there's not a lot of difference between you and...and Penny.''

''Just because I'm divorced doesn't mean I'm into...all that.''

''Obviously.''

''Besides,'' she said, distracted by the shape of his

mouth, "it's not exactly safe to play that scene nowadays."

He nodded slowly. "Very wise of you."

He was leaning close, and she had the strangest urge to reach out and touch his mouth. His lips were firm and beautifully sculpted. She remembered their warmth against her throat and felt heat rise and begin to spread within her. Her gaze traveled over his face. His jaw was dark with a day's growth of beard. She wanted to touch that, too, to see what it felt like. Jess Brannigan fascinated her. And just now he was close enough so that all she'd have to do was lean forward slightly. It took amazing willpower not to.

He did it for her. Shifting on the sofa, he was suddenly touching her, his thigh against hers. He sunk both hands into her hair and let them slide through her thick silky mane. "I see you left off those clips." His voice deepened. "I'm glad. Your hair should always be loose like this. Wild and free."

At his words, heat rose in Carly with the speed of a brushfire. The feel of his hands was at once delightful and terrifying. It had been so long since any man had even made her look at him twice. Now, with a few seductive words and subtle sensual signals, she was filled with an intense longing. What was happening? Had she forgotten that just two minutes earlier she'd vowed not to let him do this? Had she forgotten that he was precisely the kind of man she had to avoid?

At the swift pang in her heart, she put a hand to his chest. Through the thick warm wall, she could feel his heartbeat, deep and steady. She wanted to peel his shirt away so that she could touch him with nothing to impede her pleasure. He would be beautiful, she knew—hard, muscled, all male.

She was shocked and bewildered by her runaway imagination and her body's hunger. She glanced into Jess's eyes. Her breath caught in her throat; the desire she saw there was equal to her own—and more. For a second she was suspended between heading the harsh lessons of her past and giving in to what she yearned for now.

"What, Carly?" he murmured, his tone caressing her, flowing over her like warm red wine. "What is it?" His gaze roved over her face and stopped at her mouth. Slowly lowering his head, he whispered, "You don't have to be afraid of me, Carly."

Helplessly, at the first touch of his mouth on hers, Carly's lashes fluttered down, and sensation was heightened. She'd been braced for a show of dominance. Wasn't that to be expected from a man like Jess? But that wasn't what she was getting. His mouth was warm, as mesmerizing as his voice. His tongue traced the shape of her lips, as though savoring their perfection, before he put his mouth fully against hers.

He made Carly feel as though her mouth was a feast and he was a starving man. He nibbled and sucked and sipped while she trembled with the sheer pleasure of it. His mouth moved persuasively over hers, silently urging her acceptance, her participation. She felt an almost irresistible urge to move closer to the warmth of his body, to raise her arms and link them around his neck, to open her mouth and herself to the dangerous heady sensuality that he promised.

But she didn't dare. She couldn't open herself to that kind of anguish again. With an effort that was almost painful, she remained still, suspended, every cell alive and greedy, taking, while time slowed and her senses ran wild.

Then he stopped, whispering her name in a voice that was hoarse and urgent. "Carly."

Her eyes fluttered open, unfocused. "Hmm?"

"I think I hear Mike on your porch."

She made a tiny sound and turned her face against his neck. Jess wrapped both arms around her and held her close, stunned by an emotion that he couldn't identify.

She was very still against him for a long moment. Then she stirred and moved away from him. "You have to go," she said, not looking at him.

He got up. "I'll let myself out. Good night, Carly."

"Good night."

She picked up a cushion and hugged it against her heart. On the porch, she could hear Mike and then Jess's low-spoken reply. Thunder rumbled, low and distant, and it began to rain again softly. But Carly didn't move. Bewildered and fearful, she sat and stared at nothing long after their voices and footsteps had faded into the night.

CHAPTER SEVEN

GREEN, JESS THOUGHT distractedly. When she was aroused, her eyes weren't an indiscriminate smoky something. They were as green as a deep still bayou. And her hair—Lord, he loved her hair—was soft and lush and sexy as hell. *She* was sexy as hell, whether or not she was aware of it, he decided, speeding through the dark wet night with Mike. For once he was grateful for his son's habit of keeping his own counsel.

He'd never met a woman who combined that air of innocence and sensuality. For the first time, he wondered about her marriage and the reason for her divorce, then instantly veered away from the thought. That kind of thinking suggested an interest in Carly that was a little too personal. The last thing he wanted was to get emotionally involved.

There was already enough in his relationship with Carly that was unsettling. Tonight, for instance, it would have taken only a little push, and he could have had a taste of her passion. He sensed that the tight rein she kept on her emotions could be breached. If she were any other woman, he would have aimed for exactly that. But with Carly he felt indulgent and strangely protective.

He hadn't felt that way about a woman since the days of his own first love, and he hadn't forgotten the harsh lessons he'd learned as a result. He'd been naive and idealistic when he had first met Lianne, as well as indulgent, protective and chivalrous—all the things he'd imagined a man should be toward the woman he loved. In that besotted state, he'd been an easy victim.

But since that time, no one had ever penetrated his defenses. Which was why he was slightly bemused by his reaction to Carly.

She was an intriguing contradiction—warm and giving with her kids, but wary and shy with him. She slipped from slightly insecure romantic heroine into confident counselor the instant she sensed his need. He felt his harsh features soften. He wondered how many layers he'd have to peel away to discover the real Carly Sullivan. One thing he was convinced of: incredible as it might be, she didn't realize just how lovely and desirable she was.

Lost in his thoughts, he didn't notice the car that pulled alongside the Jaguar until Mike rolled his window halfway down and the deafening vibrations of heavy metal music blasted through the atmosphere. Mike called a greeting in response to the loud and rowdy suggestions issued through four open windows. Jess glanced at his son as the youths pulled ahead in a cloud of exhaust. "Friends of yours?"

"Yeah."

"From Padgett?"

"Yeah."

Jess watched the taillights of the Datsun disappear. "Nice car," he said.

"Yeah."

"Have you thought about wheels for yourself?"

In the tiny silence that fell, Jess waited. Maybe buying his kid a car could be considered a bribe, but he wasn't above a little bribery if it meant another small crack in Mike's defenses.

Mike cleared his throat. "How...uh, I mean, what did you have in mind?"

Hiding a smile, Jess savored the small success. "Well, not a Mercedes or BMW to start with," he said. He dipped his head in the direction that Mike's friends had headed in. "How about something along the lines of that little Datsun?" He glanced at Mike. "It's your choice, Mike."

He could almost feel the turbulence in Mike's thoughts. At sixteen, a car was a powerful temptation. Mike was no fool. He was probably thinking of the complications that would accompany the car—complications he'd just as soon avoid.

"There are no strings attached, Mike."

Mike turned and studied his father silently, obviously wondering whether to believe him. Jess felt a deep sadness. It hurt that his son couldn't quite accept him at his word. When Mike turned away again, Jess glanced back at him and noted his restlessness. His ankle rested on his knee, and he was jiggling his foot, something Jess himself did when he was feeling stressed. He stayed silent as he waited for Mike to weigh as many angles as he could think of.

"I was kind of thinking of a four-wheel drive," Mike said finally. "You know, nothing that'd cost really big bucks."

Jess nodded. "Sounds fine. You decide when we can go look at them. Maybe this weekend. What do you think?"

"Sure." He hesitated. "Thanks."

"You're welcome." Jess took a corner and turned onto his street. He was nervous, he realized. For the first time in too many years, Mike was going to be in his house for a couple of days, maybe more. They'd eat together, share idle conversation, squabble over what to watch on TV. No, they probably wouldn't do the latter, he thought; he was so happy to have Mike, he'd watch cartoons if his son said the word.

He pulled up in front of his house and glanced at Mike. If he had any bad feelings about being there, Jess couldn't tell. The look on his face seemed mostly curious as he took in the sprawling house. Carly's words came back to

Jess. Maybe he didn't trust his own instincts enough. Mike would come around, she had said. A deep warmth settled in him, and for the first time since Mike had moved back to New Orleans, he almost believed it.

LIFE HAD A WAY of getting complicated. Mike was only sixteen, but he'd already learned that. The weekend with Jess fell in the complicated category, he decided, mulling it over during world history on Monday morning. Who would have ever suspected that his old man would have had an unexpected attack of parental conscience and practically force him to move in while his mother and Cliff went to Vegas? Mike skewed his mouth sideways, thinking. Funny. He'd been left on his own a lot, sometimes with a housekeeper, sometimes not. But last week Jess had made all those fatherly noises and insisted on having him over at his place. Of course, it could all have been for show, he reminded himself cynically. He wished, not for the first time, that he was a mind reader. That was about the only way he'd ever know for sure if his father cared one damn thing about him.

The bell signaling the end of second period interrupted his thoughts. He rose from his seat and absently waved at two track team buddies, but he didn't fall in with them. He still had some thinking to do. The weekend had been okay, considering. Jess was definitely better company than Cliff. At least he talked to him like a person. Cliff was okay, Mike mused, but all he cared about was bank stuff—and neither mutual funds nor the future of the Dow industrials were way up on Mike's list of interesting topics.

It *was* interesting to hear about gunshot victims and drug overdoses and all that other stuff that a trauma surgeon handled every single day. It hadn't exactly been easy getting his father to talk about it, though. Mike sensed that if Jess hadn't been trying to make up to him, he wouldn't have gotten a word out of him about Crescent City's emergency department. Maybe everybody's job wasn't their whole life, the way the bank was Cliff's.

Jess had that place across Lake Pontchartrain, for instance. He talked about it easy enough. If they hadn't spent the weekend shopping around at car dealerships, they probably would have wound up over there. He was glad Jess hadn't pushed it. For some reason, he wasn't ready to go there.

Mike politely sidestepped the two freshman girls who shared the locker directly under his own, completely missing the inviting looks they sent his way. Something between him and Jess had clicked this weekend whether he'd intended it or not. Maybe there was something to this bit about blood being thicker than water. He'd have to think it through first, maybe mention it to Penny, see what she thought. But later. He wanted to work it out in his own mind first. No matter what, he still wasn't ready to just forgive and forget all the years he'd been shoved aside for whatever it was Jess had found more interesting than being a father.

He slammed the door of his locker and shifted his books to his left hand. Chemistry was coming up, and he was feeling that feeling again. As of a week or so ago, it was his favorite class, and it sure as hell didn't have anything to do with the course content. When Ms Sullivan had suggested a tutor, he'd nearly croaked. But that was before he'd spent any time with Penny. He thought of her wide brown eyes—well, not brown like his, but sort of like dark honey. And her smile. Penny was the best thing that had happened to him since he'd left San Diego.

He turned a corner and headed for a bank of lockers on the opposite side of the hall. He slowed down when he saw Penny take out a notebook and close her locker door. She turned, still unaware of him, and almost bumped into his chest. Her face broke into a smile to die for, and his heart jumped the same way it did before he took a high hurdle. As stuffy and stupid and outdated as Padgett was, it could be tolerated as long as Penny was there.

From the door of her office, Carly watched Mike and Penny bound for the chemistry lab, oblivious to everything but each other. A smile lingered in her eyes at the picture they made: Mike so dark and youthfully lean: Penny, pretty and petite, laughing up into his face. Carly envied Penny's blithe self-confidence, the easy way she wielded her feminine power. Carly's smile faded. Had she ever been that way? Once, maybe, before Buck Sullivan had silenced her feminine confidence forever. Lucky Penny. Mike would cherish her, honor each of her female gifts as they unfolded for him alone, like the petals of a flower.

She watched Mike bend to catch something Penny said, and she smiled at his expression. His feelings for Penny were there for the world to see, and when he was with her, his face had nothing of that closed guarded look it had had that first day she'd interviewed him. When he was with Penny, he was so different from his father. Carly's eyes clouded thoughtfully. There were many similarities between Mike and his father, but this wasn't one of them. Carly couldn't imagine Jess openly revealing emotion to any woman, if he was even capable of it. She refused to dwell on the reason that thought had the power to distress her.

She turned away just as her telephone rang.

"Carly?" At the sound of his voice, she went totally still for a heartbeat.

"Hello, Jess." Once on a Florida beach, she'd been caught in the wake of a huge wave, and she'd tumbled over and over. Her insides were doing the same thing now. She sat down and tried to tune out the noise and confusion of class change at Padgett.

"How was your weekend?"

"Good." She traced the shape of a crystal bird on her desk with shaky fingers. "And yours? How did it go with Mike?"

"Good." He paused, seeming to give it extra thought. "Yeah, good."

She laughed softly. "See, I told you just to trust your instincts."

"And his intense desire for his own wheels."

"What?"

"We spent the weekend shopping for a four-wheel-drive vehicle."

"Oh."

"But it's a start."

"It certainly is." She leaned back, imagining them, both so alike, making the rounds of the car dealers in town. Jess couldn't have conjured up anything that would be harder to resist.

"I have you to thank."

It took a second for reality to intrude. She'd been so caught up that for a moment she'd forgotten the real reason he needed her. "That's nonsense, Jess. I told you—"

"I know what you told me," he cut in. "But you have your opinion and I have mine. That's not why I called. How about dinner? I owe you, remember?"

She drew a deep breath. "You don't owe me, for heaven's sake!"

"I'm not talking about Mike now," he said, his tone becoming soothing. "I drank your Scotch and crashed your Friday night pizza party. I want to make it up to you."

"You bought the pizza," she reminded him.

"Details. So, how about Friday night? Are you free? Do you still have Terry staying over?"

"Yes."

"Well, will she be okay alone?"

"She's fourteen, Jess. She doesn't need a baby-sitter."

"Great. Fine. So, does seven sound about right? We have a short docket for the grand jury. I checked with Hebert."

Carly closed her eyes, still tracing the crystal wings of the paperweight while she fought a battle with herself. She was like a moth drawn to a dangerous flame. She didn't want to like Jess, but she did. She didn't want to be attracted to him, but she was. He was an eighties man—sexually experienced, sophisticated. He was going to make demands—sexual demands—that she knew from experience she couldn't hope to meet. If he really meant it and his invitation had nothing to do with Mike, then she should make some excuse and close him out of her life once and for all before he discovered she was all show and no substance.

"Carly?"

She opened her eyes and stared at the paperweight, but there were no answers to be found in its crystal depths.

"Carly, are you—"

"Yes," she said.

He was silent a second. "Dinner, right? Friday at seven?"

"Dinner," she repeated softly. "Friday at seven."

She stared at the telephone a long time after hanging up. She made all these firm-sounding resolutions about Jess only to throw them to the wind the next time she saw him or heard his voice.

She was frowning when she glanced up straight into the amused eyes of Rachel.

"A date? A real bona fide pick-you-up-at-seven date? Well, hallelujah. And this time it's not some musty boring safe type." Rachel sauntered in and took a seat, crossing her legs. "It's about time, I must say. Now, tell me all the details."

"I'm having dinner with Jess Brannigan."

"Who else?" Rachel said with thin patience. "I assumed that."

Carly looked at her. "You did? How? I mean—"

"Based on my vast knowledge of human nature, that's how, you goose! Come on, Carly, who else could it be? The tension between you two Friday night practically sizzled all the humidity out of the air."

"Oh, Rachel!" Carly slumped in her chair and closed her eyes. "Was I that obvious?"

Rachel laughed and shook her head. "Relax. Only someone who knows you through and through could tell."

Carly groaned. "Like you and Kyle and Penny." Her eyes widened in alarm. "You don't think Mike—"

"No, I don't," Rachel said briskly. "But if he did, why would he object if his father showed the good sense to fall for you, Carly? Mike likes you and, just as importantly, he respects you. He'd probably admire Jess's good taste."

"Well, it doesn't matter, really. This date isn't what you think, Rachel."

"Oh?"

"No." Carly waved a hand. "He's taking me out as a sort of thank you for helping him connect with Mike. Anyway, you should know I'm out of my league with someone like Jess...." Her glance went to Rachel, then slid away. "There could never be anything like that between us."

Rachel cocked one dark brow. "Why not?"

"I'm just out of my league, Rachel. Let's leave it at that."

Rachel inhaled with exaggerated patience. "When are you going to bury all that baggage you've been carrying around since your divorce, Carly? I don't know, and I don't plan to ask, but whatever Buck Sullivan did to you, whatever he said, can't possibly matter anymore. The man had a ton of hang-ups. He was washed up at the pro ranks, and his career as a coach has been mediocre. That alone is enough to damage the tender ego of an insecure jock. His effect on your life now should be exactly zip! Zero! Can't you put it behind you, Carly—consider the source and give yourself a second chance? Or better yet, give another man a chance to make you feel like a woman again."

Carly's expression was wry. "I don't think Jess Brannigan is the one, Rachel."

"And why not, I repeat?"

Carly looked heavenward. "I just explained why, Rachel. Jess Brannigan is interested in me only because of Mike."

"And I still don't believe it. It was you on the receiving end of those hot looks Friday night." Rachel eyed Carly for a moment or two, then added slyly, "But if that is so, which I doubt, then why didn't he just ask me out? I have a straight line to Mike, what with Penny tutoring him every day."

"Because Kyle would kill him, that's why."

Rachel looked startled and then coolly guarded. "What's that supposed to mean?"

Carly said patiently, "Be serious, Rachel. Kyle's crazy about you. You only have to look at him when he's around you to see it."

Rachel jumped up, but not before Carly had seen the soft color in her cheeks. "Come on, Carly. There's nothing like that between Kyle and me."

Carly smiled. "Would you look at this? I guess the tables are turned. Look at me, Rachel." Carly tapped her chest with a finger. "You know who you're talking to here? Next you'll be saying you don't feel the same way."

Rachel smiled faintly. "No, I won't say that."

Carly stared at her friend for a long moment, not certain whether to believe what she was seeing. Rachel always seemed to have everything in her life under control. Except for the inevitable period of anxiety after Phillip's death, Carly knew of nothing that might have given Rachel a moment's pause. She seemed to meet every challenge life dished out with almost intrepid courage. But the look on her face this moment was one of uncertainty. "Rachel?"

"You're mistaken about Kyle, Carly. He doesn't want me."

Carly was shaking her head. "Well, you sure could have fooled me."

With her back to Carly, Rachel idly straightened one of the carved birds on the mantel. "He was Phil's best friend. As I told you before, he feels responsible for Penny and me for some reason, and I've tried to tell him his protectiveness is totally unnecessary." She laughed shortly. "You know how policemen are."

"It's more than that, Rachel," Carly said firmly.

"He's never touched me."

"Well..." Carly hesitated, at a loss. "Do you want him to?"

Another brief humorless laugh. "Oh, yes."

There was odd silence for a beat or two, broken only by familiar school sounds: a slammed locker, a distant athletic whistle, the PA system paging the janitor.

"Well, I've got to run!" Rachel suddenly made for the door in a flurry—Rachel, who was never in a flurry. "Time for your gym class, and I've got a session with a parent." She waved a hand. "Hey, we'll talk later, okay?"

Carly stood slowly, frowning, intuitively certain she'd just stumbled onto something Rachel had been carefully concealing. There had been uncertainty and vulnerability and...yes, pain in Rachel's eyes when she'd said Kyle didn't want her. Carly gazed slowly around the room, thinking. Was no one exempt from pain where love was concerned? Even Rachel, who seemed to have boundless confidence and self-esteem, was no exception.

Sighing, she snapped off the light on her desk. Time for third period and the fierce aerobic workout she'd scheduled. Since meeting Jess she'd discovered the therapeutic benefits of pushing her body to its physical limits.

She headed for the gym, deliberately blanking out her thoughts. She was in sight of the gym when Terry Faust, in Padgett's khaki-and-blue sweats, stepped up alongside her.

"Hi, Ms Sullivan."

"Hi, yourself." She smiled at Terry, noting with satisfaction that the confused scared look was gone. "Ready for a killer workout?"

Terry made a face. "Not really, but I have to work off that breakfast you forced on me this morning."

Carly pretended to be indignant. "I wasn't the one who stirred up blueberry pancakes, my girl."

"No, but you had the ingredients on hand."

"Uh-huh. Tomorrow, it's half a grapefruit for you."

Terry groaned.

"With no sugar."

Terry was laughing when they reached the gym. Just before they went inside, she suddenly touched Carly's arm, her expression sobering. "Ms Sullivan—"

"What, honey? What is it?"

"I won't be there tomorrow morning," Terry said quietly. "Tonight I'm sleeping over at my sister's house. We've been thinking about family counseling—all of us, you know?"

"Have you and Debra discussed this with your mother?"

Terry nodded.

"And she approves?"

"Well, she didn't exactly say." Terry drew a deep breath, suddenly looking much older than her fourteen years. "You see, Ms Sullivan, my mom's involved with this..." She hesitated and then gave a brief laugh. "Listen to me! This isn't the time to get all involved in a discussion of my problems, is it? I just wanted to thank you for letting me stay with you and to tell you it won't be for much longer." She pressed her fingers against her mouth, her eyes bright.

Carly reached out and touched her arm. "Don't worry about that, Terry. Just remember, I'm here for you if you need me."

Controlling her tears, Terry nodded vehemently. "Running away or doing stupid things like getting in the car that night with Richie Shelton and—oh, all that—well, I won't be that dumb again, Ms Sullivan."

Carly smiled. "I know."

Terry smiled a little mistily. "So, thanks again, okay?"

"Okay."

CHAPTER EIGHT

THE EYES OF ALL twelve jurors were fixed grimly on Irene Goodman, the night clerk at a twenty-four-hour quick-stop market on the edge of an uptown neighborhood. She was a plump middle-aged woman with tightly permed brown hair and nervous hands.

"Judson Lang didn't look like a troublemaker," she said in a bewildered voice.

John Hebert glanced down at the official transcript of the woman's statement in the file he was holding. "Tell us about that night, Mrs. Goodman."

"I get all kinds that time of night," Irene Goodman said, "but I've got to where I can pretty much spot the ones that's gonna give me grief. Gerald, my husband, he sleeps on a cot in the storeroom, and I can just buzz him with this little intercom thing, and he comes right out if need be." She glanced around the semicircle of jurors. "He's big, Gerald is. That's all it usually takes, just one look at Gerald and they turn around, usually leave real fast."

Hebert nodded. "But what did Judson Lang do, Mrs. Goodman?"

"Well, like I say, he didn't look up to mischief, so I didn't buzz Gerald. He had on really nice clothes—designer stuff—and I could see his car parked outside. It was new and pretty fancy. Anyway, he walked up to the counter and didn't have nothing in his hands, so I figured he wanted cigarettes or likker, which is both behind the counter. It was about then I noticed his eyes was real red and he kept looking this way and that, nervouslike, never in one place for long, you know? 'What'll it be?' I says, and he says, 'Cigarettes.' Then when I get the cash drawer open, he whips out a pistol, quick as you please, and makes me move aside before I can buzz Gerald."

"What happened then?" Hebert asked.

"Well, Mr. Gervais, a regular—he always buys rum—he walked in the store. He's slow, because he has a cane, and when he saw this fella with the gun, he looked like he was gonna die right there. But Lang, he just yelled all wildlike for Mr. Gervais to lie down on the floor. 'And do it fast!' he told him. Then he grabbed all the money out of the cash drawer, mumbling that he had to have it and he was sorry. He was crazy acting, kinda like he might have been takin' something."

"And then?" Hebert prodded quietly.

"Well, he sorta shoved me aside and made me lose my balance. I think Mr. Gervais began to try to get up to help me, and this kid used his gun to knock Mr. Gervais's cane out from under him because without his cane and all, he...he'd be pretty helpless."

"Just take your time," Hebert said quietly. "We understand this is hard for you."

Irene Goodman sniffed and dabbed at her eyes with a Kleenex. "Well, that's about it. The gun went off—when he swung it at the cane, you know?—and the bullet hit Mr. Gervais in the chest."

A murmur rippled through the jurors.

"Course, 'bout that time, Gerald appeared from the back."

"How did Lang react?" Hebert asked.

"I'll declare, he just went crazy. He went nuts. He fell on the floor sobbing. Gerald didn't have to do nothing to just take his gun and make him stay till the police came."

She nodded knowingly. "To tell you the truth, he was real pitiful."

"HIS ATTORNEY WILL probably go for an insanity plea, even though the SOB ought to be fried," Joe West complained, removing his sunglasses and smoothing his red hair, which had been blown around during the brisk walk; the jurors were making their way back to the jury room after lunch at a nearby restaurant. Carly walked between Jess and Colonel Buckley, who was nodding in agreement with West. The jurors had debated less than fifteen minutes before indicting the preppy Judson Lang. But that wouldn't mean much to Herman Gervais's family; they were still struggling to accept the reality of his death.

"It'll probably be manslaughter," Jess said.

"We can indict these hoodlums all day, but they all find a way to get off," the colonel said, his tone heavy with disapproval. "In the Marine Corps now, we don't have these loopholes."

"But we can't afford not to have the insanity defense," Carly put in quietly. "Perhaps Judson Lang really is mentally disturbed. If so, he needs help, not the electric chair."

"Psychosis induced by chemicals," Jess said in a hard tone, "put into his body by choice."

"That's not for us to decide," Carly argued.

"Unfortunately," Jess said dryly.

Carly didn't comment. It would have surprised her had Jess taken any other attitude.

Elizabeth Cohn drew up beside them, puffing slightly from the exercise. "Well, as for me, I thought there was an interesting similarity between young Judson Lang's case and our first case this morning."

"You mean Benjamin Winslow?" Carly asked. They'd indicted Winslow for vehicular homicide. At thirty-one, with two previous arrests for driving while intoxicated, he'd been the driver of a car that had veered into oncoming traffic and collided head-on with another car, killing its sole occupant.

"There was no difference," Jess stated flatly. "Lang had had too much cocaine and LSD, and Winslow had had too much booze. The end result was two dead people."

"I'm not defending either Lang or Winslow," Carly argued. "I'm just defending their right to all of the defenses within the law."

"You mean all the loopholes," Joe West declared.

Jess opened the door of the jury room and waited for Carly to enter. "What's the difference between drinking enough Jack Daniel's to render yourself senseless and ingesting whatever it was Judson Lang took to alter his mind beyond reason?"

Carly knew when to give up. Jess persisted in seeing every case in black-and-white. She spread her hands and shrugged. "Nothing, if that's what happened. I'm just saying after hearing the testimony about Lang that he might have some psychological problems, problems his attorney will probably explore in his defense. I'm saying that's okay."

"Well, maybe you could put in a suggestion to his lawyer," Jess suggested with a little bite in his tone.

She looked around at the skeptical faces of the other jurors and sighed. Jess wasn't alone in his rigid application of the law. Most of the men tended to side with him. In Jess's case, she had to admit it was understandable, considering the amount of time he spent every day in his job coping with the reality of violence. The women, she noticed, tended to be more lenient in their judgments. It was interesting.

Once they arrived at the jury room, Elizabeth Cohn sank down into her chair with a relieved sigh. "Murder, rape, manslaughter...surely that's enough violence today," the old lady said plaintively to John Hebert. "Can't you vary the docket a bit, John?"

"Funny you should ask," John said, looking like a man withholding a treat. "There's a juicy one coming up." He waved his hands to quiet the clamor from those seated around the dais. "Ballot box tampering," he announced cheerfully, again waving his hands to subdue the collective groans going up from the twelve.

He cleared his throat and assumed an important tone. "The State of Louisiana versus Anthony 'Terrible Tony' DeLeon."

"You're kidding," Michelle Bordelon drawled in her soft Cajun accent.

"He's a wrestler!" Ron Bridges exclaimed. Ron was the youngest juror, twenty-one, a construction worker who tended to be idealistic.

"Oh, my," murmured mousy Miss Lillian Pritchard, only loud enough to be heard by Carly, who sat next to her.

"I kid you not," said John. "Terrible Tony, a local wrestler of dubious success but far-reaching fame, is accused of tampering with the election results of the mayoralty race in Bayou Bernay held last May, in which he was a candidate for that office running against incumbent Vincent Fiorello. Terrible Tony won by a slim margin—the election, not his last match," John put in dryly. "Fiorello is bringing the charges. Witnesses are two individuals from the polling station and two ladies who work part-time in the mayor's office. One is a cousin of Tony's, and the other is Fiorello's wife." He sent an amused look around the room. "There appears to be reason to look into the hiring practices in some of these small townships. But that's another issue." He rustled his papers and continued. "Tony insisted on appearing before this august body and challenging you to decide for yourselves whether he would sink to this kind of 'infamous behavior.''' Hebert looked at them over his reading glasses. "That's a direct quote."

A few titters went up from the jurors when Terrible Tony entered and made his way confidently to the witness chair. He was as tall as a tree, his 260 pounds outfitted in a flamboyant cape of blue-and-green satin panels lined with peacock-patterned silk. To complete his ensemble, he wore black boots with pirate-style cuffs. His long black hair was bound with a leather headband, and he sported a black handlebar mustache. On being seated, he sent a withering look around the room from beneath heavy black eyebrows.

"He certainly looks terrible," Carly murmured, earning an amused look from Jess.

John Hebert cleared his throat. "You wanted to personally speak to the jurors, Mr. DeLeon—"

"Call me Terrible," boomed DeLeon.

"Ah...yes. You're charged with intimidating voters, using force to keep away citizens who supported your opponent, Mr. Fiorello. Do you have anything to say in your own defense, Mr. ah...Terrible?"

"I'm innocent."

"IF HE'S INNOCENT, I'm the queen of Bayou Bernay," Carly said, still laughing.

Jess fell into step beside her, also heading for the parking lot. "You mean we finally had a defendant your liberal heart doesn't bleed for?"

"Don't try to provoke me," she countered, stepping off the sidewalk and crossing to her car. "I don't care how many character witnesses that big moose paraded before us—he's guilty as sin. He only got off this time because Fiorello's supporters were just as guilty but weren't found out. If he'd won, Terrible would have cried foul, too. It was just a question of whose methods were the most effective." She reached into her purse for her car keys and shuddered. "Did you see that tattoo on his arm?"

"I take it you're not referring to the one on his left bicep that said My Mother, My Heart?"

"Hardly." She rolled her eyes. "I meant the gross rattlesnake on his other arm that began at his wrist and curled up to his shoulder to eat a screaming woman. Yech!"

She stopped at her car and, giving way to a fit of giggles, looked up at Jess. "Guess who's a wrestling fan?"

He propped an arm on the Datsun. "Who?"

"Miss Pritchard."

"Uh-uh."

"Cross my heart. Terrible's her hero. She told me."

"Incredible."

She nodded, grinning. "I had to listen to a gushing tribute to those guys. Did you know they're fantastic athletes, male machines carefully honed to perform breathtaking physical feats, masters of split-second timing? In short, she's absolutely infatuated with male wrestlers."

Jess shifted from one leg to the other, but Carly was just warming to her subject. "She absolutely wouldn't have it that Terrible Tony only ran for mayor for the publicity. Only a besotted fan couldn't see that strong-arming the voters at the polls was right in line with his terrible image—no pun intended. He reveled in the scandal."

He chuckled, then bent to open her door for her. "I guess this means you don't happen to be a fan."

She halted, half in, half out. "Do I look like a wrestling fan, Jess?"

He shook his head. "I was afraid of that."

Still amused, she searched his face. "Why?"

Carly watched as he glanced away toward the Mississippi River, where the Delta Queen's whistle sounded, long and low and plaintive. He looked uncomfortable, something so rare that her curiosity was immediately aroused. "Why? How could I like wrestling? It's a stupid sport and everything's rigged, everybody knows that."

Meeting her eyes ruefully, he rubbed his chin. "Would you believe there's a big championship match at the Superdome tonight?"

She stared a second or two. "Well, Terrible timed his grand jury appearance just right, I would say."

"And I have tickets."

"You have tickets," she repeated, deadpan.

"Four tickets," he clarified.

"We had a date for dinner, not wrestling."

He sighed. "Guess who else besides Miss Pritchard is a wrestling fan?"

"Mike Brannigan," she said, not missing a beat.

"Bingo."

Carly rested her arms on the steering wheel and stared straight ahead. Then her mouth twitched. Jess watched her shoulders move slightly, and he thought he heard a chuckle. Then she put her head back and laughed. It was a lovely sound.

"Thanks, Carly," he said, and when she looked up at him, still laughing, he bent and kissed her.

CARLY OPENED HER DOOR that evening to three beaming faces. Granted, Jess's smile had a slightly embarrassed edge, giving her the impression that he wasn't much more taken with the sport of wrestling than she was, and Penny's face wasn't quite as bright as usual. But Mike was obviously in genuine high spirits.

Holding the door wide, she surveyed all three. "I guess there's no point in me inviting y'all in and suggesting pizza and absolutely any VCR movie of your choice, is there?"

Cocking one dark brow, Jess reached for her and pulled

her over the threshold. "Too late, you're committed," he murmured for her ears only.

"And miss the opening match?" Mike exclaimed, assuming an astonished expression. He closed Carly's door firmly and herded them all down the steps. "No way! Besides, the first event will be a treat for you ladies."

"A treat?" Carly repeated faintly.

"First up are the GLOWs," Jess said, opening his car door and seating her. He closed it, but not before Carly spotted a wicked gleam in his dark eyes.

She looked over her shoulder at Penny in the back seat. "Help me out here, Penny. Who or what are 'the glows'?"

Penny scooted over to make room for Mike. "Gorgeous Ladies Of Wrestling," Penny supplied helpfully.

"Oh, great," Carly mumbled. She shot another look at Jess as he climbed into the driver's seat. He met her pointed glance blandly. The whole thing was a farce, and she knew he thought so, too. She hadn't counted on having to endure a wrestling match all for the love of Mike, she thought, feeling a smile start. But there it was. She deliberately raised her eyebrows in a manner that promised retribution. He winked at her, then turned his Jaguar into the traffic and headed for the Superdome.

She was still feeling warmed by that wink when they climbed to their seats in the dome, each carrying an order of nachos with cheese sauce and jalapeños.

"I still owe you dinner," Jess said, watching her lick melted cheese from her fingers.

"You sure do," she agreed, then missed his reply in the roar of the crowd as the action started. To their credit, both she and Penny refrained from sexist comments throughout the spectacle of "ladies"—single-handedly or in tag teams—engaging in the sport. The crowd was wild—not that Carly had expected a level of decorum similar to that found at a golf match, but neither had she expected the out-and-out blood lust that reigned with fans growing steadily more frenzied as the bouts continued. She was torn between shock and amusement.

She grabbed Jess's forearm and squeezed it. "They're going to kill each other!" she exclaimed, grimacing when one muscled female hurled her opponent overhead, then down on the mat, and stomped on her throat.

"Nah," Mike said casually. "They're expert athletes—"

"Carefully honed machines," Jess put in, glancing at Carly with a gleam in his eye.

"Masters of split-second timing," she finished dryly.

Mike looked surprised. "Yeah, exactly."

She leaned across Jess to look at Mike. "Do you know Miss Lillian Prichard?"

"Who?"

She met Jess's eyes and laughed. "Never mind."

Finally the last GLOW match ended—to equal cheers and jeers—and the crowd's enthusiasm was rejuvenated by the appearance of two hulking male brutes.

"It's Terrible!" Carly cried, again clutching Jess's arm.

"It sure is," Penny murmured when Terrible whipped off his peacock cape and bared the full majesty of his physique.

"No, his name is Terrible," Mike explained to Penny.

"I don't care what his name is," Penny said, wrinkling her nose. "He's gross and so is his opponent. Mike, this is barbaric."

"No, Penny. These guys are really world-class athletes. Only they're showmen, too." He glanced at his dad, clearly expecting some masculine support.

Jess studied the top of his can of soda. "To tolerate the kind of punishment these guys dole out and then get up to play another day definitely takes talent."

Mike gave Jess an approving look before turning back

to Penny and Carly. "You two are kind of extrafeminine," he said, "so I guess you'll have to learn more about the sport before you learn to love it."

Carly suddenly choked on her strawberry soda and Jess, straight-faced, helpfully thumped her on the back.

BY THE TIME she and Jess got back to her house, the whole flavor of the evening had deteriorated to the absurd, as far as Carly was concerned. She couldn't help but be in good spirits—the evening *had* been fun. Previously, no sport could have been less appealing to Carly than wrestling. What was it besides two muscle-bound individuals brutalizing each other? Ugh! Before tonight, the chances of her ever attending a match had been slim to none. And then she'd gotten involved with the Brannigan men.

And she was involved with the Brannigan men. After an evening spent watching the growing camaraderie between Jess and Mike, there was no more pretending. Trying to think of Jess as just another father and Mike as just another of her students was ridiculous. Her feelings had gone far beyond that.

"You owe me. I know I said it didn't matter, but after this one, Jess Brannigan, you definitely owe me." Laughing, Carly climbed up her porch steps. "You sounded so ridiculous agreeing with all that nonsense Mike was spouting."

Jess grabbed her wrist and with a jerk pulled her up against him, grinning at the startled look on her face. "You'd better watch it, woman. All that unbridled aggression has me itching to throw my weight around. Terrible Tony knows a thing or two, judging by the swooning females in the crowd."

Still laughing, Carly returned, "Then all I have to say is, be prepared. The evening wasn't a total loss for me, either. Those GLOW-lady types had some interesting defense techniques, I noticed.''

Jess stared down into her face, easily immobilizing her. Her efforts to push against his shoulders only succeeded in locking their bodies together from the waist down.

''Forget it,'' he said, softly blowing at a wispy curl that had strayed from the confines of her barrette. Suddenly all traces of laughter faded. His gaze roved over her face, then homed in on her soft lips, which parted in sweet anticipation. He lowered his mouth, murmuring, ''You're just not the type, and you never will be....''

At a sudden noise coming from the other side of Carly's door, Jess stopped short of the kiss both were aching for. Cursing softly and explicitly, he leaned his forehead against hers. ''Who the hell is in your house?'' he demanded, flexing his fingers into the curve of her waist.

''Uh...'' Carly took a deep breath, then shook her head helplessly. ''Terry, I guess. I'm sorry, Jess. I...she...''

His arms tightened and he moved his hips suggestively against hers. He was hard and warm. Stunned, she flushed with heat and a delicious weakness. It was a good thing someone was in her house. If not, she wasn't sure what she would have done next.

He chucked her gently under the chin with his knuckles and laughed ruefully. ''One of these days, I'm going to get an opportunity to kiss you without any interruptions, but at this rate I'll be so frustrated, I may scare the devil out of you.''

A shiver snaked down Carly's spine just thinking about it. The idea of Jess wanting her with that kind of intensity filled her with conflicting emotion. It was at once both wonderful and scary. Since her divorce, an elemental caution had protected her from another devastating experience at the hands of a man, but with Jess, she seemed to have lost that caution. She felt so much a woman when she was with him. It was that, more than anything else, that drew her to him so compellingly.

"It's probably just as well," he murmured, planting a lingering kiss against her temple. "With my luck, just as things got interesting, Mike would appear." He nuzzled a line down to her jaw and stopped. "I promised him a ride home."

They stepped apart and turned as the door opened and Terry Faust smiled at them.

"Hi, Ms Sullivan. Hi, Dr. Brannigan. We thought we heard someone drive up." She held the door open and stepped back. "Hey, come on in." She laughed a little self-consciously. "It's your house."

"SO, WHAT'S THE PLAN?" Carly said, dividing a look between Terry and Debra. Jess, already familiar with her kitchen, was making coffee. Carly suspected that he hadn't had a sudden craving, but had simply wanted to give Terry and Debra a bit of privacy.

The sisters shared a strong family likeness. Both were dark haired and taller than average, with smooth creamy complexions and beautiful gray eyes. Carly guessed Debra, who was married with a small son, to be eight or ten years older than Terry. She behaved with almost maternal protectiveness toward her young sister, a pattern established in childhood, judging by the facts Carly had pieced together from her talks with Terry.

"First of all, I want to thank you for everything you've done for Terry, Ms Sullivan," Debra said sincerely. "Terry and I both know how lucky she is."

Carly smiled. "I was glad to do it, and please, call me Carly."

Debra glanced toward the kitchen and caught Jess's eye across the breakfast bar. "And we appreciate Dr. Brannigan stepping in that night at the hospital. Thank you, Dr. Brannigan.''

Jess inclined his head but said nothing.

''How are things with you and your mother, Terry?'' Carly asked.

Terry's expression was suddenly bleak, making her look very young. ''Okay, I guess. She's just got so many other things on her mind.''

''Most parents do, honey,'' Carly said softly. ''Try to remember that your mom's a person, too. She's only human and has her share of problems just like everyone else. She may be preoccupied right now, but she'll be there for you, I'm sure, if you can just have a little patience.''

''Maybe my staying with Debra will take some of the pressure off her.''

Carly felt a pang as she realized that the young girl considered herself a burden to her mother. It was especially sad, seeing as Terry had no father. Thank heaven for Debra and her strong sense of responsibility, Carly thought. She looked at Debra. ''What about counseling for the whole family? Did you mention that to your mother, Debra?''

''We did and although she wasn't thrilled, she promised she would go with Terry and me.'' Debra's laugh was bitter. ''We could tell she would have preferred to just pay the expenses, not face up to the problems we've got, but Terry and I both insisted. So she agreed.''

Carly nodded. ''Wonderful. I'm delighted to hear it.''

When Debra and Terry started to rise, Carly stood. ''You've got all your things, Terry?''

''They're already in the car.'' Terry leaned over and shyly kissed Carly's cheek. ''Thank you, Ms Sullivan. I won't let you down.''

Carly hugged her. ''You won't let yourself down, Terry. Bye now. See you Monday.''

On her way back from seeing them out, Jess met her with a glass of wine. "What happened to the coffee?" she asked, taking the wine and sipping it gratefully.

"I decided it was too late," he said, taking a swallow of something that was rich amber in color and poured over ice cubes. "Besides, while I was looking for the mill to grind it, I stumbled on a new bottle of Scotch. It was no contest after that."

She smiled. "What if I'd been saving that for somebody special?"

Looking deeply into her eyes, he held out his glass and clinked it against hers. "Then that lets me out, honey. But you, now...you definitely are somebody special, Carly Sullivan."

Carly dropped her eyes and stared into the pale yellow wine. "Not really, Jess. I'm not the only teacher who goes a little beyond my job description if a kid really and truly needs help."

He shook his head, rejecting that. "First Terry, then Mike.... Who knows how many others? What do you get out of it?"

"Do I have to get something out of it?"

"You're the psychologist. You tell me."

When it became obvious that she wasn't going to reply, Jess asked suddenly, "How long were you married?"

Startled, Carly frowned at him. "Why do you ask?"

He shrugged. "You lavish a lot of nurturing and caring on the troubled teenagers who parade through your office. It would seem more reasonable to pour all that emotion into marriage and a couple of kids." For a second, there was a stricken look in her eyes. Then it was gone. "What went wrong?"

She sipped her drink and began to walk toward the living room sofa. He followed. "It's not a very unusual story. I was married three years. Apparently, we weren't very well suited. I needed...things from him that he simply couldn't provide."

"Like what?" Had it been money or social position? No, that wouldn't explain the bleakness he'd glimpsed in her eyes. Remembering the relationship still caused her pain, apparently. "What, Carly?"

She set her glass down on the coffee table in front of the sofa and sat down, clasping her arms around her middle. "Oh, Jess, does it matter? It was a disaster, just one of those mistakes that happen occasionally. You don't realize it until it's too late."

"What did you need?" Jess persisted, surprising himself at the depth of his interest in Carly's past. He sat down at the other end of the sofa.

She refused to look at him. "I honestly don't think you'd understand."

It dawned on him that he'd never been frustrated because a woman wouldn't talk to him. If the situation had been reversed, he certainly wouldn't have wanted her probing into his head. He'd never really cared enough to develop any emotional depth in his relationships with women. It felt funny to be on the other end.

"Try me," he coaxed. "What did you need from your husband that he couldn't give you?"

"I was too demanding," she confessed with stark honesty. "My idea of marriage and his were simply too different."

She turned, her arms still folded protectively. "He was a man's man—you know, an athlete. The strong silent type," she said, her eyes almost challenging. "He found it difficult to display emotion—any kind of emotion. And he wouldn't talk to me. I wasn't very experienced. I knew there were things I didn't know, but when I tried to..." She looked away. "He just shut me out."

Her ex-husband had obviously hurt her deeply. Jess was

still, aware of an uncomfortable similarity in the man Carly was describing and himself. She was a loving emotional woman, a hearts-and-flowers-and-commitment kind of woman. She deserved someone who could give her what she needed. Jess reminded himself that he wasn't that someone.

A sharp rap on the door broke the lengthening silence between them. Both Jess and Carly looked toward the entrance, where Mike's tall slim frame was silhouetted against the gleam of the streetlight. Jess walked toward the door, wanting to leave Carly's house for the first time since they'd met.

CHAPTER NINE

ONCE IN THE JAGUAR with Jess, Mike began to rehash the wrestling match. Jess listened, but with only half an ear, responding absently. Only a couple of weeks ago, the prospect of relaxing with Mike after an evening they'd both enjoyed had seemed hopeless. He had Carly to thank for helping him make it happen. And that was the problem. Instead of the casual friendly influence in his life she'd started out to be, Carly was suddenly a major complication.

Until tonight, he'd convinced himself that her past—whatever it was—was nothing he needed to be concerned about. He'd never been hesitant in grabbing at an opportunity that was right under his nose, and the already established friendship between Mike and Carly was a golden one. Fate brought them together at the grand jury. With all the sweetness and generosity of her nature, she'd agreed to help him reestablish his relationship with Mike. It was icing on the cake that he'd wanted her from the first time he'd seen her.

Now, try as he might, he couldn't forget the look of her as she'd talked with underlying pain about her failed marriage. He'd always sensed something vulnerable, almost fragile, about Carly, and it had provoked unexpected feelings of protectiveness in him. Tonight was no exception, only the intensity of his emotion was suddenly multiplied. He'd wanted to take her in his arms and hold her. That kind of reaction was dangerous.

Jess stared out into the night. He didn't need this. He

had his priorities in order, and getting involved with Carly Sullivan wasn't one of them. First and foremost, he had to concentrate on his relationship with Mike. And he still needed Carly to help smooth the way. That alone ruled out a casual affair. There was Mike to consider, too. Jess found he didn't want to set that kind of example for his son, especially with Penny on the scene and Mike just coming to terms with his own sexuality. So far his influence in Mike's life was nothing to be proud of. He was in a position to change that now, and he wanted his influence to be for good, not otherwise.

And then there was his job. Lately he'd toyed with the idea of making a change, just chucking everything. He was definitely tired, fresh out of the professional detachment that was necessary, even vital to keep him going as a trauma specialist. In a less-demanding speciality, he'd have more time to be a real father. His mouth twisted. If it wasn't too late. At present, changing specialties was barely a germ of a thought, but the very fact that he was feeling so uncertain about his future made pursuing any serious relationship a lousy idea.

Jesus, was he having a mid-life crisis? he wondered, rubbing a hand over his mouth, blind to the midnight activity on St. Charles Avenue. He was about the right age. He definitely had all the symptoms. He—

"Hey, look at that!" Mike suddenly leaned forward, eyeing the scene on the street ahead. A police patrol car, blue lights flashing, screeched to a stop in the middle of the next block. A small crowd had gathered, and a couple of cars in front of the Jaguar slowed to a stop, forcing Jess to do the same.

"Looks like an accident of some kind," Jess murmured. "Must have just happened. The patrol car's just getting here."

Mike rolled down his window, curious to see exactly

what was happening. The crowd seemed to be focused on something at the edge of the sidewalk. "Somebody's lying there," he said to Jess over his shoulder. "A guy, I think. He's hurt."

Jess quickly reached over the seat and grabbed his black bag, the physician in him immediately alert. "Here," he said to Mike, handing him the keys and opening the car door. "You take the car and find a place to park." His brisk tone had Mike scrambling across the seat almost before his dad was out of the car.

Jess shouldered his way through the crowd, signaling to a cop by raising his bag.

"Hey, let the doc through!"

Like the Red Sea, the crowd circling the fallen body parted. Jess didn't take time to glance at the victim's face. All his attention centered on a hole directly below a plaid shirt pocket, where blood gushed out with every heartbeat. He quickly pressed the butt of his palm against the wound and reached for his bag.

"Can I help?"

Mike, winded from running, crouched down on the opposite side of the victim, meeting Jess's quick glance.

"Open my bag."

Mike obeyed and watched as Jess took something from the bag to staunch the bleeding wound. "Hand me that pack," Jess ordered. "And then press here." Mike responded, his hands, so like his father's, remarkably steady. Both tuned out the voices of the onlookers above them as they worked in concert to save a life.

"What happened?"

"She shot him."

"Who?"

"That woman over there."

"She was getting off the streetcar, and he tried to snatch her purse."

"She had a gun."

"He had one, too."

"Jeezuz, he's just a kid."

"Which means exactly nothing." The opinion was laced with disgust. "A kid can pull a trigger same as anybody else."

"Damn it, ain't nowhere safe anymore?"

Another vehicle approached, its siren shrill and piercing in the night. "Here come the EMTs."

Jess sighed and rested back on his haunches. "That'll do it, Mike." He glanced up at two white-uniformed men hurrying toward them. "Hey, Oscar, get a move on. I've patched him up, but he's shocky."

The two attendants, carrying medical apparatus and a gurney, dropped down beside the boy. "Lucky son of a gun," Oscar muttered, wrapping a pressure cuff around the skinny arm. "He gets shot and the best trauma specialist in the state just happens by."

Mike stood up slowly, his dark eyes intently following the efficient procedure of the two Emergency Medical Technicians. Both men, Mike noted, responded instantly to a couple of terse orders from Jess. One ran back to the emergency unit and appeared seconds later with a plastic IV bottle. The one called Oscar quickly set it up while Jess watched carefully.

"I see you had some help here," Oscar observed, flicking a glance at Mike while regulating the IV valve.

Jess was occupied checking the pupils of the unconscious boy. Satisfied finally, he straightened and looked at Mike—the first time he'd done so since he'd glanced up to find his son assisting. There was blood on Mike's hands and jeans. Sixteen years old and here he was on his hands and knees in the street, forced to watch another human being court death. Something fierce surged in Jess. He didn't want Mike exposed to the sordidness and brutality that he had to live with every day.

"I'm sorry you got roped into this, Mike," he said, flexing a muscle in his jaw.

Mike opened his mouth to protest, but before he could, Kyle Stratton appeared, plowing through the knot of people watching the EMTs lift their patient onto a gurney.

"Man, don't you get enough of this all day at work?" Kyle demanded. He put out a hand to Jess, but when he saw the blood on Jess's, he withdrew it with a resigned look. He greeted Mike, taking in his bloodstained jeans and shaking his head.

He flicked a professional look at the blanket-wrapped figure. "What've we got here?" he asked.

"Attempted robbery, I think," Jess said curtly, wanting to be gone now that he'd done his duty. With an upthrust of his chin, he indicated the woman talking to the two policemen in the lighted area near the patrol car. "Woman got off the St. Charles streetcar and the kid tried to take her purse. She had a gun, too. Surprised him, I guess."

"Any ID?" Kyle asked.

"I don't think so," Jess replied. "He was unconscious when I got here."

Kyle nodded briefly, glancing toward his car parked at the edge of the crowd. "No problem, I can get all this later at the station. I need to get back to Rachel. This is the last place she ought to be."

Following Kyle's gaze, Jess could see Rachel Lasseigne's dark silhouette in the front seat of a car pulled in behind his own Jaguar. He frowned, recalling Carly telling him that Rachel's husband had been shot and killed before her eyes by a street hoodlum. "You're right about that. This scene is certain to upset her." His gaze strayed to Mike, who was watching everything with keen interest. "It's bad enough even if you're used to it."

"Yeah. Rachel and I were driving by from the other direction when one of the uniforms—Earl Judd—spotted me, otherwise I wouldn't have stopped." Kyle's gray gaze lingered on the wounded man. "Earl said he thought we had a fatality."

"No, this one will make it, I think. Let's go, Mike." Jess reached for his bag, but Mike was quicker. He bent and picked it up, obviously planning to carry it for his dad.

Kyle's eyes followed Jess and Mike as they headed for the Jaguar, Mike easily keeping pace with long legs only a fraction shorter than his dad's. Brannigan, Sr. looked like a man in a hurry, Kyle observed, his gaze thoughtful. Before being assigned to homicide, Kyle had been a street cop. He'd seen a lot of violence, some of it intentional, some accidental, but all of it unsettling. He considered himself lucky that he'd been able to maintain a certain detachment in his work even after years at it. But he'd been around men who hadn't, or who, after a long time at it, had reached their limit. Call it burnout, call it mid-life crisis; the label was unimportant. Jess Brannigan was showing the signs.

Too bad. Crescent City didn't have enough people with Jess's skill to be able to lose him without feeling it. Kyle signaled to Earl Judd, who nodded, then he headed back to Rachel. Stepping off the curb, Kyle watched father and son approach the Jaguar. Without giving the crime scene another glance, Jess climbed in. But young Mike, Kyle noticed with a faint smile, was finding it hard to tear himself away. Kyle put out a hand to open his car door. Maybe one day the boy would step into his father's shoes.

"You okay, hon?" He slid onto his seat, sending a concerned look to Rachel.

"I'm fine, Kyle." She was slightly pale, and her hands were tightly clenched around the strap of her purse. Kyle noticed and cursed the Fates that had brought them onto the scene.

"I'm sorry about this." He started the car and pulled out onto St. Charles Avenue.

"Don't apologize, Kyle. This is your job. You wouldn't have stopped—even though that policeman asked you to—if I hadn't insisted." Rachel gave one final look at the crowd, then settled back in her seat. "Wasn't that Jess and Mike Brannigan I saw getting into that Jaguar?"

"Yeah, Jess happened to drive up just at the right time. Probably saved the kid's life."

"Kid?"

"Yeah, he didn't look to be over fifteen, sixteen."

"Mike saw everything, I guess."

"When I got there, he was in the thick of things."

Rachel shuddered. "What a gruesome sight for a young boy."

Kyle took the turn onto State Street. "Maybe, but he didn't seem upset. Matter of fact, he seemed as coolheaded as a veteran EMT." He hesitated a second. "Less affected by the situation than Jess, actually."

"In what way?" Rachel asked, frowning.

Kyle's gaze was fixed on a red light, but his expression was thoughtful. "I'm not sure. According to the EMTs, Jess acted as quickly and expertly as usual to patch up the victim and stabilize him for the trip to the hospital. Mike jumped in, cool as you please, and assisted. There was blood all over his hands and his jeans, but I could tell it bothered Jess more than it bothered Mike. I just sensed something in Jess's attitude—a sort of disgust with the whole thing—like he'd had a bellyful of gunshot wounds and blood and the people who cause them."

"I can imagine."

He glanced over at Rachel. She was staring straight

ahead, her chin well up, but he could see her vulnerability in the trembling of her mouth.

He swore softly. ‘‘You shouldn’t have been there, Rachel. I shouldn’t have stopped. I know it reminded you—’’ He stopped abruptly, realizing what he’d almost said.

She put out a hand without touching him. ‘‘Hush, Kyle. I can’t stick my head in a hole and pretend all the ugliness in the world has disappeared.’’

He looked into her eyes, hoping to see something to convince him that she really believed that. All he saw was the same bleakness that he found every time she was reminded of that night and the consequences that had changed her life forever. His mouth grim, he pulled up in front of her house and stopped the car.

He glanced over to find Rachel studying him intently. ‘‘Kyle, do you ever feel like Jess? I mean, do you ever just get fed up? Do you ever wish you didn’t have to see so much—’’ she waved a hand ‘‘—so much of the dark side of people?’’

He waited, wishing he felt differently about his job, wishing for her sake that he was an accountant, a lawyer—hell, a truck driver. Anything but a cop, a cop who had practically witnessed her husband’s murder and then failed to find the killer.

‘‘I get frustrated. I get impatient. I even get complacent sometimes,’’ he said slowly, looking at her. ‘‘But I’m a cop, Rachel. I’ll always be a cop, and those times when it all comes right, I know I’m doing what’s right for me.’’

He watched her, feeling a familiar bittersweet ache in his loins. She was so beautiful, her hair a dark cloud around her shoulders. Under her light jacket, she wore a vivid flame-colored sweater. A thousand times he’d imagined how it would be if Phillip’s ghost wasn’t between them. If this was an ordinary date, he’d take her home. They’d share a drink, maybe watch a little TV. And then…

He had this big king-size bed. He'd carry her to his bedroom, strip every scrap of her clothing off, lay her down on that big bed and make long, slow, shattering love to her.

It was crazy to torture himself like this. She thought of him as a friend, as a link to Phillip and her lost love. He didn't know why he kept on coming around. His job would always remind her of Phillip. Hell, his job would always remind him of Phillip. He should have prevented it somehow. Short of that, he should have found the son of a bitch who killed him. He didn't and he hadn't. Would the time ever be right to tell her he loved her, needed her?

Together they walked up her steps, then onto the porch. Rachel's arm was draped around his waist with the casual affection of a good friend. It was heaven and hell to Kyle. He wanted so much more from her.

Inside, loud rock music pulsed from the general direction of Penny's upstairs bedroom. She appeared at the top landing and smiled. "Hi, Mom. Hi, Kyle."

"Everything okay, honey?" Rachel asked, letting Kyle slip her jacket off.

"Uh-huh." She yawned widely. "I'm going to bed. G'night." Her door closed with a thud, and the music ceased.

"Peace," Rachel murmured, closing her eyes for a long moment. She turned to Kyle. "It's not too late. Do you have time for a beer?"

"Thanks." He shrugged out of his jacket and followed her to the kitchen.

"I think I'll have some wine." She went to the cabinet and opened it. Her hands were slightly shaky. She'd been thinking about this moment all day, the moment when she and Kyle would be alone.

She wanted Kyle. Saying it out loud to Carly had been like taking the stopper out of a bottle. Pent-up feelings had come pouring out. She wanted to believe Kyle felt something more for her than just friendship or some kind of misguided sense of obligation and guilt. She wanted to believe, as Carly said, that he was crazy about her. God knows, for months she'd been crazy about Kyle Stratton.

She had loved Phillip, but he was gone forever. And she was still alive, never more so than when she was with Kyle. She took down the bottle of wine and sighed. How did a woman encourage a man to cross the line from friendship to...more than friendship?

Kyle, standing behind Rachel, was intensely aware of everything about her. He felt a rush of desire so strong, it amazed him that she didn't somehow sense it.

He wondered what she would do if she knew. What would she do if he kissed her? How would she taste if he kissed her? God, the idea had tantalized him for months. That was one of the reasons he felt so guilty. Immediately after Phillip died, feelings he'd buried for years had suddenly burst free. From that moment, he had not had an easy day. He wanted Rachel. He wanted his best friend's wife.

"Let's take these into the den," Rachel said, handing him a beer and moving ahead of him with her wine. "There's a good movie on the cable channel. Somebody mentioned it this afternoon at school."

Silently Kyle followed her, and when she sat down on the couch, he hesitated only a second or two before going down beside her. He took a long sip of his beer, then pressed the chilled can against his temple, thinking that it was a far cry from the cold shower he needed. No, what he needed was to get up and walk out. He was in no shape to sit beside Rachel on a couch and calmly watch a movie.

Rachel made herself comfortable, innocently stretching out her long legs. The movie began. Kyle groaned, quickly camouflaging the sound with a hasty cough when Rachel glanced at him. It was a tale of infidelity, an intense story of betrayal and lust. The first love scene came fairly soon into the story. It was between the hero and the woman who was the wife of his business partner, and the forbidden flavor of their attraction made the scene all the more sensual and arousing to Kyle.

Watching the actors, his own imagination leaped into flame. The desire that he'd worked all night to suppress was a tight throbbing ache. His fingers tingled with the need to touch Rachel, to caress her.

It was crazy. It was insane. He was sitting there going quietly out of his mind watching two people—strangers, actors—make love. There was nothing real in the passion on the screen. It was all make-believe, nothing like the deep abiding emotion he felt for Rachel.

He closed his eyes. He had to get out. Rachel had given him no indication that she thought of him as anything other than a friend. Tonight, he simply didn't think he could keep up the pretense. Abruptly he got to his feet, muttering something about paperwork and the accident they'd witnessed. Rachel scrambled up and followed him to the door, where he said goodbye almost rudely and rushed out.

She roamed around restlessly after he left. So much for her hope that the film might have an erotic effect on Kyle. Listlessly, she picked up her wineglass and Kyle's almost full beer can and took them to the kitchen. How was it she had only lately realized how sexy Kyle Stratton was? But did she appeal to him? Was she just dreaming when she hoped for something more than friendship from Kyle?

Something, a faint sound, made her heart leap into her throat. Someone was at her front door. She put her hand to her breast. *Don't panic,* she commanded her runaway imagination. She walked to the front part of the house just as her door opened and Kyle stepped inside.

He said nothing as he pushed away from the door and

moved slowly toward her, his face an inscrutable mask of shadow and reflected light. Rachel's heart was thudding in her chest. She couldn't move.

"Kyle?"

"I meant to leave," he said, his voice low. "I almost did." He put out a hand and touched the side of her face. Rachel could feel him trembling. "I can still go, Rachel. It's not too late." His eyes locked with hers. "What do *you* want, Rachel?"

Relief and delight rose in Rachel. She smiled and stepped close to him. "You."

ALL CARLY'S FIRM RESOLUTIONS to keep Jess Brannigan at arm's length and their relationship on a platonic level had been unnecessary. He wasn't interested in her as a woman. The past two weeks had proved that.

She was dismayed to discover how much it mattered.

It was humiliating to think that just at the time she had considered lowering her defenses, Jess had lost interest—if he'd ever had any. Just at the time she'd been thinking maybe the gamble was worth the prize, he'd made it clear she'd read him wrong. He hadn't been coming on to her, after all. Looking back, she wasn't sure why she had thought he was. Probably because she was so stupidly inexperienced. Hadn't he told her so himself?

But then abruptly—Carly pinpointed it to the night of the wrestling match—there were no more stolen moments, no more kisses, no more interrupted interludes. His sensual promise to ravish her if he ever got an uninterrupted opportunity seemed forgotten. He'd been to her house a couple of times in the past two weeks when Mike was around, but never when Mike wasn't. They'd watched a practice track meet together and celebrated Mike's record-high hurdle. Unlike before, Jess now brought her directly to her door and left her there, unkissed. At the grand jury sessions, there was no difference in the way he treated her and the way he treated white-haired arthritic Elizabeth Cohn.

What bothered her most was that Jess's appeal had almost made her push aside old fears. True, she had been worrying, wondering how she was going to measure up considering her miserable track record as a lover, but she'd been slowly psyching herself up. Lord, suppose he'd guessed? When was she going to face it? As a woman, she just didn't have what it took.

"In bed or out of it, you're a miserable failure." Buck's words sliced into her thoughts, and she winced.

Thank heavens Jess didn't know how close she'd come.

At lunchtime on Monday, she talked about it to Rachel. "I guess I should have known better," she said. "Jess asked me about my marriage. He wanted to know what it was I needed that I hadn't gotten from my husband."

"What did you tell him?" Rachel pushed aside her half-eaten salad and cupped her hands around a mug of hot tea.

"I told him what was missing—communication, empathy. I'd needed things Buck couldn't give. I probably gave him the idea that I was too demanding."

Rachel looked blank. "You think he read something significant in that?"

"I sensed it, yes. He left right away."

"Because Mike was at the door," Rachel reminded her.

Carly shook her head. "No. I mean, yes, Mike was at the door, but..." She tossed an empty yogurt container into the trash can. "I don't know, Rachel. You may be right. I'm probably imagining everything, especially that he had any interest in me other than as a line to Mike." She laughed shortly. "I feel like an idiot."

"There's no reason to," Rachel said quickly. "The man doesn't know what you're thinking, Carly. Besides, you're only guessing about his reaction. There may be things going on in his life that he hasn't mentioned to you.''

''Like what?''

''It's something Kyle mentioned after we saw Jess at the site of that shooting a couple of weeks ago.'' She toyed with the corner of her napkin. ''Kyle mentioned that Jess looked fed up.''

Carly frowned, instantly concerned. ''In what way?''

Rachel shrugged. ''I'm not sure. His work is demanding, more so than Kyle's actually. Kyle isn't on the street anymore, where the real danger is, but at Crescent City, Jess has to deal daily—sometimes hourly—with life-threatening situations. A single shift without at least one stabbing or gunshot victim is rare, according to Kyle. And the responsibility falls squarely on the trauma surgeon.''

''Making Jess a classic candidate for burnout,'' Carly mused thoughtfully. ''Plus, he has this problem with Mike. It seems to be working out okay, but who knows with a sixteen-year-old?''

Rachel, a parent of fifteen years, remained silent.

''He certainly wouldn't want to complicate his life any more,'' Carly murmured.

''He can't be expected to know this, but you wouldn't be a complication in his life, Carly. You'd probably be the best thing that ever happened to him.''

Carly stood up suddenly and began briskly tidying up the mess they'd made. ''Enough about that.'' She picked up Rachel's empty salad bowl and a crinkled sandwich wrapper. ''You've certainly regained your appetite, I see.''

Rachel waved an airy hand without commenting. Still, something alerted Carly. She glanced sharply at Rachel, who failed to meet her eyes. ''So, how are things with Kyle?''

Rachel brushed some crumbs from her skirt. ''Fine.''

Carly cocked a teasing brow. ''Fine?''

"Uh-huh."

"No details?"

"Uh-uh."

Carly propped her hands on her hips. "I bare my soul and you clam up? Uh-uh, no way. So, I'll repeat the question. How're things with Kyle?"

Rachel met her eyes and blushed, to Carly's amazement. "We made love, Carly."

Carly sank back down. "Oh, Rachel."

"And it was wonderful. I love him, Carly."

Carly picked up one of Rachel's hands and squeezed it. "I'm so happy for you both. He's the nicest sexiest man I know, next to—" She scrambled up and grabbed their lunch trash. "We'd better run, Rachel. It's late."

For once, Rachel left well enough alone.

CHAPTER TEN

THE DIFFERING PERSONALITIES of the grand jurors were never more apparent than they were that Friday when they heard a case involving marital rape. No one was unmoved by the testimony of the victim, a young woman who worked as a paralegal in a prestigious law firm downtown. Caroline Simpson was still clearly shattered by the experience, and when she testified—a legal requirement for all victims of rape—even though John Hebert was extremely considerate, she broke down completely. In closed session a debate raged among the jurors over whether or not to indict Troy James Domingue.

"I don't see that it's rape when these two people have been living together for over four years," Joe West stated.

"Anytime a woman is forced, it's rape," Michelle Bordelon said quietly but firmly.

"She also has a right to choose adoption over abortion," Carly said, still outraged at what the victim's testimony had revealed. Caroline Simpson and Domingue had lived together for four years. She had told the jury that she'd wanted to get married, but although Domingue had promised—even set the date several times—he'd always backed out. He was angry when she became pregnant and insisted she get an abortion. His attitude forced her into a good long look at her life and her future, she'd informed the jurors tearfully. One night after work, she told him she'd decided to have the baby and give it up for adoption. She also announced that she was breaking off their relationship.

He immediately accused her of trying to force him into marriage. The confrontation escalated into a physical assault by Domingue.

"We only have her word it was rape," West grumbled. "She could be getting back at him for refusing to marry her."

"What about the hospital report that there was evidence of rough sex?" Carly demanded. Joe West was one of the most close-minded cynical individuals she'd ever met.

West shrugged. "Some women like it that way."

Carly threw her hands up, disgusted.

"She didn't strike me as a vindictive young woman," Elizabeth Cohn offered in her quiet voice.

Carly looked appealingly at the jurors. "I agree with Mrs. Cohn. I don't think she's lying. Looking at Caroline Simpson, you can tell she's been shattered by the whole experience. I just have a feeling—"

"We can't dispense justice on women's intuition," Colonel Buckley reminded her in a tone she knew was calculated to make her feel about eight years old.

"I just have a feeling," Carly repeated firmly, refusing to look at the colonel, "that we've been told the truth by this woman. We all know rape is an act of violence. Domingue was enraged that Caroline was going to leave him. His own co-worker testified to that. Maybe he simply let his anger get out of hand."

"Yeah, that might have been the way it happened," West said with a discerning nod.

Carly glared at him, exasperated. "Which doesn't excuse raping a woman, Joe!"

She was still fuming when the session broke up for the day. Jess fell into step beside her as she took the steps of the courthouse in double-time. "One of these days, I'm going to give that Joe West a piece of my mind. And Colonel Buckley, too," she said grimly.

"I'm not sure you shouldn't have been a lawyer yourself," Jess drawled, slipping a hand under her elbow to do what he could to keep her from breaking a leg.

"Why do you say that?" she asked, deliberately removing her arm. She wasn't indifferent to his touch. It meant nothing to him, she knew, but she hadn't quite managed to achieve the same detachment.

"More than once you've turned the tide in the jury sessions," he said simply. "And you don't always have the facts on your side."

She glanced at him sharply. "Do you think any innocent person's been indicted because of me?"

He laughed shortly. "Not exactly, but a couple of guilty ones may have gotten off."

She considered that, frowning, wondering how to explain herself. "Sometimes we don't have black-and-white evidence. Those times all we have are our own instincts. Not that it helped Caroline Simpson today," she said bitterly. "Domingue got away with it."

"There just wasn't enough hard evidence, Carly."

She cast a weary eye over a profusion of bright yellow mums planted on the perimeter of the courthouse grounds. "I know, but the woman told the truth. I know it, I *feel* it. Unfortunately, we can't indict on what Colonel Buckley calls my female intuition."

"West and the colonel had a point, you know," Jess said, glancing at her sideways. Bright autumn sunshine caught in her hair, highlighting it with streaks of gold. He felt for his sunglasses and slipped them on. Together they crossed the street and headed for their cars.

"Caroline Simpson wouldn't have been the first woman to have used pregnancy to achieve her own ends," he said. "And if her aim was to nudge Domingue into marriage and it failed, her motive in bringing this action against him might not have been so pure."

"I know all that, Jess. I'm not totally naive. I just don't believe that's the way it happened. I believe she was telling the truth when she said she told him she was going to give up the baby and put an end to their relationship, and he reacted by raping her."

They stopped when they reached Carly's car. When she unlocked her door, he said, "Try not to let it get to you. You did what you could, more than anyone else on that jury. At some point, you have to trust the system, faulty though it may be."

"The women were with me," Carly said quietly, looking over the tops of the cars toward the river. "The men..." She shook her head, then turned to get into her car. "I hate to think the men identified with that...with Domingue."

"Not so much Domingue as the circumstances," Jess suggested. "And the possibility that he was victimized by the oldest trick known to man."

She stopped, looking at him narrowly. "You too, Jess?"

He shrugged. "The evidence didn't condemn him. Unlike you, I don't have the gift of second sight."

"Don't be ridiculous! You know it's nothing like that. Don't you ever just have a gut feeling about something?" She hesitated when he didn't reply, aware with dawning insight that his skepticism could only have its source in some personal experience. But when? Why? She felt a surge of frustration. He wasn't about to answer those questions, and how could they ever understand each other without some basic communication? The answer, she knew with a pang somewhere in her heart, was that they couldn't.

She drew in a deep breath. "Well, all I can say is, I hope I never have occasion for you to believe in me—when your head tells you one thing and your heart tells you another."

His grin wasn't quick, and it was slightly crooked. "Have you decided I've got a heart?"

Carly smiled faintly. "It took me a while, but I've decided you've got one—well guarded, but it's there."

"Female intuition, I assume?"

Her eyes widened. "You mean you believe there is such a thing?"

Jess studied her through his sunglasses. Flirting with her was not the way to keep from getting tangled up with her, he reminded himself. His gaze slid to her mouth, and he tried not to think how utterly tantalizing it was. This was no way to keep things between them strictly platonic, and he'd spent the past three weeks doing his best to accomplish just that.

On those days when he didn't see her, he wandered around his big empty house, feeling edgy and restless, blaming it on the unsettled state of his relationship with Mike or his growing dissatisfaction with his job. Carly was a complication in his life he couldn't afford right now. So why did the idea persist that his life would seem a lot clearer and simpler if he could just take her to his house, lock her in his bedroom and love away the weekend with her? It was crazy, but there it was.

"Mike's taking Penny to a football game tonight," he told her, noting with a slight narrowing of his eyes that she was easing her body into the car through a slight wedge in the door, almost as though to put a barrier between them.

"I guess that means you have the night off," she said with a tight smile.

Her hand was resting on the frame of the car door. He reached over and covered it, stroking her knuckles with his thumb. "I was thinking the same thing."

"Right. I've got some errands, myself."

Puzzlement flickered in his eyes. "Errands?"

She lifted one shoulder, not quite meeting his eyes. "You know how it is for a working woman at the end of the week."

He continued absently massaging her fingers while he considered that. It was one thing for him to withdraw from her, he discovered, but another for Carly to attempt the same thing.

"When I agreed we had the night off, I meant we had the luxury of a night without teenage chaperones," Jess explained. "As for your errands, save them for Saturday morning, like all reasonable working women. For tonight, we're going to have that dinner date I promised you weeks ago." *Now that's a helluva way to put distance between you and Carly,* Jess thought.

She pulled her fingers out from beneath his and tossed her purse on the seat behind her. "Thanks, but I think I really will pass tonight, Jess." She sank into the driver's seat and looked at him, her smile cool and polite. "And, please...forget about promising me anything."

"Wait a minute!" He caught the door and prevented her from closing it. "You make it sound as though I'm taking you to dinner out of a sense of obligation or something, Carly."

"Well, aren't you? Isn't that what you meant? I certainly don't believe you have any desire to take me to dinner because you desire my company—that is, without the added attraction of Mike or Penny."

He stared at her with a mixture of consternation and anger. He'd wrestled with a whole host of conflicting emotions about this woman for the past three weeks, putting his own intense desire for her aside and now, misunderstanding, her pride was hurt. Or were her feelings hurt? There was a big difference.

She was busy starting her car, so he had to bend down to see her. "Carly, I want to take you to dinner for no reason other than that I want to spend the evening with you and you alone."

Reluctantly, she looked at him.

"What d'you say?" His dark brows lifted above his sunglasses. "Seven-thirty?" He glanced at his watch and back at her. "I'm going to put in some time at the hospital, but barring an emergency, I should be able to leave by then."

She was looking straight ahead, considering.

"Commander's Palace," he coaxed, his voice low pitched and beguiling. "The best seafood in New Orleans—oysters en brochette, redfish court bouillon..."

She smiled. "Okay, okay, seven-thirty."

THAT EVENING, long before seven-thirty, Carly was prowling around her house having second thoughts—mostly because she knew Jess would be having them, too. She reached to turn on the television, wanting to drown out her thoughts. She had not imagined his withdrawal these past three weeks. No matter what he said, she knew he was taking her to dinner because he felt he owed it to her. She hated that.

Shaking her head, she started to change the channel, then she stopped short, her hand outstretched. There was a news bulletin on, and she caught the words, "emergency room at Crescent City Hospital." Backing slowly to the nearest chair, she sank down.

A disturbance, she heard; a crazed patient, armed. As the words sank in, Carly's hand went to her chest, her eyes locked on the reporter, who faced the camera, mike in hand, Crescent City's emergency entrance at his back. Although unconfirmed, witnesses reported a fatal shooting in the trauma unit. Apparently a skirmish had followed when hospital personnel had tried to subdue the assailant. Crescent's emergency room was in a state of chaos. Patients were being referred temporarily to nearby hospitals while Crescent City and the police attempted to assess the damage and restore order. Names were to be withheld pending notification of the next of kin…

Carly's eyes closed weakly, and she clenched both hands between her breasts. Her throat tightened at the thought of Jess injured. She rejected the other more horrifying possibility and fixed her eyes on the screen. It had happened more than an hour ago. She could call…who? If Jess was hurt, where would he go? If he was one of the victims—her heart stumbled over the word—he would be hospitalized, but they wouldn't tell her anything if she called. Even Mike might not be notified for hours yet.

She sprang up from her chair and headed for the telephone. Maybe Rachel could call Kyle, and he could tell her something. He would surely know. They had said something about a possible fatality, and Kyle was assigned to homicide. Fatality. Oh, God! She pressed the fingers of one hand against her mouth to hold back a cry. Halfway to the phone, the sound of the doorbell stopped her short.

Through the glass, her eyes swept over Jess. She cried out incoherently and rushed forward, fumbling with the lock. Hands trembling, she finally tore open the door.

Her eyes flew over him in quick anxious assessment. His left temple was covered with a bandage, its stark whiteness almost obscene against his dark skin. His hair had a wind-tossed look, as though he'd pushed his fingers through it a few times. His hands were shoved deep inside the pockets of his windbreaker. If anything was broken, it didn't show. She looked up and found that he was studying her with equal intensity.

"I'm early, I guess," he said, his mouth slanted in a wry half smile. But his eyes weren't smiling. They were dark and fixed on hers.

His voice seemed to release something inside her. She

pulled the door open wide to let him in, then closed it and turned. She wanted to throw her arms around him, to run her hands all over him to assure herself he was all right. Instead, she wrapped her arms around herself to keep them from closing around him and tried to hide the tumult inside her.

"How badly are you hurt?" she said through the tightness in her throat. Her eyes were all over him, taking in the strained look of his features, the bloodstains on his shirt where his jacket hung open.

His right hand came up, then fell. "It's nothing."

"I just saw it on television."

He drew in a breath, glancing away from her. "Channel Four had a unit out there," he said vaguely, his gaze going beyond her to the living room, then back to her as though pulled by an invisible cord.

Her eyes searched his face. "What happened?" She waved an impotent hand. "Why?"

He shrugged. "Who the hell knows why? He was just another street junkie, spaced out, ready to blow." He laughed without humor. "One of my regulars, actually."

"You mean you've seen him before?" she asked, shocked.

"Too many times to count."

She stared speechlessly, then noticed for the first time that he was favoring his left shoulder. "Your shoulder... Is it hurt, too?"

He shifted as though testing it, then dismissed it. "I may have pulled a muscle."

His eyes on her face were dark and stormy, and there was something else she couldn't read. He seemed to be barely holding himself together. She sensed he was suppressing some deep fierce emotion.

"We have a date," he said.

Her eyes clung to his, not even hearing him. "I was so

scared, Jess.'' Her relief and thankfulness at seeing him safe and relatively unharmed temporarily robbed her of the uncertainty that usually inhibited her. With a strangled cry, she went into his arms.

She buried her face in the warmth of his neck, shuddering when one hand curved around her back and fiercely pulled her against his hard frame. Caught up in the sheer relief of the feel of Jess, warm and substantial, *alive* in her arms, Carly thought nothing for a few long wonderful moments.

''Carly—''

She put her fingers against his mouth, interrupting him. ''I'm sorry,'' she whispered, unconsciously running a restless hand over his back, then up past his collar, sinking her fingers into his thick black hair. ''When they said someone might have been k-killed...'' Her words trailed off helplessly.

Jess turned his mouth against her temple, feeling her whole body trembling. His arms tightened around her, straining her softness to him. ''You feel so good, Carly. Warm...soft.''

Wholesome and womanly, nurturing and loving, gentle. All the things missing from his life. The thought settled in his mind with the certainty of a stone sinking into clear water. He needed all that, needed everything she was to blank out the nightmare he'd just been through and the sickening certainty that it would be waiting for him tomorrow, and all his tomorrows. He needed Carly to banish the sick feeling in the pit of his stomach, to make him forget. He turned his face into the clean silky fragrance of her hair.

Immediately he felt the twin coils of tension and danger ease. Inhaling deeply, he exulted in the scent of her, breathed in her special essence. It always put him in mind of the inviting femininity of her house and her special perfume and...her. He caught a handful of her hair and tugged gently, seeking her eyes. She had a dazed look, but her skin was flushed, her lips soft and inviting.

"I fought a war with myself all the way over here, Carly, asking myself what the hell I was doing." His lips, restless and insistent, raced over her features. He swept a hand down to her buttocks and pressed her against him, feeling the life pulsating in both of them and glorying in it.

"Carly, feel what you do to me.... Open your mouth, honey. Just this once, kiss me...." His voice was urgent, coaxing, and his lips grazed hers. She made an answering sound against his throat. It was sweet and, to Jess, deeply erotic—all he needed to lose the last of his control.

"I need this, Carly. I need you."

Carly's lips parted under his, and his tongue plunged hungrily into the warm and honeyed depths that had tantalized him from the moment he'd first seen her. His hips surged forward, seeking the feminine cradle for his male hunger. Desire and need combined, then claimed him.

CHAPTER ELEVEN

A FLOOD OF EMOTION swept through Carly, releasing all her secret longings. She forgot the caution that had frozen her responses when she'd been in his arms before. Her uncertainty vanished in joy and relief that he hadn't been killed, taken from her abruptly and cruelly before she'd had a chance to come to terms with her feelings.

She felt his splayed hand tighten across her lower back to push her even closer to the heat and hardness of him. This time she had no desire to resist. Her shortcomings as a lover were forgotten in her need. She went up on her tiptoes, fitting herself more urgently against him. Desire, strong and compelling, spiraled through her while her hands toured the sleek masculine line of his shoulders and waist, then made their way up to clench his hair and hold his mouth against hers.

A shudder racked his body, and he made a slight sound. It was a second or two before it dawned on Carly that it had been a grunt of pain. She tore her mouth from his. "Oh, you're hurt!" Her eyes on his were wide and alarmed.

"No, wait a minute," he said as she made a move away from him. He dropped his good arm around her waist and held her tightly against him, breathing unevenly. "Don't move, don't do a thing."

She felt him put his chin on the top of her head, his body, hard and tense, fitted against hers, but it was a good feeling. It felt right and natural to hold him. Without thinking, her hands stroked his back.

"Just be still, honey," he told her in a ragged voice. "I'm about three seconds away from a total loss of control, and I don't think the time is right."

Carly felt fierce color wash over her face and was thankful she was hidden from Jess's shrewd gaze. At just that moment, the telephone rang.

She murmured something and, not looking at him, pushed out of his arms and made her way across the room to answer it. Her voice sounded shaky even to her own ears.

"Ms Sullivan, this is Mike Brannigan." There was an anxious note in the boy's voice that sent Carly's gaze straight to Jess, standing in the middle of the room.

"Hello, Mike."

Jess's dark gaze narrowed sharply.

"Ms Sullivan, did you see the news? There's been a shooting at the hospital in my dad's—"

"I know, Mike," Carly began, watching Jess come toward her. "Your father is—"

"I've tried to find out something from the hospital, and they won't tell me anything. I've even tried the TV station, but they just put me off." The anguish in his voice tugged at Carly's heart.

"I thought maybe Detective Stratton could help me," Mike said desperately, "but he's not at his desk, and Mrs. Lasseigne and Penny are shopping. Do you think you—"

Jess reached out and took the receiver. "I'm here, Mike," he said, breaking into the boy's urgent words.

"Dad!"

"I'm okay, son."

There was a moment of shocked silence. Jess leaned against the counter and allowed himself a minute of sheer unadulterated joy. He would gladly suffer another incident at the hospital to hear Mike call him Dad again. He'd come to wonder whether he would ever hear it.

Mike spoke again hesitantly. "They said someone may have been killed." His voice was unsteady, catching in his throat.

"I'm afraid so, son. It was a technician who was trying to subdue the patient."

"He was shot?" Mike inquired.

"Yes."

Mike hesitated. "There were some other people hurt, according to the report I saw."

"The other injuries were minor, Mike." Jess drew a quick breath. "Look, son, these things happen occasionally. And especially at Crescent City. We talked about this last week, remember? It comes with the territory."

"Were you one of those hurt, Dad?" Mike demanded, sounding older suddenly.

Jess looked into Carly's eyes and found them soft with understanding.

"Were you, Dad?"

"I was knicked, Mike," he admitted. "It's nothing. I was lucky."

There was another interval of silence, rife with everything still unspoken and unresolved that lay between father and son.

"You say, 'knicked,'" Mike repeated carefully. "Does that mean a gun or a knife?"

Jess's frown took on an impatient edge. "A gun, Mike, but I'm telling y—"

"Where were you shot?"

Jess turned his mouth from the receiver and swore. "Right in ER in the middle of the hall. Now, listen, Mike—"

"No, you listen!" Mike's voice exploded through the wire. Jess looked startled, and even Carly, four feet away, could tell the boy's control was at an end. "Stop treating me like a little kid, damn it! You were shot, almost killed by some sleaze bag high on crack or something. Hell, I could get that much from Channel Four! Now, I want to know where—in your arm, your leg, y-your chest..." He drew a quick unsteady breath. "Where, Dad?"

Jess hesitated only a moment before deciding to take Mike at his word. "He knicked my temple and gave me the granddaddy of all headaches," he said quietly, then added in a hard tone, "He must be a lousy shot considering the number of bullets he sprayed around before we could stop him. Still, Tim Steadman's dead, and two others were cut by flying glass when the guy went through an inside window."

"Jeezuz," was Mike's whispered response.

"I would have called you in a few more minutes, Mike," Jess told him. "I'd just walked in Carly's door and we—" His eyes found hers. "I was just telling her about it."

"I bet she was upset," Mike said, sounding more normal.

"Oh?" Some of the harshness eased in Jess's expression. "What makes you say that?" he asked, still holding Carly's gaze, who peered back, unsuspecting.

"Don't be a jerk, Dad," Mike said with affectionate disrespect, his composure restored. "She likes you, anybody can see that."

"Yeah, well..." Jess floundered, caught off guard. Finding himself being teased about his love life by his sixteen-year-old son was suddenly too much to cope with in a day that had already been taxing enough. "Never mind that," he said, taking refuge in some fatherly blustering. "Since when have you taken up swearing? Damn it this and hell that. What does your mother have to say about it?"

"Nothing, since she says a lot worse than that herself," Mike replied with candid nonchalance.

"Well, knock it off."

"Okay, Dad."

Jess wrestled with another surge of pleasure. "I'll see you tomorrow, son."

"You don't need me to stay with you tonight?"

His eyes on his feet, Jess shook his head helplessly. "I'll be okay, Mike. But thanks, I appreciate the thought."

"You watch it around those lowlife types, Dad."

"Yeah."

"Otherwise, I'll have to rethink my career choice."

"You'll have to pass chemistry or the question's moot," Jess reminded him dryly.

"Bye, Dad."

Jess hung up, smiling softly.

"Everything okay?" Carly asked from across the counter.

"Hmm?" He looked up, still smiling. "Oh, yeah. Everything's okay, I think."

"I'm glad," she said with a soft answering smile.

They stood a moment looking into each other's eyes, both aware of the significance of the way Mike had reacted to the possibility of Jess in danger. As his counselor, she should have been most concerned about Mike, but watching the quiet satisfaction in Jess's eyes, Carly knew the intense joy she felt wasn't just for her student. In fact, it was mostly for Jess.

The realization was so unsettling that she turned quickly and looked for something to occupy her hands at the kitchen sink.

"Well..." She cleared her throat and reached for the coffeepot. "Shall I make us some coffee?"

Without turning, she felt him closing in on her. His hand appeared from behind her and he took the glass pot. "No, you won't make us coffee.'' He set it down and leaned against the sink, bending his knees and his head so she was forced to look at him. ''We have a real date tonight, and I intend to keep it. I've got reservations at Commander's.''

She opened a cupboard. ''I can make us something here, Jess. You're—''

He straightened. ''Uh-uh. I've freeloaded enough. We're eating out.''

Her eyes fell to the blood on his shirtfront. ''You may have trouble getting in the front door,'' she pointed out dryly.

''I'll stop by my place and change,'' he told her.

''Don't be ridiculous, Jess. You've just come within a hair of being killed, and I heard you tell Mike you had a serious headache. I'll take a rain check, for heaven's sake.''

''No way, I—''

She was rummaging around in the cupboard, but something—some slight sound from Jess—caused her to look over at him. He turned slightly, but not before she saw the unhealthy pallor of his skin. He swayed and emitted a smothered grunt.

''Jess!'' She slammed the cupboard door shut and put out a hand to him. ''What's wrong? What is it?''

He braced himself against the counter and spoke with both eyes closed. ''Just a little pang. It'll pass.''

Alarmed, Carly moved closer, wanting to touch him. She could see sweat beading above his lips and on his forehead. ''Jess, you've got to lie down.'' She put a hand on his arm and gently urged him toward the living room.

''Okay, we'll order something from that deli on Prytania,'' he said, going with her to the sofa. ''I heard it's fantastic.''

''Forget the deli!'' she ordered impatiently, edging the

glass table aside with her foot to make room for his long legs. "Humor me, just this once, and lie down."

"I've humored you more than once," he said weakly, settling down and leaning his head back, letting his lids droop with a sigh.

"Like when?" she snapped, grabbing two pillows from the floor and arranging them in the corner of the sofa. When she turned back, he was shrugging out of his jacket. "Okay, just lie back here...easy," she crooned.

Smothering a groan, he did as he was told. "Like all those times I should have kissed you and to hell with all the interruptions," he told her, watching through the tangle of his dark lashes as she bent over him and pulled at the cushions.

She looked at him anxiously, choosing to ignore his suggestive comments. "How does that feel? Is that okay? Are you comfortable?"

He sighed. "As comfortable as I can be with a drummer playing heavy metal music in my head."

"Didn't they give you anything for it?" Carly demanded, feeling anxious and concerned. "Just because you're a doctor, do they think you don't feel pain?"

"I have something, Carly," he said calmly. "In my jacket pocket. But I don't want to take anything until we've had dinner."

Muttering a word that would shock most people who knew her, Carly reached for his jacket and took a bottle of pills out of a pocket. "Wait here," she ordered.

He made a short wry sound. "Right."

She was back inside of thirty seconds with a glass of water and two capsules. "I didn't know whether the dosage was one or two," she said, holding out a couple on an upturned palm. "The bottle wasn't marked."

"Two," he said succinctly, rising on one elbow with a

slight wince and downing them with a little water. "Thanks."

Carly waited a second or two, her eyes on his face. "Are you hungry?"

He stared at her from unreadable dark eyes. "How about yourself? Have you eaten since lunch?"

"No."

"Please call the deli. Or Chinese takeout. There's a—"

Two fingers on his lips stopped him. She shook her head, a hint of a smile on her mouth. "With those pills, you'd be better off with a light omelet, I think. I've got the ingredients and some French bread. We'll skip the wine this time."

Before he could object, she was halfway to the kitchen.

Jess followed her with his eyes. Even through a haze of pain, he admired the shape of her bottom and the saucy way she walked. It was unconscious, he knew. She'd never flaunt herself or behave suggestively. She didn't have to, he thought, settling back against the cushions and smiling lazily. All he had to do was look at her, and he was turned on.

His smile faded. Carly made him feel things he didn't want to feel. It was one thing to want to lose himself in her softness after a day like today, but he'd have to make certain it was only this one time. A few weeks spent trying to keep her in the friendship-only category had convinced him it wasn't going to be easy.

When he was with her, somehow it became more important to explore the possibilities than to keep his distance. He'd have to be careful to watch that. She was sweet and soft and feminine, and those were qualities that translated into things like commitment and caring and complications. There wasn't room in his life for any more of that. He had enough with Mike and his still-unresolved decision over what to do about his job.

He frowned, wincing when pain lanced through his temple. So, nothing had changed since he'd had this conversation with himself weeks ago. But, hell, it was hard to resist her.

He opened his eyes as he heard Carly come back into the room. She was carrying a tray and had kicked off her shoes, baring her toes, which were painted with pale peach polish. Bare toes and soft curly unbound hair. He groaned as fresh desire washed through him.

She was instantly concerned. "You're still hurting? The pills didn't work yet?"

He waved a hand and struggled into a sitting position. "They dulled it enough," he said, his eyes on the tray. It held two plates with omelets. He could smell green peppers and mushrooms. One omelet was accompanied by a tossed salad and the other by sliced fresh fruit. French bread had been toasted and lavishly spread with butter. "That looks good, but you really shouldn't have bothered."

Carly set the tray down and lifted both plates. "I was hungry myself. What'll you have, fruit or salad? It doesn't matter to me."

He moved his head cautiously and went very still, absorbing the blinding pain, riding it through. Stopping here had been stupid. Getting shot must have scrambled his judgment along with his brain, he decided with wry amusement. He should have driven straight home and crawled into bed. He'd give the narcotics a little more time to work, then maybe catch a taxi home.

"Salad," he told her, even though the throbbing in his skull had killed his appetite.

She sat down beside him. "Fine."

They ate in silence for a few minutes. Jess forced himself to chew and swallow, recognizing the classic symptoms of concussion with clinical detachment. The omelet was light and savory, the bread toasted to perfection. If he'd been able to eat it, he knew he would have found nothing wrong with the salad, either. He frowned, thinking of her ex-husband. What the hell could have gone wrong?

He put his fork down and leaned back against the sofa. He rolled his head, taking in the perfection of her profile through narrowed lids.

"Why haven't you remarried?" he asked abruptly.

She turned startled eyes to his, then began collecting their used things. "Are you finished?"

Pain stopped his half-formed nod. "Yeah, thanks." He watched the quick deft movement of her hands. "You do a fantastic omelet, so why hasn't some lucky guy snapped you up?"

"There's more to marriage than making omelets," she said, standing with the loaded tray.

His gaze swept over her tawny hair, then fell to survey the rest of her. "I can't see you having a problem with any of it," he told her, watching her walk to the tiny dining room, slide the tray onto the breakfast counter then walk around to the kitchen.

"How about coffee?"

"I don't think so," he said. "Better not push my luck. Food and caffeine don't mix well with this narcotic." He patted the place beside him on the sofa. "Come back and keep me company while I wait for it to work enough so that I can tackle the drive home."

She dropped the napkins she held and came back to him, frowning. "Do you need me to drive you?"

He patted the sofa again. "I just need you to sit down so I don't have to crane my neck to see you."

She sank down beside him, smiling slightly. "Now you sound as demanding as some of my students."

He reached for her hand. "Well, I'm not one of your students, so just relax." He pulled her close against his side and rested his chin on her head. Her hair had a fresh flowery scent that filled his senses and stirred an immediate ache in his loins in spite of his throbbing head. Something about Carly was very soothing, like a summer day. A man could become addicted to a woman like that. Her ex-husband must have been a total fool. He was still thinking about it. "You didn't answer my question."

"What question?"

"Why haven't you remarried, Carly?"

"I told you before, I tried it once and it was a disaster—three awful years."

He shifted so that he could look into her face. "You shrinks are supposed to have all the answers," he said mildly. "You're supposed to have the know-how to handle relationships, especially that most intimate one—marriage. You aren't supposed to make the same mistakes as us ordinary types." He settled back with his arm around her. "So, what did he do?"

"He coached football." She named the college and sensed rather than felt his surprise.

"Sullivan... You mean Buck Sullivan? Two and eight at the end of the season when they fired him?" He remembered Buck Sullivan—big and blond, good-looking, played in the pros. He burned hot and high before an injury benched him. Somehow Carly didn't seem the type to be turned on by a jock. She was soft and feminine, not tough enough for the monumental egos of most superathletes. He was still for a second, jolted by a feeling both ugly and elemental. Jealousy. He'd never experienced basic jealousy before.

She glanced up, then settled her chin against his forearm again. "I guess you're a fan."

"Of the team, not the coach." He hesitated and she could feel him gazing around the room. She wondered what he saw, if he thought her house warm and welcoming, her taste satisfying. Or had he found something lacking?

"Anyway, I wasn't asking about his occupation," Jess said. "I mean, what did he do to you?"

Carly stared straight ahead. "Nothing," she said quietly.

Jess frowned. "Nothing? You want to enlarge on that?"

"He didn't beat me or have an affair or fail to support me or drink too much or use drugs." She laughed bitterly. "And I didn't do any of those things, either. The marriage should have endured fifty years, right?" She made a move to get up.

His arm tightened. "No, wait a minute. What did you mean by 'nothing'?"

She sighed and settled back again. "Just that—nothing. We didn't spend any time together, we didn't ever talk, and we never played together. He had his own friends, and he never shared his work, his thoughts or his feelings. We had nothing."

Sex. It must have been good sex, Jess thought, feeling another primitive surge. *Sullivan must have been great in bed.*

"I could never tell that being married made any difference in his life," Carly said wearily. "I used to wonder if I just walked out, how many days it would be before he noticed."

Jess sat very still while an urge to crush Buck Sullivan washed over him. "You sell yourself short, Carly," he said, searching his mind for something to say that would banish the bleak note in her voice. "You've heard this before, I know, but you're lucky to be rid of him."

Even in his drugged state, the thought of Carly suffering at the hands of some thoughtless, inconsiderate, second-rate jock had Jess's fists curling. She'd probably fallen for the whole image—golden-boy looks, sports hero, prestigious coaching job—what woman wouldn't? It was a very appealing image. A new thought struck him along with a new surge of raw jealousy. Was she still carrying a torch for Sullivan?

He cleared his throat. "Uh, do you see him much? I know he's coaching at a local high school."

"No, I don't see him," Carly said softly. "And it suits both of us just fine."

Something in him eased slightly. "Nothing deader than an old love, so they say."

Carly shrugged, but something about the way she held herself seemed a little too tense to suit Jess. His hand came up to touch her hair. His fingers gently raked through the tangle of curls. "It's his loss, Carly."

She made a small sound. "Don't bet on it."

His hand stopped. "What does that mean?"

"He didn't lose anything when I walked out. There was hardly anything right about our marriage, so what was there to lose?" She inhaled deeply and her breath caught, but she continued in an even tone. "He had a list of my shortcomings, and he harped on them constantly. To hear him tell it, I was good at one thing and one thing only."

So he'd been right. The only thing they had had going for them was good sex. Jess fumed silently, amazed to discover depths of protectiveness and outrage in him that he'd never suspected. God, how he'd love to plant his fist in that cruel bastard's face. He waited until he was sure he had his voice under control before replying, "Carly, yours wasn't the first marriage based on physical attraction and not much else."

"Physical attrac—" She broke off, glancing at him with surprise. "You mean sex?" She laughed bitterly. "You couldn't be more wrong. Buck said that was my worst failing. I was totally inexperienced when we got married, and according to Buck, I was never any good at it." She waved an impotent hand. "I tried—" She broke off again, unsure whether to go on.

He waited, then gave her a little nudge. "You tried...what?"

"I can't believe I'm telling you all this," she said faintly. "I've never—"

His arms tightened around her protectively. "I thought you shrinks believed in talking everything out," he teased lightly, knowing that if she had a clue to how violent he was feeling toward her ex-husband, she'd probably clam up and not say another word. "Don't stop now, Carly. You tried what?"

After a moment or two, she settled against him again. Her voice grew husky. "I tried sexy nightgowns, romantic dinners, wine. I bought books, I consulted a psychic." She inhaled shakily. "I guess I just don't have what it takes."

Jess was still, unable to think of one single thing to say. He was used to the casual exchange of details between divorced men and women, cocktail talk. He wouldn't insult Carly with the platitudes that came to mind. Words were inadequate for soothing that kind of pain. *Damn Buck Sullivan to hell!*

"I'm curious," he said, still idly stroking her hair, seeking the softness of her nape. "What was the one thing he thought you excelled at?"

"My job, of course."

Of course. She must have thrown herself into it body and soul to compensate for her empty marriage. It was no wonder the kids were so important to her.

"You kept his secret to yourself, of course," he said, allowing only a shade of his outrage to color his voice.

"His secret?"

"That he was a lousy husband and even lousier lover."

"Oh." He felt a little of the tension leave her. She even laughed, although it was a travesty of the real thing. "I suppose I did. Of course, to the rest of the world, he looked pretty good."

Jess nodded thoughtfully. "Which made it tough when you decided to make a break." He was finding the skin of her neck incredibly delicate and satiny.

"It was—very tough," she said, warmed by his understanding. It had been extremely difficult to explain her decision to her parents, to Buck's parents, to Buck himself. There had been nothing wrong with their marriage on the surface. "I'd been feeling pretty desperate for months, but then I got pregnant. I had hoped the baby—"

He looked down at her, stunned. "Baby? I didn't know—" He broke off when a shaft of pain splintered in his head.

Carly was still for two beats, almost as surprised to hear herself mention her pregnancy as Jess had been to hear about it. She was held to him by his arm, but she scrambled out from under it and hastily stood up.

"Carly—" Jess put out a hand in a haze of pain. "What baby? Do you have a child?"

She waved a hand to indicate her whole house and laughed harshly. "Do you see a child here?"

With as much control as he could muster, Jess asked, "What happened to your child? Does Sullivan have custody?"

She laughed again, without humor. "Hardly. He wouldn't have wanted any reminders of our wedded bliss."

Jess looked confused. "Well, who then?"

"I lost the child, Jess. As with everything else in that relationship, I failed there, too. I was a miserable failure as a wife, as a lover, and ultimately, as a woman."

"A failure, in bed or out of it. Failure. Failure." Carly locked her arms around her middle as the words struck her again and again with the sting of poisoned arrows.

"Carly—" Jess tumbled to his feet and reached for her. But white-hot pain struck him like a blow from a hammer deep in his temple. He put out a hand when his knees buckled and, as through a long tunnel, heard the sound of Carly's shocked voice. The whole room tilted, and nausea welled up with sickening speed. "Carly, I'm going to be sick."

One look at him, and Carly's own distress was forgotten. She didn't need professional credentials to recognize the symptoms of concussion. "The bathroom's just over here," she said, leading him to the foyer, where a tiny powder room was tucked under the stairs.

He barely made it inside before being violently ill. His stomach heaved and rolled in a way he hadn't experienced since his college freshman days. Shuddering, eyes closed, he leaned against the wall, wincing with fresh pain from his wrenched shoulder. He stirred when he felt a cold wet cloth touch his hand, and he opened his eyes to find Carly offering him a glass of water.

"Jesus," he whispered.

"Maybe you'd better not drink it, just rinse. It might come right back up."

He shuddered again. "Thanks." He took the water and started to close the door.

"I'll be right out here if you need me," she said, looking worried.

Eyes closed again, he buried his face in the cold cloth and groaned a reply, wanting nothing more than to fall facedown on a bed and sleep. It would have to wait. Getting home was the first priority, and driving was out. He should have waited to take the damn pills. He'd get a taxi, and after some rest, the worst would be over.

"Jess?"

Carly's voice sounded anxious. He opened the door and

came out, feeling like death. She was instantly at his side. "I'm okay."

"Can you climb the stairs?" she asked, her gray-green eyes shadowed with concern.

"Climb the stairs?"

"You can sleep in the guest room."

Jess had just enough energy left to laugh softly. "Who will I have to share it with?"

She sighed in exasperation. "Don't be ridiculous. No one."

"You mean there's a vacancy at the way station tonight?" One look at her and he relented. "I'm sorry, Carly. But thanks all the same. Give me a minute, and I'll get it together enough to leave. You want to call me a taxi?"

Her mouth fell open. "Call a—"

"If it's not too much trouble."

"You can't go home, Jess! The only place you need to go is straight to bed. Someone should be with you overnight, just in case."

"I'll manage."

"No!" she said fiercely. "Not only do you have a concussion, but you're drugged, as well."

He rested one hand on the staircase railing and gazed at her. "I'm afraid I won't be able to hold my own in an argument tonight, Carly. Just tell me where."

She looked mollified. "You think you can manage the stairs?"

He lifted one brow and hiked up his mouth in a smile. "With a little help. Come here and I'll lean on you."

Wary suddenly, she searched his face. "Why don't I just stay close," she suggested. "You start up the stairs, and I'll be right behind you."

He nodded, but his dark eyes had a look in them that she didn't think was related to a concussion or drugs. Nevertheless, he climbed the stairs without any apparent difficulty, halting at the top. "Which way?" he asked, still looking ready to keel over.

She nodded in the direction of the guest bedroom. "That one. There's only one bathroom upstairs. It has fresh towels and an extra toothbrush in it. My room is there." She waved a hand in the opposite direction. "If you need anything, just let me know." Her voice was slightly breathless when she added, "Do you think you'll be okay?"

Looking into her gray-green eyes, he reached out and curled a hand around her neck, stroking the soft skin with his thumb. "You worry too much."

"You almost passed out, Jess. Anybody would react to that with some degree of concern," she replied stiffly.

"Then I'll just say thank you and promise you dinner at Commander's another time..."

"Here we go again," she said to the ceiling.

"...when I'm sure I won't upchuck it," he finished, his thumb stroking across her lips.

"Fine." Her tone was a little choked. She couldn't move. As long as he touched her, she was bound to him as though tethered with a silken cord.

Jess searched her face, his gaze going deep and dark. "Do I owe you an apology?" he asked huskily.

"For what?"

"For bringing up your marriage, forcing you to recall things that obviously still hurt."

"No, no apology."

"You're sure?"

"Positive."

"You realize that your ex-husband is a total jerk, don't you? You're not a failure at anything. You were simply unlucky in your choice."

"Thank you," she said, dropping her gaze from his. Having Jess in her house overnight was far different from having one of her teenagers, she realized. Even wounded and drugged, his appeal wasn't diminished one iota. He looked just as attractive to her rumpled and slightly battered as he had on all the other occasions she'd shared with him.

"I don't have any pajamas for you," she said, seeking suddenly to banish the intimate mood that had sprung up somehow between them tonight. Knowing that it stemmed from the rehash of her past and the scare she'd gotten from Jess's accident didn't make it any less threatening.

"I don't need pajamas," he returned, with a look that made her feel like a skittish spinster.

Immediately her imagination conjured him up in nothing but his deep tan, and she blushed, to her dismay. Taking a deep breath, she stepped back, causing his hand to fall away. "Then I'll say good-night," she said, not looking at him.

"Good night, Carly."

CHAPTER TWELVE

CARLY HADN'T EXPECTED to get much sleep that night, and she didn't. She was too aware of Jess in the bedroom only twenty feet away. Why, she asked herself, couldn't she think of him as just someone she'd simply offered the use of a bed to, the same way she'd offer a bed to a guest who had had too much to drink and was in no condition to drive? Would she be torturing herself with visions of him naked and sprawled over the whole length and width of her bed if he was just a guest?

She didn't go to bed right away, thinking he might be more seriously injured than he'd led her to believe. She washed and pressed his clothes, and after a boring hour of television, she gave up and went upstairs. She took a quick shower, one ear cocked for any noise from his bedroom, then slipped on a cream satin nightgown and crawled into her bed. The espionage novel she'd been reading might as well have been written in Russian for all the sense it made when she doggedly picked it up where she'd left off the previous night.

At two o'clock in the morning, she went in to check on him. Cautiously she listened at the door and, hearing nothing, she carefully turned the knob and went inside. Light from the window fell over the bed, outlining his long length. He was sprawled out flat on his back; one hand rested on his middle, and the other was flung wide. A smile almost materialized on Carly's mouth. He probably wouldn't be a very restful sleeping partner, she thought, then felt a rush of heat envelop her. His bed partner would probably never notice. She'd be too occupied enjoying the delights to be found in Jess's bed. For a moment Carly felt a piercing pain, knowing she couldn't be that partner.

Edging closer, she allowed herself a long look. He was deeply asleep, which alarmed her almost as much as if he'd been thrashing around in delirium. But he was breathing evenly, and something about the look of him eased her mind. His color seemed okay. His features were as rugged and firmly defined as ever. But his mouth was softer, gentler. Awake, he looked every one of his thirty-six years. Asleep, he seemed younger; the lines that bracketed his mouth were smoothed out, almost gone. His lashes were remarkable—long and thick. They added an unexpected vulnerability to his hard masculine features. She longed to reach out and touch them. Touch him.

She could see even in the dimness that his skin was darkly tanned. *He must spend a lot of time outdoors and shirtless,* she thought, admiring the smooth sleek muscles of his arms and shoulders. Her gaze took in the dense mat of dark hair on his chest, which narrowed in a straight line to a point blocked from her vision by the sheet. One leg was uncovered, bent at the knee. He was beautiful in the way of a man in his prime, as she had known he would be. Assuring herself that he was really all right, she tiptoed out.

Carly awoke in the morning just as dawn was breaking. She lay still for a moment, then heard a sound. Alarm brought her wide awake, and she sat up in her bed, clutching the blanket in one hand against her breasts. Another sound, this time the unmistakable click of the bathroom door, and she was out of the bed. Forgetting her half-dressed state, she rushed out of her room and almost collided with Jess. He was standing in the middle of the hall wearing only navy-blue briefs and a lazy smile.

He put out both hands to steady her. ''Easy, sweetheart, it's only me.''

She stared into his face, shadowed with morning beard, the harsh features slightly blurred and sleepy-looking. He appeared big and warm and...cuddly, she decided. Yes, that was it. It was so unexpected, she was at a loss for words for a moment. ''Are you okay?'' she asked, forgetting to step back. In fact, it seemed totally natural to step forward, right into his arms. She almost did just that.

''I'm okay,'' he said, leisurely rubbing her arms with both hands. ''I didn't mean to wake you. It's early yet. Go back to bed.''

She didn't reply; she simply stood looking up into his face. Jess caught his breath. She was an early morning delight, he thought, feeling a quick urgent response. Her hair was all mussed, and her skin was flushed and soft from sleep. If she kept on looking at him like that, he was going to have a hell of a time going back in that room without her.

''Does your head hurt?'' she asked, her eyes going to the bandage. His hair fell over it, glossy and dark. ''Do you need to take some more pills?''

''No to both,'' he said, having a hard time keeping his eyes above her neck. She must have hurried out of her bedroom without even thinking of a robe, he realized. And the gown she wore left nothing to the imagination. It was short, ending at the top of her thighs, and showed the full breathtaking length of her long legs. The tiny straps holding up the top begged for a whisper touch of his fingers. That was all it would take to slip the thing off and bare those beautiful breasts. They would be beautiful, he was convinced. One glance and their shape and the exquisite way her nipples beaded was already seared in his brain. ''I'm sorry I woke you,'' he said huskily, knowing he lied. Carly, fresh from her bed, sleep warm, her defenses temporarily suspended, was enough to make a man forget his principles.

Her eyes clinging to him, she shook her head. "It's okay. I heard you and I was concerned."

"You'll get cold," he murmured, and his hands began a leisurely stroking of her arms.

"No, I won't."

He abandoned her arms for the more tantalizing shoulders and spine, letting his fingers trace the delicate line down to her tiny waist and beyond. He stepped closer so that their bodies touched, just barely. "You remember last night I tried to refuse your offer to let me spend the night, Carly?"

"Uh-huh." Her hands came up and she spread both palms wide on his chest, finding his nipples almost accidentally, then shyly stroking them.

Jess reacted with a harsh intake of breath. "This is why," he said, closing the minute space between them, pressing his body, hard with his arousal, to the soft secret of her femininity. "I knew if I ever got half a chance and no interruptions, I wouldn't be able to resist this." And his mouth came down on hers.

Carly shuddered when his tongue slid into the depths of her mouth. Delight and desire exploded in her and spread out like warm honey, robbing her of the capacity to think beyond the moment. What she was feeling felt so good, so right, so natural that she didn't have to think. All she had to do was feel. And every nerve and cell in her body was alive with pleasure. She moved closer, her hands leaving his chest, instinctively anchoring around his neck.

Desire coursed through Jess with the thundering force of a freight train. He had wanted Carly from the moment he'd seen her, but he hadn't guessed how responsive, how eager she would be. Her wary shy reticence had been swept away in the force of her passion. Her mouth was generous and warm, her body supple and yielding. It delighted him and made him hungry for more.

He dragged his hands through her hair, reveling in the feel of it, silky and curling around his fingers. He shifted, tilting her head, taking her mouth in another deep hot kiss. A little moan slipped out of her, almost sending him over the edge. He knew he should slow down. This was a time for caution, for slow and easy foreplay, but even as his mind thought it, her uninhibited response sent him rushing headlong. He wanted to pull her down right on the floor, cover her body with his and show her just how beautifully talented she could be at making love. How she could ever believe she wouldn't be any good at this was beyond his understanding. He was stunned to discover how much he wanted to erase from her mind her imagined failures.

His hands fell away from her hair, down to where he could explore the soft shape of her breasts. He cupped them through the sleek satin, found the hard nubs of her nipples and stroked them. She dragged her mouth from his, gasping with the fierce sensations that came with every sweep of his thumbs over the tender crests. She trembled and arched toward him, her breath tangling with his. Her responses drove him higher, whetted his appetite for the deeper sweeter pleasures of her body.

With one deft move, he dispensed with the straps of her nightgown, freeing her breasts. He nestled the creamy weight of them in his hands and hesitated a second just to look at her, to admire the smooth ivory perfection of her.

"Oh, Carly, you are so beautiful—" he bent and softly touched his mouth to a pink tip, watching it enlarge with arousal "—so desirable."

She made a soft sound.

"It's true, you are, you are." Still cupping her breasts in his hands, he put his mouth to one and sucked strongly, triggering an answering need in the deep female heart of her. Her head fell weakly to his shoulder, and she buried her lips in the warm male skin of his neck, helpless in the dizzying surge of intense consuming passion.

A vague trickle of sanity reached beyond the daze in Carly's mind. She hadn't expected to ever feel anything like the madness that had been touched off by one simple kiss.

Madness. That was what feeling with this intensity amounted to. She had never understood that before. She'd never really known passion before, she realized, stunned. It was wonderful and terrible, desirable and dangerous. Jess was a terrific lover. And demanding. Even now he was urging her toward the bedroom. He'd expect… What would he expect? She couldn't bear to disappoint him, couldn't bear for him to discover how inept she was as a lover. Kissing was one thing, but the complete act of love required erotic skills that her failed marriage had proved were beyond her.

"Jess, please." She bent her head, pushing away from him, avoiding his seeking mouth when he groaned a protest. Quickly she tugged at her nightgown, pulling at the delicate strings with unsteady fingers.

Jess reached for her, refusing to let her slip away from him. He gave her a little shake. "Carly, don't stop now, please. I'm not going to hurt you. You know I'd never hurt you."

"This shouldn't have happened," she said, refusing to look at him. "I don't know why it happened. You know I can't…"

He frowned, leaning back so he could see her face. "You can't what?" When she didn't answer, he gave her another little shake. "You can, Carly, you can."

She twisted, trying to get free. "Stop it, Jess. Let me go! I know what you're trying to do, and it won't work."

He was still a moment, his breath slowing. Seeing the

look on her face, he sighed and released her. Instantly she darted toward her bedroom, but he was right behind her. Before she could close the door, he was inside with her. "I let you go, Carly, but I'm not leaving this room until you explain why you panicked. You want me as much as I want you. I can tell it, I can feel it. Don't deny it."

She stared at him through eyes that were guarded and unreadable. "Will you be honest if I ask you one question?"

He looked confused, but he nodded. "Yeah, sure. What is it?"

"Why did you kiss me just now?"

His eyebrows lifted. "Why?"

"Yes, why? I mean, what was your purpose?"

"Purpose?"

"Stop repeating everything I say and be honest! Please."

He tilted his head to one side, eyeing her in disbelief. "A gorgeous woman greets me at the crack of dawn wearing almost nothing, looking all sleep warm and sexy, and you ask why kissing her came to my mind?"

She dismissed that with a wave of her hand. "You don't have to try to save my pride, Jess. I may seem unsophisticated to you, but I know something about human nature. I'm not gorgeous or sexy. That's not the reason, and you know it."

Exasperation and amazement fought for dominance in him. How could she persist in thinking herself undesirable? He leaned against the door frame and crossed his arms over his bare chest, beginning to understand just how much damage Sullivan had done. "You sure as hell are gorgeous and sexy," he stated flatly. "You look good enough to eat in that little satin thing."

She immediately crossed her arms over her chest. "Will you be serious," she said, her cheeks turning pink.

He couldn't help the smile that spread over his mouth. "I am serious, Carly."

"No. You were out to prove something."

"Like what?"

She turned, rubbing her forehead with two fingers, giving him a delightful view as the gown hiked up. "I can't believe you'd do this, Jess. When I told you about... about—" she waved a hand "—everything that was wrong in my marriage, I didn't expect you to see it as some kind of subtle request for...for sex therapy."

Jess's smile disappeared. He pushed himself away from the door and faced her. "Sex therapy?" he repeated softly.

"I know what you were doing, Jess, and I don't appreciate it. I haven't spent the past three years trying to put myself back together just to have my self-esteem destroyed for the sake of some casual sex."

Jess's face seemed carved in stone. "Are you finished?" he demanded. "Is that it?"

The hand that she used to smooth a few stray curls from her face was shaking slightly. "I agreed to help you regain your son's trust, but that's the extent of my generosity. I'm not a convenient plaything, someone to toy with because I just happen to be handy and—"

"Shut up, Carly."

"And because you feel a quixotic impulse to play Dr. Ruth."

He took a step toward her. "I said shut up and I meant it, lady."

"I don't need you to solve my bedroom problems!" she said defiantly.

"Damn it, Carly!"

Her mouth fell open as he came at her. She took a step backward and felt her legs come up against the edge of her bed. She lost her balance and tumbled back, making a startled noise as he came down with her. Stunned, she found herself pinned beneath him, trapped by the warm solid weight of his body on hers. Her heart was racing suddenly and not, she knew, from physical exertion. She wasn't hurt. For his size he'd been very gentle. Before her own senses betrayed her, she began to struggle, but she might as well have tried to dislodge a ton of solid rock. He calmly threw one leg over her to subdue her wild thrashing.

"Let me go!"

"In a minute," he growled, catching both of her hands in one of his and pinning them over her head, leaving nowhere for her to look except straight up into his face. He bent over her, his dark coloring intensified by the white bandage. Intensely aware of the enforced intimacy of the position they were in, she ceased to struggle.

"You've had your say," he told her grimly. "Now I mean to have mine." For a moment, however, words failed him. His black gaze seared a path from her eyes to her suddenly unsteady lips and then swept back to her eyes again. "I don't know who's been dealt the worst insult here—you or me. I'm offended that you could accuse me of wanting to go to bed with you to give you a few lessons in sexual technique. Damn it, Carly! Is your opinion of me so low?"

Carly's lips parted, but nothing came out. She turned her eyes from his.

"It's inconceivable to me," he said in a tone of disbelief, "that you can think so little of yourself. You did the same thing when I invited you to dinner. You couldn't believe that I asked you because I wanted to spend the evening with you."

Carly stared at him, wide-eyed and wary. She wanted to believe him so much that it hurt. The pain deep inside her was actually physical. Could a man like Jess really desire her? Was it possible that he didn't really believe Buck's cruel assessment of her as a woman? As a lover?

Jess leaned back slightly to study her expression. "What are you thinking?" he demanded huskily, still enveloping her with his body. He maintained his hold on her wrists, but there was nothing threatening about him. His anger had faded.

She shook her head. "Nothing."

He looked at her, almost smiling. "Nothing. You're not going to rise up in outrage and deny everything?"

She didn't move.

"Not going to threaten to leave me in the lurch with Mike?"

She still didn't move.

"Not going to accuse me of any devious purpose if I invite you out and it's only you and me?"

She almost smiled, but still didn't move.

He bent his head and started to nuzzle a path from the curve of her naked shoulder, up her throat to her ear. "Or if I get carried away—" his voice was suddenly deep "—and try to get you in bed again, you're not going to panic?"

She did smile then—sort of. "I guess not."

"Because we will make love, sweetheart," he told her, fighting a wild urge to take her right then and there. "But not now. Not this morning. When we make love, after it's over, I don't want you to look at me with regret or resentment. I don't want you to feel you've been taken advantage of."

He nipped at her lobe, then swept the sensitive inner shell of her ear with his tongue. The desire Carly thought safely conquered only moments before rose again, quick and hot. She couldn't resist thrusting her body against his one last time and was thrilled when she felt his instant response: a sharp intake of breath, a quick tensing of his thighs. He was warm and ready, nearly naked on top of her. His skin was smooth, his muscles were hard. She wanted to run her hands over him, explore all his wonderful masculine secrets. The last thing she wanted to do was wait. What in the world had happened to Buck Sullivan's insecure ex-wife?

He bit her softly on her bottom lip. "Stop that, lady. Or I'll have to exact payment."

She threaded her fingers through the thick dark hair that fell over the bandage on his head. "Oh, yeah?"

"Yeah. And you already owe me one for falsely accusing me."

Carly lay very still, unable to believe she felt enough confidence to do this. "I'll make it up to you," she promised.

He nodded. "Uh-huh, you sure will. And I know how."

"How?"

A flicker of something came and went in his dark eyes. Only Mike could bring that look, she knew. He put his weight on one elbow, but his leg still rested across her thighs. With his other hand, he stroked the smooth satin gown where it covered her abdomen. It was an intimate gesture, but Carly didn't tense up or make any move to preserve her modesty. Jess's touch on her seemed right and natural.

"I want to take Mike to my place across the lake next weekend," he told her. "Will you go with us, spend the weekend? I'm going to tell him he can invite Penny if he wants to."

She smiled, pleased that she could read him so well. "I think he'd probably come whether you include Penny or not. But with her, it's a sure thing."

"You think so?"

"I think so."

"One more thing," he said, holding her gaze with his.

"Just so you don't jump to any more dumb conclusions, you're not there just as a chaperon."

"Yes, sir."

He rolled sideways and off the bed, catching her hand and pulling her up at the same time. He made a muffled sound of pain and rubbed his shoulder.

"You have a terrible bruise!" she said, seeing the angry purple-and-green mark on his shoulder.

He worked it up and down gingerly. "I'll be okay after a hot shower."

She reached for her robe and quickly put it on.

"I've got a few things to do this morning," Jess said, moving to the bathroom door.

"I don't think you should be pushing yourself, Jess. You were in bad shape last night. You must at least have a headache this morning. Don't deny it."

"I have been in better shape, but I promised Kyle I would come in this morning and give him a statement."

She spread her hands wide in disgust. "I know better than to argue with that macho mentality. Why do men insist on denying pain?"

He crossed his arms over his chest and eyed her. "Why do I get the idea that I'm being judged by your ex-husband's habits?"

She shrugged. "He was an athlete. I saw him injured and in pain, barely able to function but determined to work out with the team. It always seemed ridiculous to me."

The look he gave her was long and drawn out and brought a flush to her body beneath the robe. "It's the macho mentality, all right, that has me leaving you this morning, Carly," he assured her softly. "I'm already aroused almost to the point of no return. And if I stay here and subject myself to the torture of your delectable self sashaying around in those little nothings, we're going to end up right back in that bed that I was fool enough to leave a couple of minutes ago.''

''Oh.''

''Yes, oh.''

She was suddenly seized with the urge to escape. ''I'll get your clothes and then make some coffee.''

Feeling his eyes on her, she went into the bedroom he'd used and came out carrying his neatly folded pants and shirt and handed them over. ''Here you are, all clean and pressed.''

He took them and thanked her, then said, ''Carly.''

Color still high on her cheeks, she looked at him.

''One more thing. A few perfectly natural male traits are about the only thing your ex-husband and I have in common. And don't you forget it, lady.''

She fled.

SHE WAS AT the breakfast counter when he came downstairs. He saw her carefully set down the coffee she was holding and lift the newspaper slowly. Something about the way she held herself brought him quickly to her side. ''What is it?''

Without looking up she lowered the paper to the counter so that he could see it. ''You're not going to believe this, Jess. Terry Faust's mother has been arrested for murder.''

''Murder?'' He glanced down, following her eyes. The article was on the bottom half of the front page. '''Bookkeeper Charged with Murder and Embezzlement,''' he murmured, reading the caption. His eyes went to the photograph accompanying the article. A tall woman, blond and attractive, he noted absently, was being led across a lawn toward a police car. Even in the grainy photograph, he could see the marked resemblance to young Terry and her sister.

''Lila Faust,'' Carly said in a tone of disbelief. ''I can't believe it! I know Lila. She couldn't kill anybody. She's so reserved.''

Jess went to the coffeepot and helped himself. ''Sometimes it's the quiet ones who have the most explosive tempers,'' he said, resting a hip against the bar stool.

With a degree in psychology, Carly certainly knew that could be true. But she didn't think it was true of Lila Faust. She frowned, trying to recall what she knew of the woman from remarks made by Terry and her sister. Only that their mother had been distracted lately, wrapped up in her own personal problems. But enough to be driven to commit murder?

''How did it happen?'' Jess asked.

Carly glanced at the newspaper. ''Actually it was self-defense, according to Lila.'' She picked up the paper and looked at the article again. ''She's the bookkeeper for a foreign car dealership that is owned by two men, or rather, was owned by two men. It was one of the partners she shot—James Fitzgerald. This says she was working late last night when Fitzgerald came in and they argued. She told the police she was scared that he was going to kill her, and she shot him in self-defense.''

Jess shrugged. ''Not a lot of detail there.''

''I wonder where the other partner was at the time,'' Carly murmured thoughtfully.

''I'll probably know the answer to that Friday.''

Carly looked surprised. ''You're right. If the D.A. has enough evidence, it'll come to the grand jury.''

''And you'll have to recuse yourself.''

''Is that the term for sitting out because of a conflict of interest?''

''That's it.''

''Because I know the family,'' she finished, disappointed.

He downed the last of his coffee and set the cup in the

sink. ''Which is probably a stroke of bad luck for Lila Faust,'' Jess said dryly, then winced from the soreness in his right shoulder as he shrugged on his jacket. ''I don't doubt you'd persuade the jurors that she simply couldn't have done it, a nice quiet lady like that.''

Her retort was muffled by the swift hard kiss he left on her mouth. ''Thanks for the TLC.''

ON MONDAY, Lila Faust's arrest was the talk of Padgett School, faculty and students alike. All day Saturday and Sunday, Carly had tried to reach Terry at her sister's house, but there had been no answer. She'd finally given up, hoping Terry would decide to come to school, difficult though it would be to face the students and their curiosity.

''I think we've had about as much violence as we can handle around here,'' Rachel commented in Carly's office, where she'd elected to spend her midmorning break. ''First that mugging in the street, then Jess got it right in ER and now Terry's mother...'' She hunched her shoulders in distaste. ''It's enough to drive us across the lake.''

''There's no escaping it. A woman was stabbed on a jogging track in Covington only last week,'' Carly reminded her. She stirred a scant few grains of sweetener into her coffee and leaned back in her chair. ''But you're right. We do seem to be getting more than our share.''

''Speaking of the north shore,'' Rachel said, draining the last of her coffee, ''Penny says you're going to Jess's place across the lake next weekend.''

''That's the plan.''

''I know I can trust you to keep an eye on the kids,'' Rachel said, watching Carly bury her nose in her cup.

''Of course, Rachel.''

''I don't mean keeping them from drowning or falling out of a tree or not letting them play with matches, Carly.''

She drew a beleaguered breath. "I just wish that was all I had to fear."

"I understand, Rachel. Although I think you're worrying for nothing. They're good kids."

"I know they're good kids, Carly. But they're normal, red-blooded kids, too."

"I'll keep that in mind," Carly said, thinking after Rachel left that it wasn't Mike and Penny who'd need to exercise some restraint during the upcoming weekend.

She glanced up just as Kyle Stratton appeared in her door. "Kyle, how are you? What brings you here?"

"Hello, Carly." Smiling, he came inside and closed the door behind him. "I'm fine, and business brings me here, I'm afraid. But it'll only take a few minutes. Is this a bad time?"

"No, no, of course not." She waved a hand. "Have a seat, please. Coffee?"

"Thanks, no. I'm floating away in the stuff from the ten cups I've already had."

He pulled a small pocket notebook from the inside of his jacket. "I need to ask you a few questions about Terry Faust."

"Oh, of course."

"Did she ever mention her mother?"

"Frequently," Carly replied, taking her seat. "They were having difficulties. Terry was going through a troubled and rebellious period and claimed her mother just didn't understand her. That's about all I could make out of my sessions with Terry. I met Lila when Terry first enrolled, but not afterward. She never came in, although I sent her several requests."

"In writing?" Kyle's pen was poised over the notebook.

"Yes, and through Terry, too, but Lila always made some excuse. Terry said her mother was too wrapped up in her own personal problems."

Kyle glanced up at that.

"She never revealed any details, Kyle."

He leaned back, tapping his pen on the notebook. "That's it?"

"I'm sorry." She shrugged. "It's not much, is it?"

He slipped the notebook back inside his jacket and got to his feet. "No problem. Every little bit helps."

He opened the door just as Rachel was returning. For a second, they looked at each other in surprise. Then Kyle smiled as Carly looked on, everything he felt for Rachel open for the whole world to see. Carly sighed. *Lucky, lucky Rachel,* she thought wistfully.

CHAPTER THIRTEEN

THE DISTRICT ATTORNEY put the case against Lila Faust together with unusual speed and presented it to the Orleans Parish grand jury on Friday. There were only two other cases on the docket that day: an aggravated battery charge against a police officer who seriously wounded a neighbor with his police-issue weapon at a backyard barbecue, and a charge of fraud against a married couple who falsified the records of their ambulance service.

The first two cases were dispatched quickly and, as Jess had predicted, because of her relationship with Terry Faust, Carly was forced to step down while the remaining jurors and an alternate heard the evidence against Lila. It was still early in the day, and Carly decided to go back to work, but on her way out, she found Terry and her sister, Debra, in the small waiting room for members of the press and others with an interest in the jury proceedings.

Terry looked pale and shaken. She began to cry softly when Carly sat down and put her arms around her, saying nothing. Debra was smoking, her movements jerky and uncoordinated. When she reached over to stub out her cigarette, Carly saw that her hand was unsteady.

"What's going to happen to my mom, Ms Sullivan?"

"I don't know, Terry. We'll have to wait until the grand jury's verdict is announced. Even then, there are still several options for your mother."

Terry sat back and sniffed, wiping the tears from her

cheeks with both hands. "You mean she won't have to go to jail?"

"I don't know, Terry. We'll just have to wait and see."

"The police don't believe her," Debra put in harshly. "Did you know that? They're saying she stole money from the business. She was the bookkeeper, and she had the perfect opportunity. They say Fitzgerald confronted her about it, and she shot him to keep him from filing charges against her, not in self-defense."

"Mom says it was self-defense," Terry put in. "They argued and he yelled at her, threatened her."

"Who had the gun?" Carly asked.

Terry bent her head and looked at her hands. "It was in Mom's desk. She worked late lots of nights and kept it just in case."

"Was Fitzgerald unarmed?"

Debra nodded. "They say he was."

"I don't believe Mom could shoot anybody," Terry said earnestly, "even in self-defense."

Debra looked directly into Carly's eyes. "Neither do I, Ms Sullivan."

Even though Carly agreed with their assessment of their mother's nature, she knew it would do no good to say so. Her voice was soft with sympathy for the two sisters as she said, "I know it's hard for you both to imagine your mother using a gun, but none of us know what we'd do in a threatening situation. Do you have a good attorney?"

Debra was suddenly occupied with pulling out another cigarette. "Matthew Forbes is paying for the best," she said in an even tone.

"He's the other partner?"

"Among other things," Terry said bitterly.

Carly divided a thoughtful look between both girls. "He must be a good friend."

Debra lit up and turned her head, blowing smoke impatiently. ''Yeah, a very good friend.''

''Was he there that night?''

''He had stepped out to pick up something to eat,'' Debra said, not bothering to disguise the dislike in her voice.

''I take it you don't like Mr. Forbes.''

Terry and Debra exchanged a look. ''We don't think the way he treats my mom is very nice,'' Terry said. ''We wanted her to quit her job, but she wouldn't. She said she would never be able to make the same salary anywhere else.''

Debra's short laugh held no humor. ''Yeah, the pay's great.''

At that moment the grand jury clerk stuck her head in the door, and Debra and Terry jumped up. They hurried off toward the jury chambers, leaving Carly with the impression that there was a lot more to the incident that had brought Lila Faust before the grand jury than the lady was admitting.

CARLY DIDN'T LEAVE the grand jury offices until she found out what action had been taken on Lila's case. To her relief the D.A.'s evidence failed to convince the jurors that she was guilty of second-degree murder. An indictment for a lesser charge of manslaughter might have been successful, but word from the top was that the D.A. believed the evidence pointed to murder and intended to prove it. Another hearing was to be scheduled when the prosecution felt they'd compiled an airtight case against her. For the sake of Lila's daughters, Carly was thankful to hear she'd been released on bail.

''I still don't believe she actually pulled the trigger and killed a man,'' Carly told Rachel later that afternoon as they left the school together and walked to the parking lot.

"All of us have our limits," Rachel observed. "It just takes the right circumstances to push us over the brink."

"The right circumstances," Carly murmured thoughtfully. Something in those words reminded her of her conversation with Terry and Debra. Her brows came together as she tried to get a fix on exactly what they'd said that had bothered her. Or maybe it was what they hadn't said. Deep in thought, she was almost sideswiped by a red Porsche that was pulling away from the parking space next to her own.

"After the last bell this parking lot reminds me of the warm-up pits at Indianapolis," Rachel grumbled, huddling against Carly's car to let a tiny Chevette roar by. "Slow down!" she yelled.

Shading her eyes from the November sun, Carly watched a shiny black-and-silver four-wheel-drive vehicle approach at a near reasonable speed. "Isn't that Mike?"

"Looks like it," Rachel observed, adding cynically, "Penny must be with him. I can't imagine any normal Padgett student driving so sedately, otherwise."

Mike cruised up and stopped, rolling down his window and treating them to a blast of rock music. Penny leaned around him in the driver's seat and flashed them a blinding smile. "Mom! Carly! Mike just got his wheels today. What d'you think?" she demanded, forcing them to read her lips over the reverberating beat of Huey Lewis.

"Very nice." Rachel pitched her voice to carry over the din.

"Awesome," Carly offered, standing back and subjecting the vehicle to an inspection that earned her a look of approval.

"When are you going to remove the sticker price?" Rachel bent down to read the bottom line of the white shipping invoice glued to the window and thumped her fist against her breastbone. "Dear God, Jess must have lost his mind," she muttered to Carly.

Carly smiled at that. She knew that to Jess the cost of the car of Mike's choice was nothing. And it wasn't a bribe—not entirely. For him it was a way to express his feelings for his son. Too bad he didn't know how to come right out and voice them. *Maybe in time,* she thought. *Maybe even this weekend.*

"Are the two of you looking forward to the weekend?" she asked brightly.

"We sure are!" That was Penny.

"Yeah, I guess." That was Mike. He wasn't gushing enthusiasm all over the place, but Carly thought she read a gleam in his dark eyes. He was sure to be curious about the country dwelling where Jess spent so much time.

"Dr. Brannigan said we could all go together," Penny told them, obviously thrilled. "Mike's driving."

"That sounds fine to me." Carly patted the little plaque on the vehicle that carried the brand name. "This baby seems just right for the country. What time are we leaving?"

"Six-thirty or seven," Mike volunteered. "As soon as Dad can get away from the hospital. He needs to check a couple of patients, and then we're outta here."

There was no mistaking it. Mike was pleased at the prospect of the weekend. Things were working out very well for Jess, it seemed, which was no surprise to Carly. She understood better than anyone how easy it was to fall under his spell. She decided not to think about the prospect of the weekend as it related to her and Jess. He had planned the weekend for Mike. If Penny hadn't been coming along, Carly wouldn't have been included. She'd have to remember that.

BEFORE THE TIME CAME to leave, Carly spent some time thinking. The early morning encounter with Jess in her bedroom had marked a turning point in their relationship. She wasn't sure where it was going, but if his main interest in her was to help him repair his relationship with Mike, then Carly knew she was in trouble. She could no longer limit her involvement in his life to that role. Her passionate response when she'd been in his arms had told her that much.

She had been very cautious since her divorce, too much so, maybe. But Jess, she knew, had the power to devastate her. Naive she might be, but not enough to think that a man like Jess was in love with her. Was it too much to expect something from him, something that would convince her that she was truly special to him? Her bruised heart couldn't take another rejection.

That evening, her smile was ready and her pulse was racing as she opened her door to him. One look at his face, and her smile faded. Pushing the door wide, she took a step back so that he could come in. "What is it, Jess?"

He brushed past her. She sensed that something was wrong, but it didn't prevent her from noticing how good he looked in jeans and a leather jacket over a plain Western-style shirt. His boots were scuffed and worn. In them, his legs seemed longer, his thighs more powerful. She felt her heart quiver at the look of him, big and dark, totally male. He smelled like the outdoors, his after-shave and leather and…just Jess.

She closed the door, watching him when he didn't turn. He brought his hand up and rubbed the back of his neck, as though he were weary beyond words. Maybe he'd had another incident at the hospital, she thought, following him into the living room. The longer she knew him, the more she felt he didn't seem to be able to throw off the images of the broken and bleeding bodies that passed through his hands in ER. She heard him draw in a deep breath, and her heart contracted. She wished she had the right to say all the things she felt. He turned to face her.

"All ready to go, I see."

His voice was calm, but his eyes were not. They burned. Some intense feeling swirled in the near black depths. Anger? Pain? Despair? Jess was skilled at concealing his emotions, but something—some fierce, insistent force—had pushed him to his limit. His eyes roamed restlessly over the room, then swung back to Carly. Impulsively, she put out a hand to touch him.

"What's wrong, Jess?" A thought struck her. "Is it Mike?"

"Yeah." He sat down suddenly on the sofa and then with a muttered curse got up again and began prowling around the room.

"Oh, no." Carly swallowed hard, visualizing a twisted broken heap of black-and-silver metal. She covered her mouth with her fingers. "Is he… Is it…"

He glanced over his shoulder, frowning at the stark whiteness of her face. "No, God forbid, no. Not that." He swore again and covered the space between them in swift strides. He pulled her into his arms and held her head against his chest. One hand stroked her shoulders and her spine. "He's not hurt, honey. I'm sorry, I didn't mean to give you a scare like that."

She raised her head to look at him. "What then? What happened?"

His mouth thinned and he gazed beyond her, his features harsh. "He can't go, Carly. She let me think everything was fine until the last minute, and then she killed it."

"Can't go? Killed—" Carly shook her head, totally confused. "What? Who?"

"Lianne, that's who!" He pulled away and cursed viciously. Pacing, he dragged his fingers through his hair.

He curled his other hand into a fist and repeatedly thumped it against his thigh.

"She let me think... *Damn it to hell!* She let Mike think she had no objection to him spending the weekend with me, and then at the last minute—" he threw Carly a look that revealed all the rage and resentment he felt "—she announces with regret—*with regret!* Do you believe that?—that her parents, Mike's grandparents, are coming in for the weekend and are counting on him being here."

"He doesn't see them often," Carly guessed, unable to think of anything that might stem his rage or ease the bitter resentment that seethed in him.

"They live in Arizona and it's Papa Bill's birthday," Jess explained, his tone heavy with sarcasm. "'He's an old man and might not have many more.' That's a quote."

"How old is he?" Carly asked faintly.

"Sixty-one, for Pete's sake! Sixty-one and hale and hearty. He plays eighteen holes of golf every other day of his life." He flicked a drape open and glared out into the night, a study in fury and frustration. For long moments, he stood there before bringing his eyes back to hers. His voice had calmed a little when he said, "She engineered the whole thing, Carly. I was a fool for not suspecting it. It's just the kind of thing she would do. I ought to know. She pulled it often enough when—"

He stopped himself. "Hell, just forget it. You don't want to hear the disgusting details. Other peoples' old war stories are boring." When he looked at her, the corner of his mouth was twisted in a mirthless smile, and his dark eyes were bleak. He walked over to the sofa, where Carly had sat down, and he slowly sank down beside her. "I'm just so disappointed, Carly."

She put her hand over his. "I'm so sorry, Jess."

He nodded and threaded his fingers through hers. Then he lifted them, still joined, to his mouth. "Mike was disappointed, too,'' he said, murmuring the words against the back of her hand. ''He was in a hell of a fix for a kid. He couldn't tell me how disappointed or frustrated he felt because he's so damned loyal to Lianne. A kid shouldn't have to cope with that kind of crap, Carly.''

''Fortunately you understood his feelings without him having to spell them out.'' There wasn't much comfort to be found in the situation, but Carly made a stab at it.

''I understand because it's so familiar. My folks were brilliant at playing me off against each other.'' He tucked her hand in the curve of his neck and shoulder, as though attempting to block out the pain and bitterness of those memories.

His skin was warm, and Carly felt an answering warmth rise up inside her. She had to bite her tongue to hold back the words of love that would have truly comforted him.

''I almost gave him up rather than subject him to this kind of cruelty, Carly.'' His voice was laced with steel when he added, ''I won't back off again.''

''It'll be okay this time, Jess. He's old enough to work this out for himself.''

He shifted, bending his knee and turning so that he could look into her eyes. ''I didn't realize how much I was looking forward to this weekend until it was all off.''

''There will be other times, Jess.''

''For Mike, yes,'' he said, stroking her knuckles with his thumb. ''I was looking forward to showing you my place, too.''

She looked down quickly, afraid he would see the joy she knew must have been revealed in her eyes.

His clasp on her hand tightened. ''Can we still go, just the two of us?''

She did look up then, searching the dark unreadable gaze fixed on hers. A thousand questions formed in her mind, but the only one she asked was, ''When?''

"Tomorrow morning," he said instantly. Was he relieved? Pleased? She sensed some of the taut emotion easing in him. "Early."

Her smile blossomed and she nodded. "I'll be ready, early."

He stood up, still holding her hand, and pulled her to her feet. "Great, now get your coat," he instructed. "We're going to have that special dinner I've been promising you ever since the day we met."

She flicked a glance over him and then down at her jeans. "We're not dressed for anyplace special."

"This is New Orleans, lady. There are plenty of special places where we can eat in jeans." He gave her the slow smile that turned her insides and her will to mush. "Besides, anyplace is special when I'm with you."

"I'll get my coat."

MIKE DROVE AROUND a long time after calling his dad. He didn't want to call Penny—he wanted to tell her the bad news in person. Bad news. When he put it like that, he felt a little twinge of something—guilt, he decided. He knew he shouldn't begrudge his grandparents a measly weekend. He could do the weekend at Jess's place across the lake anytime, he told himself, ruthlessly pushing down something he refused to acknowledge as disappointment and a sort of simmering resentment. Covington was only...what? Thirty, forty minutes away at the most. His grandparents lived in Phoenix, Arizona, for Pete's sake. It was Papa Bill's birthday and he was pretty old. As his mother said, he might not have too many birthdays left. Mike would have plenty of time to go to Covington. Besides, Papa Bill and Mama Jo were just about the only grandparents he had. Jess's folks sure didn't count. A card with money in it on his birthday and at Christmas was the extent of the attention he received from those two. They were the same kind of grandparents that his dad used to be as a parent, he thought bitterly.

He just wished he'd known about the weekend a little sooner. Calling it off at the last minute like this made for all sorts of complications. Not only did it ruin his and Penny's plans, but his dad's schedule at the hospital was messed up, and Ms Sullivan was left high and dry. He wished his mother—

He downshifted the Dakota and overtook a pickup that was crawling along. He didn't want to think anymore about the way this whole thing had happened. He knew his mother didn't understand how much he and Penny had been looking forward to the weekend. Not because they were all that curious about Jess's place, he reminded himself quickly, but because they would get to spend hours and hours together without having to worry about any curfew or midterms or studying or pretending he still needed tutoring in chemistry. He'd easily mastered chemistry once he'd put his mind to it, but neither he nor Penny could see the sense in telling anybody that.

No, he couldn't say any of that to his mother. Especially since the weekend had been planned by his dad. If he mentioned anything to his mother that even halfway reminded her of Jess, she really got ticked off. She really seemed to hate— He broke off that thought because it gave him another kind of twinge—an ache, sort of, in his chest. Why did life always have to be full of complications?

ON THE WAY HOME from the restaurant that night, Carly felt the last of her doubts about Jess slip away. Not about loving him. Her doubts had nothing to do with whether or not she loved him. She knew she did. What had taken her so long to accept were all the risks that went along with loving him. There were so many that it was probably a miracle that she had even found the courage to try. In the dark, her mouth twisted in a wry smile.

She sat beside him in the Jaguar wrapped in her own thoughts. He'd been subdued tonight, not quite able to throw off the mood that had settled on him. He was far more vulnerable than he appeared, she knew, and his vulnerabilities appealed to something deeply feminine in her. The contradictions in him attracted and intrigued her. A woman could be with him forever without ever peeling away all the layers. When she had sat across the table from him in the quiet restaurant he'd chosen, Carly had made a conscious decision to trust him. He had said they would be good together, and he wouldn't hurt her. The truth was, she wanted to be with him more than she was frightened of being hurt. Tonight she would let him know she was ready to make love with him.

Deciding it was one thing, she thought, realizing with a start that she was home, but how did a woman actually let a man know she was ready to go to bed with him? They stopped and she got out of the car quickly. As she walked beside him up the steps to her door, her thoughts churned like the lake on a windy day. Now that the decision was made, she was eager to make it happen. But she was nervous. She wanted to please him so much. She hadn't felt this kind of anxiety since her honeymoon. What if she...? Before the thought could form fully, she quickly banished it.

"I'll pick you up around seven," Jess said as she unlocked the door. "That's not too early?"

Before she opened the door, she said, "No, no. That's fine. Uh, would you like some coffee? Or a drink? Scotch. I've got Scotch."

He looked at her quizzically for a moment, then nodded. "Yeah, that sounds good."

Relieved, she pushed the door open and watched him

shrug out of his coat, then hang it up. When she made no move to take off her own coat, he reached for it. As his fingers brushed her neck, Carly jumped as though she'd been zapped by a live wire. She was getting more nervous by the minute.

Jess was aware of it, but he didn't understand it. It had taken him a while to settle down tonight, but after a few minutes of Carly's sympathy and understanding, things were soon back in perspective. It was after he'd calmed down, about midway through dinner, that he became aware of her distraction.

In the car, she'd hardly said a word, twisting the strap of her purse with tense fingers. He didn't think she even noticed when he simply stopped making any effort to talk. Was she having second thoughts about going with him tomorrow? The depth of his disappointment surprised him. He wanted her there. He needed her there.

Maybe she was having second thoughts because she didn't trust him. He hadn't made any secret of the fact that he was looking forward to the time when he got her into his bed, but he wasn't going to push her. He thought she'd believed him when he'd told her that. He hoped she would soon overcome her hang-ups, but he could wait until she was ready and willing, a condition he'd been in longer than he liked to think about.

"What's wrong, Carly?"

Keeping her back to him, she wrapped her arms around her middle. "Nothing." Her voice sounded forced, too bright. "Why do you think something's wrong?"

"You seem nervous."

"No, I'm not. I'm fine, really."

"Are you sure?"

"No, uh... I mean, yes, I'm sure."

He frowned and put out a hand to touch her hair, then dropped it.

"Your drink," she said in a rush. "I'll get it."

He stopped her with a hand on her arm. "In a minute."

She didn't turn. "Coffee or Scotch? You didn't say."

"You hardly touched your dinner."

She looked to the ceiling. "It was delicious. I love shrimp scampi—it's my favorite."

"Have you changed your mind about going with me tomorrow?"

"No, of course not."

"Because you don't have to worry about anything, Carly," he told her quietly. "Nothing will happen if you don't want it to. I just want you to see my place."

"And I want to see it. I know it will be lovely."

He touched her hair. "Turn around and tell me that, Carly."

She turned slowly, her eyes going to his, all her uncertainty and anxiety and nervousness there for him to see. His heart sank. He should have realized that the thought of a weekend alone with him would cause her to panic. Especially after that scene last weekend. He searched frantically in his mind for words that she would believe, aware suddenly that wanting sex with Carly wasn't a good enough reason for losing her. He was chilled by the thought without really understanding why.

"You can trust me, Carly," he said, curling his fingers around her neck. He didn't pull her into his arms, although he wanted to—every instinct was urging him to. Instead he looked directly into her eyes. "I want you to visit at my house this weekend. I want to walk around the place with you. I want you to tell me what you think of it."

Some of the anxiety faded from her eyes. "I'd like that."

"We'll just hang out, check out the neighborhood."

"Okay, I—"

"It's got a gazebo. Did I tell you about the gazebo?"

"No, but I—"

"Maybe we won't leave here so early. We could even come back Saturday—not stay the night."

"No! Jess—"

His thumb caressed the sensitive skin under her ear. "I'm not taking you there to have sex with you, Carly. I swear it. I want to make love to you, you know that, but not this weekend, sweetheart."

"Oh." Her eyes fell away. Now that he'd paused and she could get a word in, she found there was nothing to say.

He stopped his caressing and looked at her sharply. "What is it? What are you thinking?"

"Nothing."

"That was what you wanted to hear, wasn't it? Until you know how you feel—"

Carly took a deep breath. "I do," she said.

"You do?"

"I know how I feel right now, Jess." She read the confusion in his expression and didn't wonder at it. She must have sounded like the inexperienced, unsophisticated, hopelessly behind-the-times would-be lover that she was.

He was absolutely still, his hand at her throat, his gaze locked with hers. Not a muscle moved as he waited.

She cleared her throat. How was she to say it? she wondered frantically.

"Are you planning to tell me?" he prompted softly.

"Jess, this is so..." She looked away. "I've never done this before, Jess. I never dreamed I would do this," she said in an incredulous tone.

"Are you trying to say you want to make love, Carly?"

Her eyes closed and she nodded mutely.

"Are you sure?" It was the last thing he expected.

Distressed, she cried, "Oh, Jess, of course I'm sure. It's what I've been trying to say for the past five minutes, but you wouldn't let me get a word in. I know I botched it all up. I didn't taste a thing I ate for dinner. I spent the whole trip home in the car trying to think how to tell you. I'm no good at this. I told you I didn't know anything about—"

His other hand joined the one already around her neck. Keeping her at arm's length, he bent at the knees so he could look right into her eyes. "Are you sure?" he said again.

She felt ridiculous and totally out of her depth. "What's the matter, you want to back out?"

The look that leaped into his dark eyes almost stole her breath away. "Not on your life, sweetheart." His arms went around her, pulling her close against him. The moment he had realized what she was saying, an incredible feeling had come over him. He felt about ten feet tall. He'd never dreamed she would find the courage to actually take the first step.

"When, Carly?"

She looked up into his face. "I thought...tonight," she whispered.

"Tonight," he repeated.

"But if you've got something else—plans—I understand perfectly."

He shook his head, smiling slightly. "You've got to be kidding."

She searched his face, trying to see something besides passion and anticipation, needing it, but his dark eyes were as unreadable as ever. Anxiously, she said, "I just want to tell you not to expect too much, all right?"

His gaze took in the flushed look of her, all the way down to her throat. Her hair was curled around her face, her skin smooth, her mouth soft and inviting. Desire for her came, swift and urgent. He bent and pressed a hot fierce sweet kiss on her mouth, then withdrew. "And I just want to tell you not to expect too little, all right?"

She buried her face in his shirtfront. "I almost believe you when you say things like that."

He caught her hand, pulled her into the living room and posed her in front of the sofa. "You'd better believe it, lady. But don't take my word for it. After this night, you're gonna see for yourself."

CHAPTER FOURTEEN

"STAY RIGHT THERE." Jess quickly put a match to the kindling in the fireplace. When he was satisfied with the fire, he turned, still on his haunches, and held out a hand to her. Carly went to him and knelt down beside him on the soft deep pile of the white rug, looking at him hesitantly, apprehensively. Long-suppressed needs burned inside her. She wanted to put her hands to the buttons of his shirt, strip him down and look at him, but her hands seemed like lead at her sides.

"Relax, honey," he said, touched, as always, by her vulnerability. Still on his knees, he stroked her soothingly: her arms, her neck, her back. He felt her reach out, touch him at his waist, clutch a handful of his shirt and hang on. The mixture of trust and caution inherent in the gesture triggered a host of emotion in him. It was suddenly important to him—vital—that the experience be good for her.

He leaned toward her and kissed her. His touch was gentle and persuasive. He made love to her mouth alone, taking his time, patiently coaxing a response from her.

Carly's lips softened and yielded to the tender overtures. He tasted as he always did to her: dark, musky, delicious, irresistible. Heat suffused her whole body as her pulse accelerated.

He drew her closer to him, then began dropping little kisses over her face, holding back from the deep hungry ravishing of her mouth he wanted. She moaned quietly. At the sound, he cradled her face in his hands and slanted his mouth over hers. Feeling her response, he opened his mouth and coaxed hers wider, plunging his tongue in the warm sweetness. Instantly he imagined being sheathed by the warmth of her femininity and was rocked by a surge of desire that almost overwhelmed him.

His lips still clinging to hers, he began unbuttoning his shirt. It came as a surprise to him to discover that for the first time ever his partner's pleasure took absolute precedence over his own. Yanking the tail out of his jeans, he let the shirt hang open. "Touch me, Carly," he said in a low rough tone. "I want to feel your hands on me."

Her eyes flicked to his, then to the dark curling hair that covered his chest. Tentatively, she placed both hands flat on it, seeking out the tiny male nipples. Under her fingers, they tightened, pebble hard. She leaned forward and impulsively touched one, then the other with her lips.

Sucking in a harsh breath, Jess hauled her fully into his embrace. "I can't take much of that, lady," he said hoarsely, driving his fingers into her hair and bringing her mouth up to his. He kissed her wildly, hungrily, his tongue driving deep. Carly felt a radiant burst of pleasure at the knowledge that she'd provoked such a response in Jess.

"Take this off," he said suddenly, grasping the bottom of her sweater and pulling it over her head. "I want to see you, Carly." He tossed it aside, his eyes fixed on her.

He moved his hands along her sides until his palms were cupping her breasts. Shaking his head, he shot her an apologetic look. "I'm sorry, honey. I'm trying to go slow, but you're just so sweet and soft and I've wanted you so long."

Smiling, she felt her confidence growing. She unhooked her bra and it fell away. He put out both hands and cupped her again, flicking his thumbs over her nipples. She gasped and pressed herself against him, wanting the satisfaction of his weight crushing her softness. Sensing what she needed, Jess shrugged off his shirt and gently tumbled with her to the rug, covering her with his body.

She moved her hands to his hair, dreamily sifting through the rich dark thickness, then smoothing her palms down his back, delighting in the feel of him.

"Ah, Carly...so sweet." He trailed a line of kisses over her breasts, raking his teeth gently against her flesh. Then he bent and enveloped a nipple, drawing on it deeply. With a little cry, Carly's head fell back while she luxuriated in the pleasure that spread through her. His hands and mouth felt so wonderful. He was introducing her to sensations she'd never dreamed she could feel, encouraging her to go where she'd never been. She had needed this so much. She felt alive and real and unafraid—all woman.

Impatient now, Jess quickly stripped her down to her bikini panties—a scrap of silk and lace. Then, kissing every inch of her as he uncovered her, he peeled them off. She was perfect, sleek, unmarked by her pregnancy. All the damage was inside her, he thought, thinking of the child she'd lost, feeling a rush of compassion. It hurt him to think of her pain, but he could try to assuage some of that. Now. Tonight. By showing her how precious she was. Quickly he stood and shed his own clothes, and then he came to her.

Chanting inside his head that he had to think of her needs first, Jess squeezed his eyes tightly closed. He inhaled the musky heady womanly scent of her passion and bent to taste the skin of her stomach. He felt the tremor that went over her, but was beyond words to reassure her. Instead, he encircled her with his arms and rested his face against her belly, staying still for a long moment.

Carly's muscles contracted when his tongue dipped into her navel. She drew in a shuddering breath, not sure what to do next, only aware of a need to give him...something. For her, the act of love had always been too quick, mechanical, unimaginative. It took time to come to this mindless state of pleasure, she realized.

Whispering endearments and encouragement, Jess's palm swept down her concave abdomen and settled on the mound of her femininity, cupping it. In no hurry, he trailed his fingers through the tawny triangle at the apex of her thighs, then sank his fingers into the wet warm heart of her. A moan ripped out of her and into him as his mouth took hers in a deep dark erotic kiss. Dimly she heard words of love breathed hotly against her skin. She tossed restlessly, thrashing her head back and forth, reaching, reaching....

"Let go, sweetheart," he murmured hoarsely, his thumb relentlessly stroking. "Don't hold back. Let go, let go..." The words were a dark refrain that swirled through her senses along with the passion and need he'd fired in her. Tension peaked, then splintered, breaking into a million bright shards, leaving her rocked with sensations and gasping for breath.

Her eyes, dazed and stunned, found his. Jess smiled. He'd wanted to see her like this, still floating in her own pleasure, her body pliant and yielding. Then his smile faded. He moved up over her and lowered his body fully onto hers.

"Are you ready for me, Carly?" he asked tightly, doggedly hanging on to the last ounce of his control, on fire to bury himself in her.

"Yes, yes." She was all woman now, restless and wanting. Positioning himself, he thrust once, going deep into her. She cried out and he froze.

"Don't stop, don't stop," she begged, pulling him down to her, seeking his mouth.

She was tight, so tight. And hot. Desire pounded in him, thick and hard and unreasoning. Returning her kisses avidly, he forced himself to resist the primitive urge to plunge again and again into her welcoming warmth. But she wrapped her legs around him and dug her fingers into his shoulders, arching urgently. He began to move in her, slowly at first. He felt the tremors take her again, and he was lost. With a final mighty thrust, he gave himself up to the dark mindless luxury of fulfillment.

Neither spoke. The only sound in the room was the shuddering, slowly decreasing rhythm of two people breathing. Beneath the seductive weight of Jess's body, Carly floated in a sweet deep languor, as though her veins flowed with melted honey and her bones had no substance whatsoever. In stark contrast, her thoughts raced. Never, never had she expected anything like this. Bits and pieces of the past hour flashed in her mind like isolated frames of a fast-moving film. Was that her? Could that sensuous uninhibited *responsive* woman possibly have been her?

She felt the weight and power of Jess's body on hers with a sense of delight, and ran a palm over his sweat-slicked skin from shoulder to buttocks just because it felt so wonderful to touch him. His face was buried in the tangle of her hair. A few strands stirred against her ear with each breath. His hand gently caressed her breast. She sensed in him the same supreme satisfaction she was feeling. She had given him that, she thought with a little thrill. But he'd given her more. Never had she felt so much a woman, a complete woman. She savored the feeling, hugged it to herself fiercely.

Jess planted a soft fervent kiss on the side of her neck. "You were fantastic, wonderful, beautiful," he murmured, his lips brushing her skin with every word.

Closing her eyes with sheer happiness, Carly squirmed, enjoying the little shivers that were shooting through her. "So were you," she said, basking in the warm satisfied feeling. She hadn't disappointed him!

He chuckled softly, shifting to one side to prop himself

up on his elbow and study her. "'Don't expect too much,' huh?"

They faced each other, Carly's head resting on her arm. But at his words, she scooted closer and turned her face into his chest. His musky manly scent mixed with hers. It stirred more emotion when she was already on emotional overload, still breathless and reeling. "You aren't any more surprised than I am," she said with wonder in her voice.

Jess angled his head back slightly to look in her eyes. "I wasn't surprised at all, lady. I recognized a natural the first moment I ever saw you."

She returned his look a long moment. "Is that really true?"

He narrowed his eyes as he thought back. "It was the day we were summoned for the grand jury. You had on a sort of dull gold outfit with a skinny skirt that outlined your cute little fanny." With his right hand, he made a meandering inspection of the fanny in question. "Your hair was pinned back, and I thought then how I'd like to see it like this—" he threaded his fingers through it "—wild and free. It was that same dull gold. You were that color all over, like a sun-kissed fantasy woman."

Carly considered that, speechless with pleasure, her hungry heart savoring the incredible fact that this self-contained, utterly sophisticated man would actually tell her something so wonderful.

"Now you look not only kissed, but loved."

Carly wondered if too much happiness could strike a person dumb. Mutely, she reached out to brush her hand over his chest, just for the joy of touching the springy curls and his warm flesh.

Returning the caress, Jess swept one hand up over her breast and throat, then buried it in her thick tawny hair. His gaze roamed over her naked body on the lush white rug. She was flushed in the afterglow of love. "You remember that first night when you offered me Scotch and sympathy?" He lifted both eyebrows, and Carly nodded.

He glanced at the rug, then back to her, squinting, his eyes growing distant with recollection. "That night, I looked at this rug—soft, white and inviting—and I had this fantasy.... I could see you nestled in this white fur wearing only a smile." He touched a gentle finger to the corner of her mouth, which was barely turned up, then leaned down and kissed that tiny start of a smile. "You look even better than my fantasy."

She put her arms around his neck and hugged him tightly. "How do you know just what to say to me?"

Resting his chin against her temple, he thought about that. "I don't know. I've never been good at saying the right things to the people who mattered to me."

Inside herself Carly savored the revelation, however inadvertent, that she mattered to him.

"You're not the only one who did a little fantasizing."

She felt him smile against her temple. "Oh, yeah? And when was this?"

"Last weekend when you spent the night here."

His hands started wandering again, exploring the intricacies of her spine and fanning out to find the twin dimples on her hips. "I wasn't fantasy material that night, as I recall."

"It was the middle of the night."

"Hmm, this is getting interesting."

"I went in to check on you."

He chuckled softly. "Like the conscientious little caretaker you are."

She hid a wry smile. "It was probably just an excuse to look at you, because that's what I did."

"Was I decent?"

Speaking in a husky voice that told him she was seeing

it all again, she said, "You were all sprawled out with the sheet pulled way down to here." Slowly she drew a line with one fingernail low on his stomach, smiling when his muscles went tight.

Jess's voice was a little gruff when he found it. "Was I smiling?"

"You were asleep."

"I ask," he said, "because what I was dreaming that night could have put a smile on the face of a dead man."

"Oh? What were you dreaming?"

"Let's just say you figured in it prominently, lady."

"I thought you were beautiful," she told him softly, idly twirling her forefinger in the whorl of dark hair that surrounded his navel.

His hand caught hers and stilled it. "Carly..." He groaned when her leg found just the perfect nestling place against his newly stirring manhood. "Whoa, darlin', keep that up and you'll start something that just may take us hours to finish."

She stared up at him. "Don't we have hours?"

He sat up and pulled her with him, placing a fierce—and to Carly, all too brief—kiss on her mouth. "Yeah, we have hours and hours—the whole weekend. And I want to spend every minute of it with you." He kissed her again. "Across the lake." Again he kissed her. "At my place." And again. "Okay?"

Before she melted into a puddle at his feet, she gave in.

JESS'S PLACE IN COVINGTON turned out to be nothing like Carly expected. Oak trees and magnolias dotted the deep expanse of lawn from the road up to the house, which, in the moonlight, looked like something out of the past. It was built on two levels. The lower had originally been designed to accommodate flooding, but it was now closed in. Split stairs curved up to the front porch on the main level, where beautiful oak double doors with inlaid leaded glass ovals opened directly into a large front room. The dining room and kitchen were beyond that. To the left was a stairway leading to the lower level.

She could see the house was old, but it had been carefully restored recently. She had assumed that Jess had owned the house a long time, or that it had been a Brannigan family retreat, but now she wondered. It didn't seem very lived-in, but it had an air of timelessness and tradition about it. All it needed was a family.

As soon as they stepped inside, Jess put her things in a guest bedroom, then started a fire in the front room. She wondered about the bedroom. She'd assumed they would share one, but she decided not to say anything. She was uncertain about the etiquette in these things. It was very late, but she wasn't particularly eager to go to bed—at least not alone. Neither, apparently, was Jess. He had a bottle of wine open and a sizable fire going.

"Tell me about your house," she suggested, taking the long-stemmed wineglass he offered her, then sinking into the deep cushions of the sofa in front of the fire.

He poked unnecessarily at the fire, stirring up a burst of flame that highlighted his rugged features. Unbidden, she thought of his face after they had made love. He'd lost that closed guarded look. He'd been peaceful, serene. He was always so intense, she thought, melting with love for him.

Instead of joining her on the sofa, he sprawled out on the rug, thrusting out his long legs, crossing them at the ankles and leaning against her knees. He'd rolled back his shirtsleeves, baring strong muscled forearms. Her eyes traveled slowly over him, enjoying the "mellowed out" look, to use a phrase from her students.

He tasted his Scotch, then made a short sweep of the room with his glass. "What do you think?"

"About your house? I didn't expect anything like this."

"What did you expect?"

"Oh, you know." Her gaze traveled beyond him to the twin stained glass windows on each side of the fireplace. "When you said you had a place in Covington, I assumed it would be something new—probably in an exclusive area, possibly custom designed. I never expected something old and—" she shrugged "—and homey."

"I almost bought exactly what you described," Jess told her, allowing his gaze to drift around the room. "Then one afternoon I was out driving around and I saw this place. The trees, the land, the house..." His eyes narrowed, unfocused. "I don't know what it was about it, I just know that it seemed to have something I wanted. Needed." He shot a look at her. "Does that sound ridiculous?"

"Not at all. I think you're lucky to find something you need in a piece of land and a house and trees."

"Don't forget the barn."

She looked delighted. "You mean there's a barn, too?"

"Looking just like something from an Andrew Wyeth painting."

"Do you keep horses, too?"

"No horses. Only two vintage cars."

"In a barn?"

He shrugged. "Why not? They're a lot neater than horses. I've never had to muck out the stall where I park my Corvette."

She gazed at him with a look of discovery. "Now it all fits," she said, nodding knowingly. "A '57 Corvette—a classic, right? And your Jaguar, also a classic, although I don't know much about classic cars." She smiled at him. "Don't get offended, but I assumed you bought the Jaguar already restored, but you did it yourself, didn't you?'"

"I like working with my hands."

Of course. Carly studied the clean strong lines of his

hands, visualizing them skillfully and diligently treating the traumatized in Crescent City's emergency room. Instantly that image faded, and she saw herself naked and pliant under those same hands while they stroked and teased and caressed her body. She was suddenly breathless and warm, and not because she was too close to the fire.

She cleared her throat. "Why did you want a place in the country?"

"So I could run from reality," he answered, drawing himself up on one knee and resting his wrist on it. "The same reason a lot of people leave the city. Sometimes I need to get totally away. I've only had this place a few months—the restoration work was mostly done when I bought it—but I love it here. I wish I—"

She waited, brows raised expectantly. "You wish...?"

He rattled the ice in his glass. His voice had a dark hard edge to it when he replied, "I don't know, it's just something I fantasize about when I've had to patch up a few too many bullet holes or stab wounds in a week."

"Do you ever think of changing your job?"

"Sometimes." In one motion, he was on his feet. He moved over to the tall window that framed a moonlit scene so peaceful it could have been a postcard. Clamping a hand behind his neck, he stared into the darkness. Carly got up and went to him.

"I don't just think of it sometimes," he admitted, lowering his hand to her face. He traced the line of her cheek with his finger all the way to her chin, then cupped her neck in his palm. "I think of it constantly."

Carly curled her fingers around his wrist and looked at him, confused. "So, what's the problem? You're a physician. You can set up a practice anywhere. You have a fine professional reputation and a beautiful place to live. Why—"

"Maybe I should get out of it altogether, Carly."

She stared at him. "Out of medicine?"

He pulled her into his arms, sighing at her softness, letting her warmth and womanliness flow into him. "It's crazy, isn't it?"

She was still, except for her hands, which caressed his back, giving him the comfort she sensed he needed. "Oh, Jess, not crazy, not if you're really certain it's your profession you want to give up and not the situation you're in because of your profession."

They stood there quietly, not saying anything for several moments. Carly stroked the taut muscles of his back, feeling it when his tension eased. Jess rested his chin on the top of her head. "Guess what?" he said with a soft half laugh that she could tell was directed at himself.

"Hmm-mmm?"

"I'm feeling like one of your screwed-up adolescents again, spilling my guts. I've unloaded on you again."

She rubbed her nose against his shirtfront. "Not unloaded...shared."

His arms tightened around her, fitting her against him all the way down to her toes. "It's no wonder you've got such a great success rate."

She laughed softly. "My students don't get quite this much personal attention."

He shook his head helplessly. "Carly..."

She lifted her gaze to his, and with a wrenching moan, his arms went around her and he hugged her tightly. She whispered something against his neck—he never knew what. Blindly he sought her mouth, kissing her deeply, hungrily. Desire, banked like the glowing coals of the fire, was instant and hot.

He swung her up into his arms and carried her to his bed.

CHAPTER FIFTEEN

IT WAS A BEAUTIFUL crisp November morning, at least by Louisiana standards. Carly discovered, to her delight, that the windows in Jess's bedroom were actually French doors that opened onto the gallery overlooking the grounds on the south side of the house. A few hundred yards away, the surface of a small pond glinted like a gray pearl. At the edge, a snow-white egret stood on one leg and dipped its long beak into the water, fishing for minnows.

"Okay, I'm done." Fresh from a shower, Jess appeared at the door in jeans and a navy sweatshirt.

She turned and smiled into his eyes. "I was just admiring the view."

"Yeah, me, too." His gaze swept over the tawny cloud of her unbound hair and lingered on her breasts—also unbound—in a soft pink sweater. He stepped through the French doors and walked up to her, then bent down and touched his mouth to hers.

His lips were cool but soft. He tasted minty fresh and smelled like soap. Carly made a small sound of pleasure, and when his arms immediately went around her, she felt his heat and hardness. She anchored her own arms at his waist and opened her mouth to the gentle invasion of his tongue. He took his time, leisurely exploring her inner warmth while his hands explored her body. After a time—which could have been a minute or five or ten, Carly didn't know or care—he buried his face in her hair.

"That was delicious," he murmured fervently, wondering what had ever made him think he could resist Carly. Even a simple good-morning kiss made him want to take her by the hand and lead her straight back to the bed they'd just left. The interlude on the rug—however mind shattering and satisfying—had been only the beginning. Upon sweeping her up and taking her to his bedroom, he had proceeded to lose himself in her. Passion had flowed out of her freely and surprisingly fiercely once she'd discovered the sensuous woman inside her.

It had been a night of discovery for him, too. He'd become jaded and cynical after too many years of casual affairs and women chosen precisely because they presented no threat to anything in his life, personally or professionally. He'd believed himself incapable of the kind of feeling he'd discovered while he'd made love with Carly. He threw a protective possessive arm around her and pulled her close.

"Are you cold?" He leaned back and looked at her. "Come on, let's go inside. I made coffee while you were dressing, but breakfast is still up for grabs." He contented himself with briskly rubbing her arms, then urged her ahead of him along the gallery, around the back of the house to another set of French doors that opened to the kitchen.

"This house is wonderful, Jess," Carly said, walking into the blue-and-white kitchen and falling in love.

"It has possibilities," he agreed, glancing around, his head to one side, as though he were considering something.

Carly followed his gaze. Everything was immaculate, but to her female eye, strangely empty. The whole house cried out for someone to live in it, to clutter it with the little things that transformed a house into a home.

Together they made breakfast. There wasn't much early morning chatter—something else they had in common?

Again she felt a sense of the rightness of being with Jess, and her eyes went soft. She was still breathless and slightly dazed from the night of love and was perfectly content to savor it in silence.

After breakfast, they explored the house—every nook and cranny of both levels—then the carriage house, which had been converted into a garage, and finally, the gazebo and pond. Jess found himself grinning a lot, taking pleasure in Carly's obvious delight with the place. Her reaction was almost as important to him as Mike's. Maybe more so, he thought, although for the moment he chose not to examine the reason for that. How could he until he sorted out what it was he felt for Carly? There was a sweetness about her that could become habit-forming. At one time, he would have shied away from that. Now he was eager to uncover all the layers that made up the special woman she was. Aside from the passion they shared, being with her brought him a sense of peace and contentment the likes of which he'd never known.

They had lunch on the patio. Only then did they notice the weather.

"Looks like a front coming through," Jess said, squinting at the overcast sky through the widespread limbs of a massive oak. He got up and grabbed her hand. "Come on, I want to show you the barn before it starts to rain."

"This is wonderful, Jess," she said, her voice hushed as they stood just inside the huge old structure.

"That's what you said about the house and the gazebo and the old carriage house," he teased.

"And the pond," she murmured, her eyes taking in everything. It was dark inside, but it smelled like all barns. She told him so as he turned on a light.

"There haven't been any animals in this barn for over ten years," he informed her, pretending to be insulted.

She laughed. "I didn't mean that smell. I meant hay and old wood and sunshine, you know."

"Old wood?"

She socked him on the arm. "You know what I mean."

"I don't know about old wood, but hay, maybe," he conceded. "Look up there." He pointed to the loft, where bales of hay were stacked. "When I bought the place, this barn was being leased as storage space by a local farmer. I told him there was no hurry in removing it." He surveyed the upper level. "Actually, I kind of like it. What's a barn without hay?"

"I don't know, but are those things the vintage automobiles you were talking about?" She pointed at two shoddy-looking cars, each occupying a horse stall.

"You got it." He surveyed them with pride. "That one's a '57 Corvette and the other's a '49 Studebaker."

She eyed the Studebaker. "I think my grandfather junked something that looked just like that when I was about three years old."

Jess shook his head. "Too bad."

Carly looked at him. "One man's trash is another man's treasure, I guess."

Jess grinned. "I love it when you get profound." He leaned over and kissed her on the mouth, unable to resist another minute, then circled her waist with his arm. "C'mon, the wind's kicking up, and it's getting dark. It's a long jog back to the house in the rain."

She took one more look around, her gaze straying to the loft. "Anything else up there?"

He chuckled, shaking his head, and led her over to the ladder. "You've inspected this place more thoroughly than I did when I bought it."

She put her hands on her hips. "You mean you've never checked up there to see if there are any treasures, like Confederate money or old trunks with—"

"With what?" he asked, his black eyes amused. "Skeletons?"

She shrugged. "Whatever."

"Only one way to find out." He put his hands on her waist and gave her a boost up the first few rungs of the ladder just as a mighty boom of thunder rocked the barn. "Wait a minute!" He dashed to a shelf and grabbed a blanket.

"What's that for?" she asked from her perch midway up the ladder.

He shrugged and gave her a bland look.

Laughing, she scrambled to the top of the ladder with Jess indecently close behind giving her bottom numerous unnecessary boosts. She swatted at his hand, then settled for simply holding it once they reached the top. "Nothing interesting up here," Carly observed with disappointment, seeing at a glance that there was only hay in the loft.

Jess looked around. "Sorry, no Confederate money or skeletons."

They both flinched at a fierce streak of lightning and the crash of thunder that followed it.

Urging her along, Jess moved over to a wide window and surveyed the landscape. "Here it comes."

They watched the rain approach in a sheet from the direction of the pond, quickly advancing over the green lawn and the gazebo past the house to the barn. In seconds, it was a downpour. "We're stuck now," she said, enjoying the drumming sound of the rain on the tin roof.

Jess grinned down at her, a devilish light in his dark eyes. "Yeah. Stuck in a hayloft in the rain." He placed his hands at her waist and began backing up slowly, pulling her with him.

"What'll we do now?" she demanded huskily, catching his shoulders to keep her balance.

He gently drew her down onto a pile of the fragrant hay

and, lying down beside her, he threw a leg over her thighs. "I'll try my dead-level best to think of something," he told her, his voice dropping to a low fervent tone.

She moaned when his hands slid up under her sweater and cupped her breasts. Instantly they swelled and her nipples hardened. Carly gazed into his eyes and smiled. He tore his eyes from hers and pushed the sweater up.

"Beautiful," he murmured, bending to kiss first one then the other while his hand went to the snap of her jeans.

A bolt of lightning flashed, and on the heels of that a boom of thunder literally shook the barn on its foundations.

They didn't notice.

"I CAN'T BELIEVE this is me," Carly said much later, idly sifting her fingers through the hair on Jess's chest. They were lying entwined on a bed of hay, sated. Pieces of clothing lay where they'd fallen after being hastily stripped away.

Jess grunted and placed a kiss on the side of her breast, then stretched out a long brown arm to pull the blanket over them. Rain still drummed on the barn roof, but the fury of the electrical storm had passed on.

"I'm like a stranger to myself," she observed when he was again settled beside her.

He looked at her. "Does that bother you?"

She shook her head. "No. I just can't believe this—how can I put it?—*capacity* has been inside me all this time and I never knew." She leaned over to kiss him. "Thank you."

He caught her chin between his thumb and forefinger and looked her in the eye. "You want to hear something even harder to believe?" His brows went up to prompt a nod from her. "When I discovered how little confidence you had in yourself as a woman, that was something I couldn't believe."

He let her go, and she settled back on his shoulder. "There are reasons."

"Yeah, Sullivan has a lot to answer for, but fortunately you see him now for the jerk he is, right?"

She smiled against his smooth skin. "Right."

Jess was silent a long moment. "Can I ask you something?"

He felt her nod and he moved his palm over her soft stomach. "Would you tell me about your baby?"

She went instantly still.

"If it would be too painful—"

She flattened her palm on his chest. "No, it's okay," she said huskily. She started to get up, but his arms tightened around her.

"Stay here, please. I want to hold you."

She drew a deep breath. "He didn't, you know. Buck," she explained when she sensed he wasn't following, "didn't hold me. There was no mutual comforting between us over the loss of the baby, as you might expect. I woke up after it was over, and he was just standing there beside the bed. He told me, straight out—point-blank. I didn't even believe him, at first. My labor had been hard, but I didn't suspect...that. I remember I put my hand on my stomach and it was empty. My baby was gone." As though reliving it, she brought her hand over his where it lay on her stomach, and Jess clasped it tightly.

"It was as though my mind just switched off then, went blank. He said a lot of things, I don't even remember a lot of it. I was no good in bed, he said, no good as a wife, so he should have known I'd screw this up, too." She felt Jess tense with anger.

But she did remember it. It was fixed in her heart and mind as though etched with acid. *"A failure in bed or out of it.... Face it, Carly, you just don't measure up as a woman.''*

It wasn't true. With a deep sense of peace, Carly knew it wasn't true. Jess had given her that, and it was a precious gift. She reached up and kissed his jaw, as though he were the needy one.

''I know now that Buck was being pressured from the athletic director about the team's losing season,'' she said. ''He'd already gotten the word that he was going to lose his job, I think. I guess he just struck out at the person closest to him, which was me. He couldn't very well punch out the athletic director.''

''How can you even think of defending him?'' Jess growled, looking into her eyes, unable to hide the fury in his own.

She shook her head, smiling without humor. ''I'm not defending him. I've had a long time to think it all out.'' Carly focused on a point beyond his shoulder. ''How can I explain? I'm a counselor by profession, Jess. It's my nature to want to understand human relationships, people. I'd chosen to live the rest of my life with this man, and it was a terrible mistake. For my own peace of mind, I needed to try to understand him.'' Her eyes came back to his. ''Does that make any sense?''

He threaded his fingers through her hair and pushed the curls back from her face. ''As long as you aren't carrying around any more emotional baggage from it,'' he conceded, searching her face for signs that she had truly managed such a feat.

''It's going,'' she said with a smile.

He studied her a long moment. ''Fine.'' He settled back and once again tucked her in the lee of his shoulder. Then he said gently, ''Was the baby a boy or a girl?''

''A beautiful little boy,'' she told him, the husky tone

back. "He was long—twenty inches. Eight pounds. Joseph Matthew."

"What happened, sweetheart?"

"They never knew. I had a lot of trouble getting pregnant. My periods were erratic, so I took the Pill for therapeutic reasons—I still do. I told you last night, remember?"

"Barely," he said dryly. "I had a frantic thought last night at just about the point of no return. You might not believe this, but I'm very careful about birth control. I haven't lost control like that in...well, in about seventeen years, to be exact."

"It didn't have anything to do with my medical problem," she said, picking up after a few moments. "It was just one of those things—oxygen deprivation."

He nodded thoughtfully, mentally reviewing his knowledge of obstetrics. "I'm sure you were told it's rare and won't happen again."

"Yes."

He shifted so that they were face-to-face, and he allowed his gaze to wander over her features.

"You know something?" she said suddenly.

He leaned back, focusing on her clearly. "What?"

"I've never told anybody all that."

"No one?"

"Uh-uh."

"What is this? You're the psychologist, the one who's supposed to be aware of the therapeutic effect of letting it all out."

"Well, I never did, and I feel sort of...liberated." She smiled at him. "Thanks. Again."

He tucked a wayward curl behind her ear. "Anytime. It's the least I can do considering all the times I've dumped on you."

"I told you, Jess Brannigan, it's not dumping, it's sharing."

"Yes, ma'am."

Her gaze went behind him to the open window. "It's stopped raining."

Jess craned his neck to look over his shoulder. "So it has."

"Are you hungry?"

"Are you kidding? After that marathon you just put me through?"

"Exactly," she said with a sly smile. "How about if I fix us two of those gigantic steaks I saw in the freezer?"

He flung off the blanket and stood up. "Excellent idea." He swung her up into his arms, ignoring her squeals, and headed for the ladder.

THE WEEKEND WAS a revelation to Carly. Being the sole focus of a man's attention was something totally new and thrilling to her. She basked in Jess's obvious infatuation with her, and in the knowledge that he found her desirable and fun to be with. Whenever she saw a glint of male appreciation in his eyes, she glowed and thrilled in the knowledge that she was a woman capable of attracting a man like Jess.

But she was a realist, too. All that day and through Sunday, she was prepared for him to seek a break from her, to get a little weary of her as a constant companion. Like most men he was bound to need some time to himself. That lesson she'd learned from the many hours she'd spent alone while Buck was with his cronies in bars, or anywhere else where Carly wasn't. There was, she reminded herself, a Corvette and a Studebaker in Jess's barn. Restoring cars was a thoroughly masculine hobby, to her way of thinking.

But it never happened.

The more they made love, the more Jess seemed to want it. His appetite for Carly never seemed satisfied. After they'd eaten the steaks she cooked Saturday night, they satisfied their appetites for each other. She awoke Sunday morning to find him hungry for her again. Much, much later, they showered together, a new and delightfully erotic experience for Carly. When she said as much, she could tell from Jess's reaction that he was truly shocked by how unimaginative her love life had been.

Once they finally got around to making breakfast, they carried it out to the gazebo, and after consuming every crumb of it—making love was hungry work, Carly discovered—they promptly devoured each other. She was seeing a side of Jess that sealed her fate. He was relaxed and unguarded, affectionate, teasing. Sunday afternoon, when they were gathering their things to make the drive back across the lake, he suggested impulsively that they stay over another night and return to the city early Monday morning. Their jobs and their everyday lives seemed far away.

On Sunday night, the phone, which had not been picked up since they had arrived Friday night, rang as they were starting to eat the Chinese stir-fry they'd concocted together. Carly answered it and handed him the receiver.

"Jess, it's the hospital—an emergency."

THEIR IDYLL ENDED with the phone call. Gone was Carly's teasing affectionate lover, banished before her eyes. In his place was a tight-lipped harsh-featured Jess. They threw their things together and secured the house, and in minutes, they were in the Jaguar bound for the city.

"Did you get any details?"

Jess shrugged. "Only that some nut had entered a bar with a gun and shot up the place. Crescent City has three of the victims."

"Is anybody dead?"

"Three."

She shook her head helplessly. "It's incredible. Why—"

He laughed softly, harshly. "That's always the big question—why?"

She sat silently, her gaze fixed on the brightly lighted bridge that spanned Lake Pontchartrain like a long white ribbon. Carly shivered. She always felt a little apprehensive crossing the causeway at night, surrounded on all sides by the vast dark waters of the lake. She didn't need to look at Jess to know what he was feeling. The tension in his shoulders, the clipped way he spoke—even the tight controlled way he handled the Jaguar—telegraphed his feelings as clearly as if he'd shouted them.

"I'm sorry about this, Carly."

She stared at him. "My God, Jess. You're a doctor responding to a situation totally beyond your control. How could you think you need to apologize for something like this?" She watched him scrape a weary hand over the dark stubble of his beard. "You're not a workaholic, Jess. I could never resent the demands of your work."

He stared at her, then turned back to the road. "It's me, sweetheart. I resent it. I resent it like hell, and I feel guilty as hell for resenting it. How's that for real screwed-up reasoning? You think I don't realize how our plans to spend a little more time together, make love another time or two, measure up beside three lives hanging in the balance?" He rubbed the back of his neck, then brought his hand down hard on the steering wheel. "Well, I do know. Our plans are totally insignificant."

Carly didn't attempt to answer that. What was there to say?

"You know what I'd like to do, Carly? I'd like to turn

this car around, point it due north and keep right on going."

"That's running away, Jess."

"Damn right."

She shook her head helplessly.

"I'd take you with me, of course."

She glanced at him quickly and found that his harsh features had eased slightly. He was looking at her.

"Would you come?"

She leaned back. "I assume this is just fantasy?"

"Hell, yeah, it's fantasy. I don't have a snowball's chance of getting out of this mess."

"Then I'd go."

He laughed softly and reached for her, curling his hand around her neck and pulling her over for a quick hard kiss. "You're something else, Carly Sullivan, do you know that?"

She settled back in her seat with a little smile. "I know crazy talk when I hear it."

"I guess."

Jess put on a little more speed, and the Jaguar ate up the road with the powerful efficiency of its jungle namesake.

"We'll probably get this guy before the grand jury in a couple of weeks," Carly said quietly when the lights of the city finally materialized on the black horizon.

"Not this one." Jess slowed in compliance with the decreased limit. "After wasting half the bar, he killed himself."

THE WHOLE CITY was outraged over the shooting incident. The gunman, a former mental patient, had been recently released by the state. The authorities had claimed he was capable of making it in the real world. According to the television news Carly heard, the three victims who had been sent to Crescent City had survived. Carly breathed a sigh of relief, thankful that Jess wouldn't have to cope with more death.

On Monday night Rachel came over and found Carly sitting on the sofa, halfheartedly studying a student file open on her lap. She had heard nothing from Jess since he'd dropped her at her place the night before and headed for Crescent City. He'd been at the hospital twenty-four hours straight. She was beginning to get an idea of the demands his work made on him—timewise as well as emotionally.

Rachel held up a bottle of Chenin Blanc and raised her eyebrows expectantly. Carly promptly closed the file and dropped down on the rug while Rachel reached above the breakfast counter for two glasses.

''Where's Penny tonight?'' Carly asked, taking the wine and settling back against a floor cushion.

''There's a track meet.''

''I forgot. Cheering on Padgett's finest, I assume.''

''Of course. Mike's sure to sweep the competition,'' Rachel said, sprawling out on the sofa and balancing her wineglass on one knee. ''Even making allowances for Penny's bias, the kid's good, really good.''

''Jess will hate to miss him.''

''Mike understands. He told me his dad has been at the hospital since last night. He seems to be fascinated with Jess's speciality.''

Carly stared thoughtfully into her wine. ''As much as Jess wants Mike's respect and approval, I'm not sure he'd encourage him to go into trauma medicine.''

''I take it the two of you found time to talk a little this weekend.''

''I wish I could help Jess. He's very dissatisfied.'' She glanced up suddenly. ''What do you mean, we found time to talk?''

Rachel took a generous swallow of her wine and then waved the glass. "Don't mind me. That's not criticism—it's envy."

Carly looked blank. "You lost me."

"Just be thankful you and Jess can manage time alone without the complication of two teenagers," Rachel explained. "I was almost as irritated as Jess when his ex-wife nixed the weekend plans. For a different reason, of course." She smiled and lifted her glass in a salute. "Still, I can be glad you two finally got together, honey."

"Rachel..." Carly's face was pink.

There was little repentance in Rachel's shrug. "So, when does Jess plan to reschedule the weekend?"

After a second or two, Carly grimaced sympathetically. "Not right away. He told me his weekends are tied up at the hospital for a few weeks. Mike's in school during the week, naturally, so going then is out. It'll be a while, Rach."

They were both staring dejectedly into the fireplace when the doorbell rang. Carly stood and walked toward the door, her gaze on the two silhouettes framed in the oval glass.

Jess and Kyle.

Her heart beating a little faster, she opened the door.

Kyle grinned ruefully and held up a huge paper bag bearing the name of a Chinese take-out restaurant. She grinned back at him. Then, as though pulled by a magnet, her eyes went to Jess and her smile changed, softened. The collar of his denim jacket was turned up, and his hands were deep in his pockets. His dark gaze locked with hers.

"Hello, sweetheart."

CHAPTER SIXTEEN

CARLY CLOSED THE DOOR as soon as the two men were inside.

"Rachel's in there," she murmured vaguely to Kyle, with eyes only for Jess, who was staring at her just as intently. Dividing an amused look between the two of them, the big detective chuckled and made his way to the living room.

"You look tired," she said, running hungry eyes over Jess's dark features. His mouth was bracketed with deep lines, and there was a tense strained look about him.

He raked a hand through his black hair with weary fingers. "It's been a long day." They stared at each other. "I should have called..."

She shook her head. "I knew you were tied up. The news said all three men survived."

"Yeah." He glanced toward the living room. Kyle said something in his deep voice, and Rachel laughed. Jess covered Carly's cheek with one hand. "I want to kiss you. It seems like a year since I kissed you."

Carly went into his arms.

His kiss was hungry, intense. Carly whimpered softly, the woman in her sensing his need. She was helpless to deny him anything.

"Hey, Jess! I've got more Chinese here than I can handle. You want some?"

Jess groaned and kissed her once again. "Later," he

murmured, and hugged her briefly. Then they fell into step, close together, and went into the living room.

Between the two of them, Jess and Kyle wolfed down the contents of the take-out cartons in fifteen minutes flat. Both had been on duty more than twenty-four hours, surviving mainly on coffee.

"Kyle, what's new on the Lila Faust case?" Carly asked, handing him a can of beer and then sinking onto the rug beside Jess, who was sprawled in front of the fireplace on one elbow and nursing a Scotch. A double.

"Carly..." Jess's tone held mild reproof.

"I know you can't tell me anything because you're on the grand jury, but Kyle's a public servant. I'm exercising my right to know."

Kyle chuckled. "There's not much to know. Since the grand jury didn't take any action, the investigation's ongoing, as per orders from the D.A. That's about it."

"No new leads, huh?"

Jess rolled his eyes. "You think Lila's innocent, right, sweetheart?"

"I don't think it's very likely she killed anybody," Carly said.

"She confessed, Carly!"

"She had opportunity and motive," Kyle offered in his slow soft voice.

"But have you checked out all the other people who might have wanted James Fitzgerald dead?"

"'All the other people'?" Rachel repeated blankly. "What was he? A terrorist or something?"

"Not exactly," Jess told her dryly. "He was a businessman, pure and simple."

"Aha!" Carly sat up abruptly. "What if he wasn't?"

"Then we'll soon find out," Kyle stated confidently. "The D.A. won't be so hasty the next time. The case against Lila appeared to be open-and-shut, and they jumped the gun. You can bet they'll be searching for irrefutable evidence against Lila or anybody else who might have wanted Fitzgerald dead."

"What do we know about the other partner—" she waved a hand "—Matthew Forbes?"

"Some of it's privileged," Kyle replied, "but frankly there's not much more than you can get out of the *Times Picayune*."

"Did Lila herself appear before the grand jury?" she asked Jess.

"No. As the accused, she wasn't required."

"I took her statement," Kyle said.

"What did you think?"

"I thought it very likely she shot Fitzgerald in self-defense."

Carly squirmed impatiently. "I wish I could talk to her!"

Jess's arms went around her waist, and he hugged her against him. "You can't be mother confessor and counselor for the whole world, Carly."

"I know, Jess," she said. "But I just—"

"Have this feeling," he finished, reaching around her for a few grapes, which he proceeded to feed her.

She leaned back against him, chewing. "I just wish I didn't have to sit out, for Lila's sake."

"We'll try to muddle through without you," Jess teased, his mouth at her ear.

"The grand jurors should request her testimony. John Hebert might persuade her lawyer to let her testify on her own behalf," Carly said thoughtfully.

"Why?" Kyle wanted to know.

"Just to...read her, if you know what I mean." Carly poked Jess with an elbow to stifle his opinion, but it didn't work.

"Carly's very big on intuition and vibes," Jess explained. He rested his chin in the curve of her neck and shoulder and added wryly, "Actually, she's pretty good at it. She even managed to win Colonel Buckley over a couple of times."

"But not Joe West," Carly said with mild disgust.

Jess chuckled. "No, not Joe West."

Kyle gazed at Carly thoughtfully. "You really feel that strongly that Lila didn't pull the trigger at all? They were quarreling—there's evidence of a scuffle."

"I really do. There's more there than she's telling, I know it, Kyle."

Kyle finished off his beer and stood up, pulling Rachel to her feet with him.

"I'll look into it."

"DON'T GET YOUR HOPES up," Jess said later as they were tidying up. "The woman has confessed. She would have been indicted Friday for manslaughter except for the fact that the D.A. is obsessed with pinning a murder-one on her. With a tad more evidence, we'd have had no choice."

"She didn't do it, Jess."

He sighed and appealed to the ceiling. "And what do you base that on, Carly? The fact that you're personally acquainted with her? That you know her daughters, and they're nice kids?"

"I've just got a feeling...."

He rolled his eyes. "The D.A.'s got evidence, and will get more. You heard Kyle."

"Okay, I've got a theory."

"A theory."

"What if somebody else killed him, Jess?"

"Well it stands to reason that if you don't think Lila did it, somebody else had to. The poor bastard's definitely dead."

"Jess!"

He bit into a fortune cookie and looked unapologetic.

"What if she's taking the blame for someone else?"

"You are really grasping at straws, Carly."

"Well, what if she is?"

He stared at her. "Like who?"

She shrugged. "Who else would want him dead?"

He looked mystified. "You tell me. It's your theory. Even if someone did, why would Lila want to take the blame for somebody else?"

"It's a fact that the courts are more lenient on women."

"But why would she even put herself in that position?"

Carly spread her hands and shrugged a shoulder. "For love, maybe."

"Pardon me?"

"Maybe she'd do it for her lover."

"Her lover?" He snorted, obviously discounting the whole idea.

"Well, why not?"

He laughed shortly. "No woman is that generous, sweetheart."

She studied him, frowning slightly. "Do you really believe that?"

"That a woman would be generous enough to sacrifice herself, chance the very likely prospect of a jail sentence, all for love?" His brows rose skeptically. "In a word—no, I don't believe it."

"Some pretty wonderful and unselfish sacrifices have been made in the name of love, Jess," she said quietly.

He was silent a beat or two. "Let's don't talk about this tonight, Carly."

Holding his gaze a moment longer, she nodded and hung up the dish towel. She glanced at the tiny ribbon of paper that he'd pulled out of his fortune cookie. "What's your fortune?"

His mouth slanted up at one corner. "Wait'll you hear.

'Better to trip with the feet than with the tongue,'" he read ruefully.

"Hmm."

"Have I just done that, Carly?"

She took the step that erased the distance between them and closed her eyes when she felt his arms go around her tightly. "You can't force yourself to believe in love, Jess. Either it's inside you, or it's not."

He turned his face into her hair and inhaled deeply. "Carly."

"Hmm?"

"Nothing, just... You feel so good, smell so good." He bit her earlobe softly. "Taste so good."

He was tired. She could feel it in his shoulders and in the way he rested his head against hers. He smelled like antiseptic and after-shave and Scotch. He was cynical and single-minded, needy and vulnerable. And she loved him.

"I've been thinking about you," she murmured against his chest, letting her hands move gently over the taut muscles of his back. "I was hoping you'd come by when you could manage to get away from the hospital."

"I went home and took a shower," he said, giving in to the seduction of her hands, to the sheer luxury of totally relaxing his guard. Idly his hands played over her smooth shoulders and her spine and then went lower, outlining her full shapely buttocks. "My bed looked too big and too lonely. All I could think about was getting to you, touching you, making love to you." The sound that came out of him wasn't quite a laugh. "It seemed far longer than twenty-four hours since I left you."

She leaned back and looked at him. "Let's go upstairs."

HE DOESN'T LOVE ME.

Carly lay awake in her bed, her body still entwined with Jess's in the aftermath of loving. She turned her face to the window and stared out at the moonlit world. Tonight there had been an urgent, almost desperate quality to Jess's lovemaking. He'd begun undressing her on the stairs, tossing her clothes aside willy-nilly. Ever intuitive, she'd responded with a wild abandon. By the time they were both naked and on the bed, she'd been hot and languid, mindless with the sensations that washed over her in the wake of his hands and mouth.

Then their passion had slowed. Demand was replaced with gentle yearning. The need to rush subsided, and in a sweet fierce surge, he'd penetrated her, sunk into her hot velvet softness while passion swirled around them, over them, in them, taking them together to the peak of satisfaction.

Not a word had been spoken. His breath had been ragged and uneven in her ear, his body drained. With the last of his energy, he'd fitted her body to his, nestled his face against the soft cushion of her breasts and then eased into a deep exhausted sleep.

It was odd, Carly thought, the feeling of physical satisfaction. With the right person, it was easily achieved. Unlike the needs of the heart.

He didn't love her.

He needed her. Not only to smooth the rocky road to mutual understanding with Mike, and not just as a sounding board for his ambivalent feelings regarding his profession. No, he was drawn to her in a way that had nothing to do with any of that. In spite of their differences, something in each of them meshed perfectly with something in the other. With her, he'd found a measure of peace in his turbulent life. She had sensed it at the farm and again tonight. For a while he'd managed to push out of his mind whatever it was that had been demanded of him in the past twenty-four hours. For that, he'd needed her. As for

Carly...well, he had released the woman in bondage inside her.

But he didn't love her.

Carly stroked the curve of his shoulder. Underneath the smooth skin, he was hard and fit. She loved touching him. Listening to his deep slow breathing, it came to her how much she'd like to spend the rest of her life like this, night after night, forever holding Jess close while the fire of desire cooled between them.

But he didn't love her. She accepted it. She would settle for whatever they could share as long as it was meant to be. She bent and kissed his hair. In minutes, she, too, was asleep.

"WHAT'S YOUR SCHEDULE like next weekend?"

Jess. Carly leaned back in her chair, smiling. It never failed. Her heart jumped whenever she heard his voice, whether on the phone or across the dais in the grand jury sessions or murmuring against her skin while they—

"Carly?"

She snapped back to reality. "Uh, I haven't thought about it."

He laughed softly. "You haven't thought about it. Well, get yourself together, lady. It's Thanksgiving. Does that ring a bell?"

She sat up with a jerk. "It does ring a bell! Rachel's going to skin me. We're invited to her house, if you can make it. Penny is hoping Mike will be free, and of course Kyle will be there. How's your schedule?"

She heard his sigh, and her smile wilted.

"I wish I could, sweetheart, but it's impossible. I've got a skeleton crew in ER that day, and I'll have to stand by. Mike is obligated to spend the day with Lianne and her parents, who are back in town, but he's coming to the farm with me on Saturday. Finally. So, how about you? Can I interest you in a weekend in the country?"

She heard the smile in his voice. "You know you can," she told him softly.

He made a noisy kissing sound to thank her, and she closed her eyes, visualizing his beautiful mouth and the talented things he did to her with it.

"Same to you," she said huskily.

"I think I can get away early tonight," Jess told her. "We'll grill some steaks. I'll do the work."

"Mike's bound to be next door," she reminded him.

"I know. I'll bring a couple of extra ones for him and Penny." He chuckled wryly. "The kid never passes up a chance to eat. I wonder if he goes home and eats again."

"Probably," she said, knowing the teenage male's capacity for food.

"It's okay. I like coming home to you and Mike."

Coming home. Carly realized he didn't mean it literally, but she couldn't help the little leap her heart made. Although she knew he didn't feel the same depth of emotion that she did, it was obvious he took immense pleasure in their relationship.

For Carly, the past weeks had slipped by in a golden haze. They had spent as much time together as their busy schedules had allowed; Jess's was especially demanding. It had been quality time, whether spent alone or shared with Mike, and of course, Penny. The teenagers' romance was still going strong. To Mike, Jess made no secret of the fact that he was involved with Carly, but he was discreet. Carly suspected he wanted to set a good example. He wanted Mike's respect along with his love.

"Penny will be disappointed that Mike can't make it for Thanksgiving," Carly said.

"The Brannigan men will be unavoidable on Saturday,"

Jess retorted, his voice low, filled with sensual promise. "How does that sound?"

"I can't wait."

On Saturday, Mike played chauffeur. Under the amused eyes of his dad, he took charge of loading up the Dodge and had hustled everybody into it by six-thirty that morning.

Then, like Carly, he fell in love with the old house and barn. Watching him, Jess felt another small piece of his life settle into its proper place.

"He likes it," Jess said, his eye on Mike and Penny disappearing into the old barn.

"How could he not?" Carly handed him a box she'd pulled out of the Dodge and turned to get another one.

"What are we unloading here?" Jess tucked the box under one arm and grabbed two sacks.

"Oh, just some stuff." When she had what she wanted, she climbed the steep stairs to the front door and said over her shoulder, "Put it down in the kitchen for me and then go show Mike around. I know you're dying to."

In the kitchen, Jess looked over the "stuff" they'd hauled in. "Don't go to any trouble, Carly. I didn't bring you here to waste your time in the kitchen."

"Or to chaperone," she said, smiling. She gave him a playful shove toward the back door. "Don't worry about me. Get on out there and show those two what a wonderful place this is."

Halfway to the door, he reversed and headed back to her. "Forgot something," he growled. Reaching out, he grabbed her, swept her backward over his arm and kissed her senseless. Then he stood her carefully on her feet and nodded with male satisfaction at her flushed dazed countenance. "See ya," he said cheerfully.

MIKE CLAIMED the Corvette over the Studebaker when Jess made the offer. Fifty-fifty on the labor to restore both the cars, Jess proposed, and Mike could take his choice. To Jess's amusement, Mike had viewed the seasoned automobile with the avid look of an entrepreneur sizing up a project that promised vast profit. Watching him industriously sanding rust from the chassis, Jess decided it didn't appear that the job would be much like work to Mike.

His son was good with his hands. Jess smiled as he recognized the mixture of pride and pleasure for what it was. He felt a thrust of pain thinking of all the time he'd missed with Mike. It could never be retrieved, but he swore to himself he would enjoy every moment he had with his son for the rest of his life.

Jess leaned against the stall gate. Bright November sunshine was pouring in the open barn door. Squinting, he crossed his arms and let his gaze drift over the gazebo and beyond it to the pond. Then his eyes settled on the house. Penny was helping Carly fix dinner. He felt such a blossoming of emotion that he had to look down at his boots and shake his head.

He'd never known this kind of happiness. He felt like a man who had been half-alive. For years, he was just realizing, that was exactly what he had been. He had lived each day and savored none of them. He had guarded against anything that might have disturbed the emotion he kept under lock and key. He had taken care to avoid anything that would make a ripple in the even tenor of his days. Or nights. Half-alive.

He brought his gaze around to his son, now down on his haunches jacking up the Corvette, and a surge of love tightened his throat. Even without the problem of his career settled, the important things were on track finally. Mike was coming to respect him, maybe even love him a little. Carly was... He couldn't put into words exactly what Carly was. In his mind he was totally committed to her.

Not since his marriage had he thought in terms of a single woman. Now he couldn't seem to think any other way. He needed Carly to smooth the rocky road to peace with Mike, but he wanted her for herself even more. He was beginning to dream of a future with her.

He blinked as fantasy merged into reality and Carly stepped out of the house and walked toward him in her graceful stride. He pushed away from the stall to meet her.

"Can you two tear yourselves away from this to eat?" she asked, coming right up to Jess and smiling into his eyes. There was a smudge of flour on her cheek and her tawny curls were wild—she'd obviously ventured too close to the kitchen fan. She was flushed and bright eyed. He restrained himself, greeting her with a loose affectionate hug when he wanted to throw her down and ravish her right on the spot.

Mike scrambled up from under the Corvette. "I'm famished!" he told them, wiping his hands on a rag and looking beyond Carly toward the house. "Where's Penny?"

"She's putting the finishing touches on the table." She looked at Jess. "Can you break away?"

"I'm not doing anything but watching Mike work. C'mon, let's go." He glanced over his shoulder at Mike. "Leave your tools out if you want to, Mike. You can get back to this after dinner. Your choice."

"Hell...uh, heck, yeah. I'm hungry." Mike tossed the rag aside. "Let's go."

Jess looped an arm around Carly's neck and fell into step with her. Mike ran up to his other side.

"I hope you didn't go to much trouble," Jess told Carly as they crossed the patio and entered the house through the back door. "I've got sandwich makings and frozen stuff on hand."

"Hey, something smells terrific in here," Mike said enthusiastically.

Penny appeared at the dining room door wearing a wide smile. When they reached her, she stepped aside. "Ta-dum!" she said, sweeping her arm out dramatically.

Behind Carly, Jess stopped in his tracks. "What...?"

The table was set for a traditional Thanksgiving feast. Half a dozen slim tapers cast a soft glow over the old-fashioned dining room. A baked turkey occupied center stage, surrounded by dishes containing everything from glazed sweet potatoes to cranberry sauce. Crystal and silver winked and gleamed in reflected candlelight.

Jess stood transfixed, taking it all in.

"Geez," Mike said.

"Isn't it neat!" Penny squealed.

"You didn't celebrate Thanksgiving yet, did you?" Carly asked softly, watching Jess's face.

He shook his head.

"Well, now you can."

"YOU'RE FULL of surprises, lady."

Satisfied that the fire was well and truly lit, Jess dusted off his hands and went down beside Carly on the sofa. He pulled her into the curve of his shoulder and nestled her bottom in the V of his thighs, smothering a groan at the inevitable tightening in his loins. These days it seemed he was always in a state of readiness.

Carly relaxed against him and smiled. "How could you be surprised? You helped me unload it. There were enough boxes and sacks for the siege at Vicksburg. What did you think was in them?"

He shrugged, resting his chin on her shoulder. "I sure didn't think it was a five-course dinner, complete with silver, china and candles."

"Six courses, but who's counting."

He chuckled and kissed her on the ear. "Did I say thank you?"

"Only fourteen times."

"Well—" He shook his head. "I loved it."

The teasing note was gone from her voice when she said, "I thought you would. That's why I did it. So you and Mike would enjoy your first Thanksgiving together again."

The fire leaped and danced behind the grate, and they both stared into it for a few minutes, enjoying the first moments they'd had alone that day. Jess glanced around suddenly. "Speaking of Mike, where is he?"

"In the barn. I heard him trying to con Penny into helping him do something on that Corvette."

Jess sighed, then reluctantly eased Carly away and stood up. "I'd better go out there. I remember how it felt to be sixteen and randy as hell." He laughed when he saw Carly's gaze drop to the crotch of his jeans. He bent over and kissed her mouth. "I recall it vividly, since I go around feeling the same way today."

He was still smiling as he crossed the dark expanse of the lawn and headed for the barn. He hadn't been exaggerating about his desire for Carly. It grew with every passing hour. He wanted to make love to her. He wanted to say thank you. He'd already found that he could express with his body all the things he couldn't express aloud. It wasn't so much the effort she had made to fix the Thanksgiving dinner for him as the thought of it. He'd never known anything like the feeling that had come over him as he'd stood in that doorway and gazed at that table, Mike on one side of him and Carly on the other.

Unfortunately, Carly couldn't be in his bed this weekend, not while Mike and Penny were there. He couldn't very well flaunt his relationship with Carly and expect Mike not to be influenced. He *could* see to it that his son didn't fall into the same trap that had set him on the course to a life of loneliness and isolation.

He stepped through the big double doors of the barn and looked around. There was no sign of Mike and Penny. The light was on in the empty stall. Mike had obviously done more work after dinner. No effort had been made to tidy up the tools, which lay scattered around. He bent over and picked up an electric sander. Frowning, it occurred to him that Mike might not have had any instruction in caring for tools. He couldn't see Clifford Landry puttering at a workbench, and the man was the only masculine role model Mike had had until recently. The thought sent a shaft of guilt and pain through him. He would—

A brief indistinct sound ended the thought abruptly. He looked down the barn's long center aisle. Beyond the occupied stalls were several other cubicles, empty mostly. A couple of them held more hay, but he—

He stepped to the opening of the last one and pulled himself up sharply. Mike and Penny were lying on a bed of hay. Mike's leg was thrown over Penny's thighs. In the dark stillness of the barn, the sound of the boy's labored breathing was magnified. His hand was under Penny's shirt, and he was kissing her wildly, his hips moving in a thrusting cadence as old as time and all too familiar to his father.

"Mike!" Jess's voice was as harsh and abrupt as a machete and just as effective in separating the two kids. Penny shoved Mike aside and lurched to a sitting position. Mike turned to face his father and recognized the signs of parental outrage in Jess's wide stance and fierce expression. Even in his surprise and embarrassment, Mike was careful to shield Penny.

"What the hell is going on here!" Jess demanded, catching Mike by the shoulder and hauling him up on his feet. Behind Mike, Penny scrambled to her feet, frantically adjusting her clothes, a mortified expression on her face.

She turned away from them and stared at her fingers, which were twisted into a knot and trembling.

Jess pulled Mike away and faced him furiously. ''I asked you a question, Mike,'' he said through gritted teeth, his soft tone menacing.

Mike's gaze was steady. ''I think you know what was going on,'' he responded.

In another instance Jess might have been impressed with the boy's composure under attack. ''I want a straight answer, Mike.'' He put out a hand to restrain his son and glanced at Penny's bent head. ''Penny, go to the house and wait for us there, please.''

Penny whispered a tortured reply and bent to scoop up her jacket. As she brushed past Mike, he caught her by the arm. ''It's okay, Penny. I'll see you in a minute.''

As soon as she was gone, Jess rounded on Mike again. ''I'm still waiting for an answer, Mike. What the hell did you think you were doing?''

Mike's gaze did not waver. ''Penny and I were making out.''

''Making out.'' Jess had managed to get a grip on his temper, but at Mike's calm statement, it surged forth again in a red tide. ''It looked like more than making out to me. You were on the verge of— Do you realize what can happen in a situation like this, Mike?''

''Nothing would happen. I'd never let it happen.''

Jake raked his fingers through his hair. ''Yeah, I saw how in control you were just now.''

''I was in control. It was no big deal, nothing Penny and I haven't done before.''

Instantly alarm bells went off in Jess's head. ''I thought you had more respect for Penny than this. She's a guest in your home, Mike.''

''I do respect her, and this is not my home.''

Jess was suddenly weary. ''Take my word for it, Mike.

You don't play with fire like that. You and Penny will only get burned."

"I would never hurt Penny. I love her."

Jess drew a deep breath. "You love her."

Mike's look was defiant. "You heard me. I love her."

Jess turned away, struggling with impatience and exasperation. "You don't know what love is, Mike."

"Look who's talking, *Dad*," Mike filled the word with scorn. "Seems to me I'm not the one in this family who doesn't know what love is. You wouldn't know love if it came bottled up and labeled."

"Jess—"

Jess turned blindly and found Carly at his side, her eyes taking in at a glance the tense situation. "Why are my two favorite men in the whole world out here in a drafty old barn? There's a perfectly good fire going to waste in the house and perfectly charming female company to go with it."

Jess and Mike stood rooted to the spot looking anywhere but at each other. Jess's mouth was grim. Mike's features, so like his dad's, were devoid of expression.

Carly looked from one to the other and mentally counted to ten. "So, how 'bout it, you guys? It's chilly out here. Let's go inside and warm up. How's that sound?"

"It sounds like the voice of sanity," Jess said quietly, falling into step beside Carly. "Let's head on out, Mike." He motioned the boy ahead of him, watching with a troubled look on his face as Mike hesitated and then turned and walked out of the barn, his young shoulders squared and his chin jutted out.

Carly sighed. It was going to be a long night.

CHAPTER SEVENTEEN

"HOW MUCH DID you hear?"

Carly watched Jess prop both hands on the mantel above the fireplace, bend his head and fix his gaze on the flames. Penny had retreated to her bedroom. Mike was slouched on a recliner in the glassed-in sun room with earphones clamped over his head, ZZ Top blasting in his ears.

"Enough," she said.

"I couldn't believe it when I found them."

"Couldn't believe what?"

He raised his head to stare at her. "That they were— That wasn't harmless stuff they were into, Carly. Mike was riding high, and that's not a pun. That's the kind of stuff that gets kids in trouble. In a little while, who knows what might have happened?"

"Mike and Penny are pretty levelheaded, Jess. I don't think they're into promiscuous sex."

He snorted. "Are you saying they're too young to have sex?"

"Certainly not. They're biologically capable, but I don't think they've crossed the line from a very natural and spontaneous exploration of their sexuality to heavy sex."

"Are you serious?"

"I think you overreacted, Jess."

"Over—"

"Yes, overreacted. Why, do you suppose?"

He turned now, to face her directly. "Take it from me, Carly, I'm not overreacting. I'm speaking from bitter experience. Mike and Penny are young, no argument there. But he's infatuated with Penny, crazy about her. And I emphasize crazy. I've been there. You can't understand the fierce urge to satisfy the frustrations that just build and build and build in a man—even one as young as Mike—when you're involved in a relationship and are too young to exercise control."

"I think I understand basic human instincts, Jess."

He waved an impatient hand. "It's more complicated than that, damn it!" He looked in the direction of the closed door behind which Mike was holed up. "Mike's crazy about Penny. Things happen. I don't want him to make the same mistakes I made, Carly."

Carly crossed her arms over her middle. "What do you mean by that?"

He pushed away from the mantel and began prowling around the room. "I... Let's just leave it at that. I know what I'm talking about. Women have a lot of power—sexual power, emotional power. They learn at an early age to take advantage of it. They can use it to punish a man or to trap him."

Carly was frowning and had gone slightly pale, but he didn't seem to notice. "I've learned from experience how to avoid that, Carly. There have been women, but they've all known the rules. I'm up-front at the outset, so there can be no surprises. That way, nobody gets hurt and everybody lives to play another day."

Carly closed her eyes and turned away. "You can't orchestrate human emotions, Jess."

"It's worked for me so far."

Harsh words. A harsh philosophy. Carly swallowed as a deep sense of foreboding settled over her. "What are you telling me, Jess?"

He halted midstride in front of her. "I was only nineteen when Mike was born—eighteen when Lianne got pregnant.

Do you think the pregnancy was planned?'' His mouth twisted. ''Hardly. At least not by me. When it comes to conceiving, women hold all the cards.''

''Birth control is a joint responsibility,'' Carly said through lips that barely moved.

''She lied!'' He clamped a hand around the back of his neck and looked as angry as he must have been sixteen years earlier. ''Lianne lied, Carly. We were dating, not engaged. I'm not saying she was entirely to blame. She didn't hold a gun to my head and force me to have sex with her. She just encouraged it in every way. She teased and promised and flirted. And she told me she was on the Pill. Four months later, she told me she was pregnant.''

He was staring beyond Carly to the wide window that overlooked the moonlit surface of the pond. His gaze was fixed on the scene; he was quite unaware of the shocked, too still expression on Carly's face. ''It took me a while just to digest it,'' he said, his voice dropping to a low rough tone. ''I was in my sophomore year—premed. Hell, marriage was as far from my mind as it would be from a nineteen-year-old kid's today. I know now Lianne planned it all. She wanted to be the wife of a doctor,'' he ended bitterly.

He moved to the fireplace and kicked at a log in the dying fire, sending up a shower of sparks. ''She deliberately deceived me about birth control, knowing when she announced the pregnancy that I'd do the honorable thing.'' He glanced into Carly's face. ''I didn't mean that the way it sounded. I wanted to give my child my name. I even intended to be a good husband and provider. I had the hots for Lianne, and I conveniently labeled it love. As I mentioned, I was pretty young, a real jerk.''

He sucked in a long labored breath. ''Things rocked along—and that's a pretty apt term, because the reality of two kids trying to make a marriage work in college and med school tends to make things a little rocky. But I'd made my bed—'' his mouth twisted ''—and I told myself I was forced to sleep in it. Lianne, on the other hand, wasn't hung up on principles and fidelity. The role of physician's wife was appealing, but she hadn't reckoned on the long hours and the interrupted nights. So she started looking around.''

He looked at Carly, who sat on the sofa, unmoving, gazing down at her hands. ''I was in my residency and Mike was about six when she selected Clifford Landry as her next victim. This time she was older and wiser and did a little homework before leaping. Landry's profession checked out as more conducive to the life-style she'd chosen. She's a beautiful woman,'' Jess said coldly—it was a mere statement of fact. ''He went willingly enough into her web.''

''You make her sound like a monster,'' Carly whispered, shocked.

''Isn't the cold calculating manipulation of lives monstrous?''

''Why did you let her keep Mike?''

''It soon became obvious that she intended to play us off against each other if I didn't keep a very low profile. I couldn't stand the thought of him being hurt and bewildered and manipulated as a kid, when he could be free of that kind of pain if I backed off. I didn't guess, couldn't know, that Mike would see it as abandonment.''

Carly raised her eyes to his. ''You're going to have to talk to him, you know.''

He shook his head. ''I can't say these things to him about his mother. He loves her. In her way, she's been good to him.''

''You don't have to reveal the secrets of your marriage. There's no reason for him to know he's been used to punish you for years. But you should go in to him now—

tonight—and explain why you reacted so harshly about him and Penny. You can give him the benefit of your experience without telling him Lianne actually plotted to entrap you.''

Jess raked both hands through his hair. ''I'm not good at this kind of thing, Carly.''

She gazed at him steadily. ''You can't bring yourself to speak from your heart, even for Mike's sake?''

He wiped his palms against his thighs and stared in the direction of the sun room. It didn't take a psychology degree to understand his own son. He knew what Mike was doing—losing himself in the music pouring into his ears. Jess had done it often enough himself—hundreds of times, in fact. Not with music, but with his work.

''I'll see you in a little while,'' he murmured to Carly, his thoughts centered on Mike and the talk that was long overdue.

CARLY WATCHED as Jess left to go to Mike. She sat unmoving on the sofa a long moment, her hands resting protectively on her stomach. She stared into the dying fire, her thoughts tumbling over each other. Every bitter cynical word said by Jess in the past hour echoed in her mind like shock waves resounding in a closed chamber. She felt as though she'd been sleeping for a long time and was just waking up. And the awakening was painful.

She had been living the past two months in a dreamworld. From day one she had known Jess was harboring unresolved anger toward his ex-wife and his parents. But she truly hadn't suspected the depth of his bitterness, the deep resentment he harbored against women in general. And his cynicism… God, he would never truly trust a woman, never truly commit himself, wrapped up as he was in the belief that love was basically a myth.

She shoved her hair away from her face and sighed wearily, thinking back to the discussion they'd had about Lila Faust. He'd ridiculed her notion that a woman would sacrifice herself for love. It was natural for him to doubt that, she realized now, since he didn't even believe in love. When it came right down to it, there was only one person in the world whom Jess truly loved—Mike. The fire still radiated heat, but Carly felt chilled.

Her hands caressed her stomach, shielding and protecting another unplanned child of Jess's. She was pregnant. Or at least she had a strong suspicion that she was. She wasn't certain how it had happened, since she'd been taking the Pill to regulate her cycle for several years. Who could explain it? She was just one of the unlucky one or so percent of users. But there was no way she could view a pregnancy with anything but joy. Losing her baby had left a bleeding gaping wound in her heart that could only be healed with another child. So she had hugged the knowledge of her condition to herself, savored it. That it would be a child created out of the love she and Jess shared made it all the more precious to her.

She'd decided not to mention the baby. Although she had come to believe that Jess loved her, he'd never said the words. Given time, she'd reasoned in a happy glow, he would recognize his feelings. She shook her head sadly and walked slowly to her bedroom. It was time to wake up and smell the coffee.

JESS MADE HIS WAY thoughtfully through the dimly lighted dining room and beyond to the living room where the dying embers of the fire glowed softly. He felt good. With the new understanding between him and Mike, the words hadn't been nearly as hard to find as he'd feared. Not too long ago, he'd seen only resentment and suspicion in Mike's eyes. Because of their expanded understanding, Mike had been willing to hear him out. Jess didn't kid himself. Without Carly he might never have bridged the gap. At the very least, it would have taken a long, long time.

He approached the sofa from behind, expecting to find Carly curled up, waiting for him. She'd probably fallen asleep, he thought, a smile playing at the edge of his mouth. It faded when he found the couch empty. He'd looked forward to having a drink with her and telling her about his talk with Mike. And then maybe loving her a little. Or a lot. He felt a twinge of amusement. Three minutes earlier he'd been basking in the feeling of satisfaction that came with being a father. Now here he was chafing under the restraints that came with responsibility. Disappointed, he quickly banked the fire and put the screen in place.

"HI, SWEETHEART."

"Hello, Jess."

Jess pinned the receiver between his shoulder and jaw, leaned back slowly and let the sound of Carly's low-pitched husky voice flow over him. It was almost as soothing as the touch of her hands. He closed his eyes and thought how skillfully they could melt away the tension that tied him in knots.

"How's it going?"

"Oh, fine," she said, then added politely, "And you?"

He opened his eyes. "SOS," he replied.

"SOS?"

"Same old...uh, stuff." He heard her laugh. Her laugh, too, was husky and as sexy as hell. He rubbed idly at his beard, recalling that he'd skipped shaving this morning. He'd stepped out of the shower, and his beeper had begun shrieking. "Mike has a track meet in Hammond. I thought we could go and afterward, stop for something to eat that isn't pizza.'' He chuckled. ''I only managed that by letting him drive his new wheels. You and I will be alone.''

''I'm sorry, Jess. I've got a stack of work to do that I've been putting off. It just won't wait another day.''

''Are you sure?'' he said, frowning slightly.

''I'm afraid so. Maybe some other time.''

Jess hesitated a second or two. ''Look, if it's not too late, I'll drop by after the meet. What time do you think you'll be ready to wrap it up?''

She cleared her throat. ''Well, I don't know. It could be very late. Paperwork piles up. You know how it is.''

He was quiet for a minute. ''There was something I wanted to talk about this weekend, but the time got away from me. How about—''

''I really can't, Jess.''

He was very still, his gaze fixed on the ceiling. ''I would try to con you into lunch tomorrow, but I don't think I can break away here. So, how about dinner tomorrow night?''

''Just a minute, Stephanie.'' She'd muffled the phone, speaking to a student, he assumed. ''What was that, Jess?''

''Dinner,'' he said. ''Tomorrow night.''

''Um, I'm afraid not. I'm working with the Padgett dancers for a Christmas show. We'll be practicing nights.''

Jess groaned. ''How many nights?''

''Who knows? They're not exactly *Solid Gold* prospects.''

He sat up abruptly. ''Damn, Carly!''

''I've got to run, Jess. A student's waiting.''

Jess stared a moment at the dead receiver, then hung it up carefully. It was no longer a suspicion. Carly was avoiding him. It had been a long time since he'd been brushed off by a woman, but the feeling was like riding a bicycle. You never forget it.

What the hell was going on? She'd made some excuse not to see him Monday night and then again Tuesday night. Whenever he called, she was polite but slightly cool. *Distant* was a better word.

He leaned back again, frowning thoughtfully.

All in all, the weekend had been a success. He still got a little misty over the Thanksgiving dinner and had yet to figure out what he could do for Carly to let her know just how much it had meant to him. But best of all, the weekend had given him the opportunity to clear the air with Mike. The only thing that nagged at him was something he couldn't put his finger on. Something had been bothering Carly. He'd sensed it all day Sunday.

Damn it, he didn't want this. Just when things were falling into place with Mike, Carly was turning temperamental. He scowled, trying to pinpoint the change. He shook his head, at a loss. Maybe she needed a little space. Maybe the intensity of their relationship was more than she'd bargained for. For some reason, he felt a little anxious thinking that. There was something satisfying and right in his relationship with Carly. He couldn't believe she didn't feel it, too. He'd give her a little space. There was the grand jury, of course. He'd see her Friday and try to get to the bottom of it.

THE GRAND JURY met Friday, but Carly was absent. Jess took his seat behind the dais and stared with surprise at her empty chair.

John Hebert breezed in at ten o'clock exactly, introducing the first case without giving Jess a chance to ask about Carly. It was the first week in December, and in spite of the Christmas season, the docket was full: two rapes, two murders and one vehicular homicide.

"So much for the season of peace and goodwill," one of the jurors muttered.

"What happened to Carly Sullivan?" Elizabeth Cohn asked Hebert at the first break. Although Joe West had

Jess cornered, Jess managed to tune him out enough to hear Hebert's reply.

''Ms Sullivan was excused from this session,'' Hebert stated. ''She had personal business out of town, I understand.''

''I wonder if something is wrong,'' the old lady said with concern. She glanced over to catch Jess's eyes. ''Jess?''

To Elizabeth Cohn's way of thinking, Jess would know better than anybody about Carly. But his dark scowl discouraged any questions. The old lady quickly turned the conversation to another subject.

For the rest of the session, Jess could barely control his impatience. He was distracted and short-tempered. The instant the jurors were dismissed, he was out of the chambers. He called Carly from the first pay telephone he found.

He drew a relieved sigh as her voice floated over the wire, then swore and hung up when he realized it was her answering machine. What the hell was going on? Why would she go out of town without even mentioning it? And why hadn't she left some kind of message for him? God knew he was easy enough to reach at the hospital. He spent nine-tenths of his life there. Maybe he could get something out of Mike. He got in the Jaguar and gunned it out of the parking lot.

But Mike didn't know anything, and neither did Penny. Baffled and now filled with a sense that something was seriously wrong, Jess called Rachel. Carly had accompanied one of Padgett's students to Dallas for a scholarship interview at Southern Methodist, Rachel informed him. Her flight had left early that morning, and she was due back Sunday. No, Rachel didn't know exactly what time Sunday. Late, she suspected.

Jess hung up, feeling stunned and bewildered and hurt. Yes, hurt. She'd left New Orleans for a whole weekend—

a three-day weekend—and she hadn't even thought to mention it to him. A deep sense of foreboding settled in his stomach. He wouldn't have gone across the lake overnight without telling Carly, he realized. She'd come to be that much a part of his life. Almost like a—

Stunned, he sank down into a chair. Like a wife. A mate. But apparently Carly didn't feel the same way. His face grew thoughtful, his eyes narrowing in an effort to sort out how he could have been so far off base. Had he been wrong in assuming that she felt something special simply because he had? Was Carly with him only to help him with Mike? Certainly it had started out that way, but it hadn't stayed that way very long. If he and Mike had never come together, he would still want Carly, need Carly.

He stood and began to pace the floor. They had to talk. He nodded, relieved to have made a decision. He'd be waiting for her Sunday night when she got in. Communication. She was always preaching it to him. It had worked with Mike. It would work with Carly. It had to.

"HELLO?"

"Carly?"

Carly sank unsteadily into a chair. "Hello, Jess."

"Carly." For a second, she could hear relief and some other emotion in his voice. "You're home."

"I just got in."

"Did you get my message?" He laughed shortly. "Messages. Did you get my messages?"

She cleared her throat. "Yes."

"You don't return my calls anymore?"

"Well, it was so late. I know what long hours you—"

"Never mind," he said. "But just in case it ever comes up again, it's never too late for me to take a call from you, Carly."

Her eyes closed weakly.

"Carly?"

"Yes?" she whispered.

"Can I come over?"

She shook her head, blinking back tears.

"Carly? We need to talk, sweetheart."

"Umm." She swallowed with difficulty. "I don't think so, Jess."

There was another moment of silence. She knew him so well she could sense the emotion in him, could almost feel it surging through the phone lines to her, over her, into her. "Well, how about lunch tomorrow? Can you get away for just a little while?"

"I really can't."

"Dinner, then," he said.

"Thank you, but the dance team—"

"I forgot," he said, sarcasm creeping into his tone. "When is your next free moment—morning, noon or night, Carly? I'm flexible."

Carly stared at the floor, squeezing the receiver until her fingers ached. "I really don't know, Jess. The time before Christmas holidays is hectic at Padgett. Final exams and SCATs, the dance thing and—" she waved a vague hand, ending lamely "—and all."

"Sounds like you're all booked up," he said, his voice now dripping sarcasm.

"It does seem that way," she said, forcing the tremor from her voice.

"Tell you what, Carly," Jess said in the coldest tone she'd ever heard him use, "you let me know when you can work me in and I'll see if I'm still flexible." She flinched at the sound of the receiver crashing down.

Head bent, Carly clutched the telephone against her breast and fought to hold back her tears. His voice had sounded so good to her. She had missed him so much. She replaced the receiver with a hand that trembled. Her throat ached and so did her heart. She had made the only decision possible, she told herself, but it was so difficult.

She'd spent the time in Dallas thinking and rethinking her decision. She'd set up a dozen scenarios in her mind to tell him she was pregnant, imagining how he'd react. All of them had ended the same way. He'd never believe it was an accident. His resentment over Lianne's "trick" was as bitter today as it had been when he was nineteen. Today he was not an inexperienced teenager, but a man well established in his career. He enjoyed a freewheeling sophisticated life-style. He would not be amused over an accidental pregnancy. He would see her as an unscrupulous woman out to trap him. Something inside Carly was devastated at the thought of him believing her to be that kind of woman.

There were other things that worried her aside from her pregnancy and how Jess would react to it. The differences in their personal philosophies were too great. She was deeply troubled over the things he'd said Saturday night about women. And love. She had wanted him so much that she simply hadn't allowed herself to see him as he was. How long would her love survive when he didn't even believe there was such a thing? Any relationship with Jess would be devoid of all the things she believed in.

And that she could not accept.

CHAPTER EIGHTEEN

CARLY TOLD HERSELF often during the next week that she had been through other personal crises, and she could handle this one. But she hadn't counted on it hurting quite so much—or missing Jess so much. In the weeks they'd been together, he had settled totally into the fabric of her life. Cutting him out of it was like tearing a gaping hole in her heart. Telling herself she'd done the only thing she could was no comfort at night, when she longed for the feel of his body against hers, yearned for the sound of his voice. She wondered if he missed her as much as she missed him.

She did see him briefly at a track meet on Wednesday, but although he gave her a long cool look, he made no effort to come near her. Mike broke the division's pole-vault record that day and rushed over to his dad, grinning widely. Carly watched Jess squeeze the boy's shoulder and give him the classic male slap on the back, but then, as though he couldn't help himself, he caught Mike up in a fierce hug. He might not love anybody else, but he loved his son. As she watched their two dark heads mingle, Carly's throat ached with the pain of something precious lost.

By Friday, and the next grand jury session, Carly's need to see Jess was so intense that she was almost sick. She dressed carefully in a vivid tangerine sweater dress that complimented her tawny coloring. Her stomach was in a knot all the way to the courthouse. By the time she pushed open the door to the jury chamber, she actually thought she might have to make a run for the bathroom. Pregnancy and nerves didn't mix well, she decided.

But Jess wasn't there. An emergency at Crescent City, Hebert informed the jurors. Carly sat very still, rocked by a mixture of disappointment and relief.

They were in session steadily until midafternoon, when Hebert announced that the D.A. had planned a second attempt to indict Lila Faust. The evidence would be presented to the grand jury the following Friday.

"It's a tough case," Hebert told them candidly. "By the woman's own admission, she pulled the trigger. She still claims it was self-defense, but the D.A. remains unconvinced."

Carly couldn't contain her impatience. "John, I know I won't sit in on this particular case, but there's nothing that says I can't discuss it off-the-record in here, is there?"

He shook his head. "Not really, Carly. But neither I nor the jurors can reveal privileged information. You know that."

"Right, I understand. Here's what I want to know—has anybody questioned Lila's daughters?"

He flipped through some papers. "Terry, age fourteen and a married sister, Debra. Yes, their statements are in the file."

"Could the grand jurors request their testimony in person?"

"Well, sure, if they believed they might get something other than what's already on record. Why? Do you think they know something they haven't told us?"

She looked uncertain. "I just—"

"—have a feeling!" several of the jurors finished, laughing at Carly's wry expression.

Hebert smiled. "Because your track record's been phenomenal, Carly, we'll subpoena the daughters."

Carly left, satisfied that at least she'd made some contribution toward helping untangle the affairs of Lila Faust. Life could be so cruel. Terry and Debra, who had been through so much, now faced the possibility of seeing their mother tried for murder. Unless... Carly had some ideas for questions to be put to the two girls. She'd mention them to Jess—

A pain every bit as sharp as the real thing flared in her chest before fading to a dull ache. When was she going to be able to think his name without feeling this way? She slid a palm down and held it against her stomach. She had an appointment next week to see her doctor, but she didn't doubt what she would hear. Her breasts were slightly enlarged, and she'd been feeling queasy in the mornings. The day before she'd dashed to the bathroom just in time when Rachel had offered her a chocolate doughnut. She hadn't even bothered with a pregnancy test. She'd been through the early stages before. Joy bloomed inside her. In spite of everything, she could never be sorry about the baby.

The weekend loomed in front of her, and on an impulse, she decided to spend it gazing at the waters of Lake Pontchartrain from Rachel's family's summer cabin in Mandeville. Rachel promptly agreed, informing her with a soft smile that she and Kyle had spent the previous Sunday there. To no one's surprise, Kyle and Rachel had set a date to be married. Carly was happy for her, though she couldn't prevent a twinge of envy. Sometimes, it seemed, the course of true love did run smoothly.

As she was leaving Rachel's, she saw Mike park his four-wheel drive on the street. He was doing so well. She couldn't help a little burst of pride. He'd finished up first-semester chemistry with a B, bearing out Carly's professional opinion that he could master any subject he put his mind to. Of course, his developing interest in Jess's profession probably had a lot to do with his improved performance in chemistry. She smiled softly. Or maybe it was

Mike's growing respect and love for his dad. She was glad they were "tight," to use a word from her student's vernacular. Jess wouldn't ever have to fear losing his son again.

JESS HUNG UP the phone carefully, cutting off Lianne in the middle of a speech he knew she'd rehearsed carefully. Clifford Landry's company was sending him to London for six months, and she was taking Mike with them. Old resentments rose up and nearly choked him. He sat for a moment struggling, his thoughts in turmoil, and then he vaulted out of his chair. He seethed as he paced back and forth in his office. His body was wired with the need to strike out violently. She couldn't do this. He wouldn't let her take Mike away from him again. To England, yet. Damn it to hell!

Six months, she had said. Landry's assignment was temporary, she'd assured him. Living in a city rich with culture and history and sophistication would be beneficial to Mike. She'd already made arrangements for school. In six months, they'd be back in New Orleans. A wonderful opportunity for Mike, she had said, sounding sweetly reasonable, maternally concerned and flatly inflexible.

This time, he wouldn't just sit still and let her drive a knife into his back, Jess vowed. He'd get a court order. He'd get a statement from Mike's school saying that uprooting him right now would be harmful. More than harmful. He'd press them to say it would be downright disastrous.

Carly. She would know— He groaned and bent his head, shaking it. Everything was falling apart. He needed her. He woke up at nights wringing wet with sweat, his dreams so erotic and so full of hunger for her that he honestly wondered if he was losing his grip. For the hundredth time, he wondered what he had done. How had it all gone wrong? Why had she suddenly decided she didn't want to be with him? Why wouldn't she talk to him, tell him straight to his face?

He reined in his thoughts and drew a deep breath. Now was not the time to get distracted thinking about Carly. He'd already made up his mind that he would win her back, but he would do it carefully, gently, the right way this time. She was a woman to be wooed. But first things first. He'd finally faced up to his career burnout, and he'd already taken the first steps to fix that. Although she didn't know it, Carly played a major role in his new life.

He stood in the middle of his office and forced himself to calm down. Lianne had learned long ago to disguise her iron will under a cool sophisticated veneer. He'd take a leaf out of her book. He couldn't win any concessions from her if he couldn't look at her without wanting to throttle her. Communication. Carly's favorite peacemaking tool. He wasted a moment wishing he could turn this one over to Carly and let her work her skillful know-how on Lianne, but this time he was on his own. He'd have to go to his ex-wife and try to reason with her. Mike couldn't be taken from him for six months. Mike couldn't be taken from him ever again.

MIKE STORMED OUT of the big house on Prytania and headed for his car. The past year had been a bitch, and now this! Just when he's making a place for himself, his mom announces they've got to go to England. *England.* For six whole months! What the hell was he going to do in England? He could barely get past the accent. When he watched some of those British comedies on TV, sometimes he couldn't even make out what the actors were saying.

He slammed the door, started up the Dakota's engine then squealed backward. Old Mr. Guilliot next door was sitting on his porch swing. Mike saw him cup his mouth and yell something, but he cut out in a flurry of street gravel and left the old man standing up and waving his fist.

Mike rubbed a hand over his mouth. This was the worst thing he'd had to take yet. It had been bad enough leaving his friends in California. Then his mom had insisted on Padgett when he would have ten times rather gone to a public school. And his dad. Damn it, he was just getting to know his dad. Some of the stuff he'd believed about his dad wasn't true; he knew that now. Being around his dad, he could see that things weren't always what they seemed. Lately, he'd been wondering about the divorce. But although he had questions, he'd decided to just leave it alone. He had them both now. He lived with his mom, and he could see his dad whenever he wanted to. His dad had time for him now, and Mike liked the stuff they did together. He liked the place in Covington, and he wanted to finish fixing up the 'Vette. He sure as hell couldn't do that in England.

He leaned on the gas and headed for the lakefront. It would only be six months, his mother had said. Accepting the assignment would mean another promotion for Clifford, she had reminded him, making him feel like crap for not wanting to go along with the plan.

And Penny. Just saying her name made him go weak inside. He didn't want to leave Penny for six months. He loved her. Whether the adults in his life believed him or not, he did know what love was, and he loved Penny. She was like sunshine in his life. He didn't know if he could stand not seeing her every day.

What the hell was he to do?

CARLY WAS ON the point of leaving for her first-period gym class on Monday when she looked up to see Rachel and Penny enter her office. One look at them, and she tensed with instant alarm. "What is it?" she asked Rachel.

"Mike has run away."

"We thought you might have heard from him," Penny said.

Carly moved to her desk and sank into her chair. "No, no, I haven't." Her first thought was for Jess. He would be frantic. "What happened? Why would he run away?"

Penny looked confused. "You mean Dr. Brannigan hasn't told you?"

Carly looked at her. "Told me what?"

"Mike's stepfather has a six-month assignment in London," Rachel explained. "His mother is insisting that Mike go with them. Apparently Mike was extremely upset. He called Penny."

"When was this?"

"Yesterday," Penny explained. "He said he'd been driving around and that he would get back to me. He said he had some serious thinking to do." Penny's eyes were troubled. "When he didn't come home last night, his mom called me. She wanted to know if I could think of anyone who might know where he would go, but nobody I called knew anything."

Carly looked at Rachel. "What about Jess?"

"He was as torn up as Mike, especially when Mike couldn't be found. He seemed to think you might know something, but I told him you couldn't possibly, that you were at the summer cabin in Mandeville, and Mike didn't know about it."

"He must be worried sick," Carly murmured. Her heart ached for him, knowing how this would tear him apart. She stood up suddenly. "I think I should go—" A rushing sound filled her ears. She'd already discovered that she couldn't even get out of bed suddenly anymore without bringing on a quick dizzy reaction.

''Carly, you're white as a ghost!'' Rachel was by her side in a second. ''Here, bend over. Put your head between your knees.'' She glanced up at Penny. ''Penny, go get Carly a cup of water.''

''Yes, ma'am.'' Penny yanked open the door and looked around helplessly in the outer office for a cup or a glass while Rachel crouched beside Carly.

''Carly, are you pregnant?''

Penny stopped in her tracks, dividing a wide-eyed look between her mother and Carly. Rachel glanced up at her stricken daughter.

''Penny!''

Penny dashed away and in the teacher's lounge she filled a cup with water. Balancing it, she almost collided with Mike striding down the hall toward the guidance office. He still wore his jeans and shirt from yesterday.

''Mike! Where have you been? Everybody's been looking everywhere for you. Kyle even has a bulletin out for your four-wheel.''

''I know, Penny, and I'm sorry.'' Mike looked down. ''But right now I need to talk to Ms Sullivan. I didn't even stop to change.''

She caught his arm and herded him toward the guidance counselor's office. ''Where were you, Mike? Your folks are frantic. Your *dad*—'' her voice dropped ''—your dad was really upset, Mike.''

Mike considered that. ''No kidding?''

She pushed open the door with an exasperated sound and hurried to hand her mother the cup, Mike trailing a step behind her.

''I'm okay now, Rach. Please.'' Carly took the water and sipped it to please Rachel. Over the rim of the cup, her eyes widened. ''Mike!'' She set the cup down and promptly forgot it.

Mike had the grace to look sheepish. ''Hello, Ms Sullivan, Mrs. Lasseigne.''

Penny tugged at her mother's sleeve. ''Mom, Mike needs to talk to Carly.'' She looked at Mike. ''I'll wait for you out here, Mike.''

''I'll use the phone in my office and call your mother, Mike. She's frantic.'' Rachel gave him a motherly pat on the arm and waited until Carly's color had returned to normal before leaving with Penny.

''Sit down, Mike.''

He did, looking ill at ease.

''You're in hot water, Mike. I guess you know that.''

He nodded. ''I'm sorry I just disappeared like that, but I was so fed up with everything. I needed to think it all out before I faced everybody.''

He rested his big hands on his thighs and looked her straight in the eye. ''I don't want to go to England, Ms Sullivan. Not for six months or even six days. I want to stay here, but my mom's really got her mind made up. I thought you might be able to help me.''

''Have you talked to your father about this, Mike?''

''Uh-uh.'' He glanced down, then looked up again a moment later. ''I don't know if he would want me.'' He shrugged. ''I mean, I don't know if he would want me living with him, being around all the time—you know.''

Carly felt a pang in the region of her heart. She wanted to tell Mike how much his dad would love to have him live with him permanently, but that was something Jess should tell him. ''Why don't you just ask him, Mike? He may not realize how much you want to stay with him. He may think you'd welcome six months in England.''

''How could he think that? We've been spending a lot of time together. How could he think I'd want to move again? I'd never see him. It would be like when I was a little kid all over again. Clifford Landry has been good to me, Ms Sullivan, but Jess is my father.''

''What do you think your mother will say about this, Mike?''

He looked uncomfortable and slightly guilty. ''She's not going to like it.''

''Then that's something else you have to work out.''

He stared at her a long moment, as though turning something over in his mind. ''I've been thinking about my mom and dad a lot, Ms Sullivan. It's funny, but now that I'm a little older, I can see them as people, the way I see you and Mrs. Lasseigne and Detective Stratton. You know what I mean?'' When he saw her nod, he went on. ''I don't know why they got a divorce, but when Dad talked to me last weekend, he told me a lot about how it was when they first got married and how tough it was—how he buried himself in the books, studying all hours, and how Mom had to more or less entertain herself. Then after I was born, she had me to take care of. Dad was really careful not to say anything critical about my mom.''

Carly nodded, saying nothing.

''My mom's real critical of my dad,'' Mike said, as though the admission were difficult. ''She says things about him that made me think ever since I was a little kid that he wasn't a good person. But I've been around him a lot. He is a good person, Ms Sullivan. You know that—I don't have to tell you, because you know him better than anyone and he loves you. But my mom...well, she hurts him.'' Mike's young voice trembled. ''She never passes up a chance to hurt him. Why does she do that, Ms Sullivan?''

Carly forced her thoughts away from Mike's innocent observation that Jess loved her. How she wished it was true. ''I don't know your mother, Mike, so it would be unfair for me to speculate about her feelings. I do know that sometimes in the aftermath of a divorce, there are deep feelings, feelings that we hold inside. But emotions are funny things, Mike. They are going to escape one way or another. If your mother has leftover pain from her marriage to your dad, it might come out in a very human desire to make him feel that pain, as well. Do you understand?"

As Mike nodded, the telephone on Carly's desk rang. She murmured an apology and picked it up. "Yes?"

"I understand my son is in your office, Ms Sullivan," came the voice of Lianne Landry. "Please, may I speak with him?"

"It's your mother, Mike." Carly extended the phone and got up to go as Mike took it. He covered the mouthpiece.

"No, stay. Please, Ms Sullivan." He watched her sit back down. "Hello. I'm sorry, Mom." He nodded. "I was at Dad's place across the lake." He paused while she replied. "He didn't put me up to it, Mom." A pause. "If he called, I didn't know it. I spent the night in the barn." He held the phone slightly away from his ear. "Yeah, the barn, Mom. I slept on the hay." Pause. "Dad has blankets. I wasn't cold." Another pause. "I'm not afraid of animals or prowlers at Dad's place, Mom." Pause. "Look, Mom, I know I should have called, but—" Pause. "I worked on the 'Vette and did some thinking." Pause. "You know what. I was thinking about having to go to London. You know I don't want to."

He listened a few moments. Carly could hear the steady babble of Lianne's voice, the tones rising and falling—accusing, cajoling, commanding. Mike suffered it stoically, shaking his head at times, too still at others.

"Mom..." He waited but Lianne didn't let up. "*Mom*..." He held the phone out from his ear and looked patiently at the ceiling. When she finally stopped, he said nothing. He just waited. Carly was struck by how much he looked like Jess at that moment. He was going to grow up to be a man to be reckoned with, she suspected, wishing that she could be some part of his life when that time came.

"Are you finished, Mom?" He drew a deep breath and locked his gaze with Carly's, as though to draw support from her. "Okay, here's what I want to say, what I went to Dad's place to figure out. Now, before you jump all over me, Dad doesn't know anything about this. I haven't talked with him at all, so what I'm going to say is strictly from me. Okay?"

Lianne's reply this time was mercifully brief.

"I want to stay here and live with Dad when you go to London, Mom. I'm almost seventeen years old. I think I'm mature enough to make a decision like this. I don't want to hurt you or to cause you and Dad to have another fight over me. I think we should try to put all that behind us." His eyes still locked with Carly's, Mike dropped his voice a pitch lower and softened. "I love you, Mom." He swallowed. "I love Dad, too—wait, Mom. I do, I love him, too. I want to stay here with him while you go to England and do what you have to do."

His eyes fell as he listened quietly to Lianne's reply.

"Mom, please, don't make me choose."

CHAPTER NINETEEN

MIKE LEFT CARLY'S office and went straight to see his dad at Crescent City. As usual, he felt a stirring of excitement upon entering the hospital. He dodged a gurney being wheeled out from one of the emergency cubicles and stared with keen interest at the patient, taking in the pallid complexion and the eyes heavy with sedation. An IV bag dripped a life-giving fluid, and the medical team—two women and a man—had an urgent air about them. *Heart attack,* Mike hazarded, wishing he could hang around the place more.

He went into Jess's office and found him standing at the window, gazing over the rooftops to the murky waters of the Mississippi River. "Hi, Dad."

Jess wheeled around. "Mike!"

"Yeah, I thought I ought to come see you in person," he said. He was only a little nervous, considering. It struck him, belatedly, that his dad might be mad enough to half kill him. "In case you wanted to break my neck or something."

Jess shook his head, smiling slightly. "You're right. At the very least I ought to bend it some. And I would except I'm too relieved that you aren't dead in a ditch somewhere." He walked over and playfully punched Mike's shoulder. "When I see that 'Vette again, I'd better see some progress to show for a whole night's work."

Mike grinned. "How'd you know where I was?"

The humor faded from Jess's expression, and he grew thoughtful. "Your mother called me, son."

Lianne's voice had been cool, unemotional as she had inquired whether it would inconvenience Jess to have Mike living with him for the next six months. *Inconvenience him!* She supposed he was old enough to make his own choices, Lianne had said, sounding as though she thought just the opposite. If Mike wanted to throw away this opportunity, then so be it. Jess had put down the phone and stared at it in disbelief.

Emotion, fierce and intense, had churned deep inside him. Not the rage and frustration and resentment Lianne usually provoked. Shock, yes—hell, yes. But mostly just plain unadulterated happiness.

He'd looked longingly at the telephone, and again he'd felt the loss of Carly in his life. His first impulse had been to call her, to tell her all about it, to celebrate the deep satisfaction he felt knowing his son would be living with him.

"Do you really want to stay with me, Mike?"

Mike gave him his best straight look. "Is it okay?"

"It's okay." Jess's voice was gruff. "It's more than okay. It's...well, son, let's just say you made my day."

Mike laughed self-consciously. "I would have been up a creek if you'd refused, huh?"

Jess squeezed his son's shoulder, wishing he could find the words to convey the intense emotion he felt.

"I went to see Ms Sullivan, Dad. We talked it over. She kind of helped me see some things a little clearer—things about you and Mom and how people act when they've been hurt, and all.

Jess dropped his gaze to his feet, wondering at Mike's instinct to seek out Carly. *It must run in the family,* he thought. He rested a hip against the edge of his desk and said to his son with perfect understanding, "She's a wonderful lady."

It was Mike's turn to stare at his feet. "Uh-huh, she is."

Sensing something, Jess's gaze narrowed. "What is it, Mike?"

"Penny waited for me outside Ms Sullivan's office. She and her mom had been talking about me when I showed up at Padgett."

"We were all worried," Jess murmured, watching Mike intently.

"When I got there—to Padgett, I mean—Penny was getting Ms Sullivan a glass of water." He looked up directly into Jess's eyes. "Ms Sullivan had almost fainted."

Jess looked startled. His eyebrows came together in a dark frown.

"She's pregnant, Dad."

Jess felt the blood drain from his face. His heart thudded suddenly in his chest. If he hadn't been leaning against his desk, he would have had to sit down. He shifted his gaze from the knowing look in his son's eyes, shaking his head.

"No," he murmured, not to Mike, to himself. "No."

"She is, Dad. Penny heard her mother talking to her about it."

Jess's gaze burned with fierce naked emotion. "Penny must have misunderstood," Jess insisted, his voice hoarse. "Carly said—" He broke off, aware even in his shock that what he'd been about to say was indiscreet. His gaze locked with Mike's. One brow was raised sternly. "Mike, I know I don't have to remind you that Ms Sullivan's private life should stay that way—private. Understand?"

"I understand, Dad."

"I'll take care of this," Jess said firmly.

Mike cleared his throat. "Are you mad at Ms Sullivan?"

Jess looked startled. "Hell, no."

"The last time you were with her was the Thanksgiving weekend, when you gave me that lecture about sexual responsibility," Mike said meaningfully.

Jess sucked in a patient breath. "Mike—"

Mike shook his head. "I'm not thinking what you think I'm thinking. I just wonder if your views about stuff like that might have made her back off, kind of take a long look at what she should do," Mike said hesitantly, as though he were working it out as he went along. "There're lots of things single women can do these days." He stopped and waited for his father to meet his eyes.

Jess nodded, his expression bleak, too distraught to appreciate the irony in the role reversal between him and Mike. His son was sounding very much like a concerned father. "I hear you, Mike." He dragged his fingers through his black hair. "I'll take care of this."

Mike nodded, and without saying another word, he walked toward the door. He turned back to look at Jess. "Take care, Dad."

FOR THE SECOND TIME that day, Jess sat at his desk stunned and speechless. Carly was pregnant and hadn't told him. It was almost too incredible to believe. But possible. They hadn't used any birth control, because she'd told him she was protected. He shook his head. Why would she tell him she was protected if she wasn't? The suspicion that was forming in the back of his mind wasn't pretty. She'd lost one baby. She was great with kids, a natural mother. Would she deliberately use him that way?

He jumped up and went to the window. No, she wouldn't. Maybe some of the women who had drifted in and out of his life might have, if they'd been given the chance. But not Carly. He'd stake his life on her honor and her integrity.

He frowned, and again, he tried to fix on the elusive

thread. But again, he couldn't find it. He thought back, trying to pinpoint when Carly had begun to avoid him. It had been sometime during the Thanksgiving weekend, but when exactly?

His face grew thoughtful, his eyes narrowing even more. He'd been ticked off because of Mike and Penny. Carly had accused him of overreacting, but he'd explained his reason. Lianne's treachery still haunted him. He'd said a lot of things about Lianne and women in general, he recalled now, feeling slightly uncomfortable. But an unplanned pregnancy for a kid like Mike would be a disaster. No one knew that better than Jess.

What if Carly had known then that she was pregnant? Dear Lord! He swung away from the window and began pacing. He'd said some pretty hard things. He gripped the back of his neck, groaning as he recalled some of them. Everything fit. She'd gone upstairs without waiting for him. Later, he'd sensed something, but he'd been preoccupied with Mike, not Carly.

Remorse struck him like a fist in his stomach. No wonder she'd backed off. But he hadn't meant all those things to apply to Carly. Never Carly. She was a woman to be cherished, a woman to love. The woman he loved. Without even realizing it, his feelings for her had grown into the real thing.

Going to bed with him had been an act of faith and trust for Carly. She had withdrawn because he had destroyed that trust. She thought she'd made a mistake upon hearing the thoughtless remarks he'd made that Saturday night.

God, what had he done?

He started for the door to go to her, then stopped, backtracking to his desk. He couldn't go charging over to her and throw her secret in her face. She would be more than justified in telling him to take a flying leap. He didn't want her thinking he wanted to marry her out of a sense of responsibility or duty. He didn't want her thinking he wanted to marry her for any reason except that he loved her.

It seemed like an eternity until Friday, the day of the grand jury. Before then, he considered and discarded at least ten different ways to approach Carly. The longer he waited, the more uncertain he became. He'd always been self-confident with women, even arrogant. He'd never wanted a woman he couldn't have. Now he was plagued by all kinds of doubt. He'd become a stranger to himself. With Carly, there was too much at stake. The peace and satisfaction that she brought to his life—happiness itself—hung in the balance. He couldn't bear to face the prospect of a future without Carly.

She wouldn't see him, wouldn't take his phone calls. There were, however, two places where he would be certain to see her: at Padgett, where they were sure to be interrupted, and at the grand jury where they had no privacy. Still, the latter was the better choice, he decided.

He arrived early at the courthouse and decided to wait for her in the lobby by the elevator. By two minutes before ten, he faced the fact that she was not going to be there. He felt a sense of desolation so deep that it was an ache in his belly. Had she managed to get excused for the remainder of the grand jury term? It was difficult, almost impossible, but it could be done, in the case of extreme hardship, a family emergency, illness. Pregnancy.

All along he'd convinced himself that what he needed was some time with her, and after a few minutes of explaining himself, she would see that everything was going to be all right. All he needed was a second chance. Suddenly he was afraid he would never get that chance.

"Hello, my man." Kyle Stratton clapped him on the shoulder. "How's it going, Jess?"

"Kyle." Jess nodded with an air of distraction. With a

final keen look around the crowded lobby, he entered the elevator with Kyle. "You got a case for us?"

"I owe your lady for this one." Kyle tapped a folder. "The grand jury's hearing Lila Faust's case again today, and thanks to Carly, I've got something I think just might clinch it." He shook his head. "Unfortunately, it doesn't look good for Lila. Carly's going to be disappointed."

"If Lila's case is up today, Carly's excused," Jess said, more to himself than to Kyle. After a moment, he said, "Carly was convinced that her suggestions would help clear Lila."

Kyle shook his head. "Just the opposite, I'm afraid. But I shouldn't be talking out of school." The elevator whooshed open, and he headed for the D.A.'s private office.

CONTRARY TO KYLE'S PREDICTION and the D.A.'s hopes, Lila Faust was cleared of murder that day, and Matthew Forbes, the dead man's business partner, was indicted, instead. Lila's daughters made a dramatic impression upon the grand jurors. With a few gentle questions from Elizabeth Cohn, fourteen-year-old Terry revealed that her mother and Matthew Forbes were "involved." Terry's older sister, Debra Tanner, then filled in the details for the jurors.

Her mother had fallen in love with Forbes, according to Debra. He had paid the rent on her expensive uptown apartment, furnished her with unlimited credit cards, bought her a car and taken her on exotic trips. He had even paid Terry's tuition at Padgett—with funds stolen from the firm and his partner, James Fitzgerald.

"Do you believe your mother would have confessed to shooting James Fitzgerald if Forbes had asked her to?" Mrs. Cohn asked Debra in a gentle voice.

"I do," Debra said, adding simply, "She loved him."

"Don't congratulate me," Mrs. Cohn said later, beaming at the stunned jurors as Debra Tanner left the chambers. "Save it for Carly Sullivan."

Jess glanced at her sharply. "What about Carly?"

Mrs. Cohn allowed herself a small self-satisfied smile. "She called me this morning and suggested that we try to persuade Debra and Terry that it would be in their mother's best interest to answer all questions put to them by the jurors. Apparently she suspected Lila had asked the girls to keep some things private."

"Such as the fact that she and Matthew Forbes were lovers," Michelle Bordelon said in her sultry voice.

"Which explains how Lila managed to live so lavishly on her salary," Mrs. Cohn said, thoroughly enjoying herself.

"That secret account in Lila's name that Detective Stratton uncovered actually consisted of the funds Matthew Forbes was stealing. Lila didn't even know it existed," Art Milhouse said.

Mrs. Cohn shook her white head sympathetically. "Carly had talked with the two girls, and they'd dropped hints about their mother's distraction over some personal problems. Carly didn't think Lila was the type of woman to steal money. But she did think she was the type of woman to...well, to love too much."

"It was stupid to take the blame for killing him," Joe West said, disgusted.

Michelle shrugged languidly. "He convinced her the courts were more lenient on women."

"Humph! A waste of the taxpayer's dollars," Colonel Buckley said with a disapproving frown.

"Forbes must have thought the police would buy the self-defense angle," Ron Bridges, the youngest juror, guessed. After ten weeks, his idealism had been badly shaken. "Lila would not have been prosecuted, and he would have gotten off scot-free."

"A tangled web, indeed," Miss Pritchard said primly.

"Indeed," Jess murmured. He'd been unusually quiet during the jury's deliberations on Lila's case, content to let his mind drift with thoughts of Carly. From the beginning she'd guessed that Lila had been motivated by love. He felt a stirring of pride mixed with love, no longer surprised by her uncanny insight. She might have been excused from Lila's case, but her influence had determined its outcome.

Suddenly he ached to see her. He'd managed to curb his impatience, thinking that she'd be here today. The past week had been hell. It was almost more than he could handle to have to sit still and listen to a full docket of murder and mayhem when his future with Carly was still jeopardized.

The jurors broke for lunch, but Jess had little appetite. He couldn't rid himself of the fear that Carly was slipping away from him. Instead of the crawfish bisque the jurors were tucking into with enthusiasm, he wished for Scotch. Depressed and apprehensive, he braced himself for a long afternoon.

Carly was at her seat on the dais when the jurors returned from lunch. Jess, lagging behind, not wanting to endure another several hours of testimony, was the last to enter the chambers. Dazed, he stared at Carly, who was smiling and utterly beautiful in a vivid blue silk dress. She was surrounded by her fellow jurors congratulating her on her part in unraveling the mystery of Lila Faust.

Over Mrs. Cohn's white head, Carly's gaze collided with Jess's. The babble of voices around her receded until it seemed there was only the two of them, alone. He was looking at her with anger and determination in his dark eyes. And something else. Hunger? Vulnerability?

She was breathless and weak suddenly. She leaned back in her seat, tearing her gaze from his as John Hebert rapped smartly on a tabletop. And the jury was in session. Carly would not recall a single case from that afternoon. Jess and the determined set of his jaw, the dark hot promise in his eyes, overpowered everything else in her mind. By the time the jury had completed the docket, her heart was thudding with a mixture of excitement and sheer nerves.

She sprang from her seat as though propelled by an explosion and headed for the door. She heard Jess call her name sharply. Her heart thumping wildly, she glanced backward as he took a purposeful step in her direction. But Hebert halted him with a word. It gave her time to dash for the nearest staircase and disappear.

Her heels clicked loudly on the concrete as she quickly descended. One floor, two, three. Cautiously she opened the door onto the main level. She stepped out and made a startled sound as she felt hard fingers curl around her arm.

"Hello, sweetheart."

"Jess." Her skin was flushed, and she was breathing rapidly. Without releasing her, he guided her away from the crowd to a secluded corner of the courthouse lobby. When he stopped, she looked up and found his night-dark gaze fixed on her.

"We have to talk."

She sent a quick look toward the courthouse doors and freedom. "Um, I…I have an appointment."

"I'll go with you," he returned in a flat voice, "and wait."

She looked up into his eyes, and her protest came out as a tiny sound. He slid his fingers from her arm down to her hand and twined his fingers with hers. "Better yet, you can cancel your appointment and come with me." His voice had dropped to a low enticing lure. He was close, so close. She was intensely conscious of his thighs brushing the silky material of her dress.

"No! I mean—"

"You mean you won't," he said, frustration and something else flaring briefly in his eyes.

She looked away. "All right," she conceded quietly. "I mean I won't."

"Why, Carly?" His tone brought her head around. There was bewilderment and pain in his voice. She stared at him, torn apart by her own fears and the desire of her heart.

Tell him. Tell him you need something he's unable to offer. Tell him you need his love and trust, not just his body. Tell him you'd curl up and die inside without it.

Tears sprang into her eyes, and she looked away. "Oh, Jess..." She tugged at her hand, but he held it fast. "Just leave it alone, can't you?"

"What have I done, Carly?"

"Nothing." She sniffled, then repeated in a whisper, "Nothing."

"Well, is there someone else? Have you met—"

She shook her head vehemently. "No, there's no one else."

He shrugged helplessly. "Then is it my work? Because if that's it, it's going to change shortly. I wanted to talk to you about it, but you've been avoiding me, I've—"

"It's not your work, Jess."

He leaned back on his heels, studying her intently, even though she refused to look at him. "It's me, then. Am I too...too jaded for you, Carly?"

"No!"

"Too dull? Too cynical? Too moody?"

"No, no, no...."

"Is it Mike? He's a typical teenager, but things are good between us, Carly. He won't be—"

She did look at him then. ''Mike? How could it be Mike? I love Mike,'' she said passionately, ''almost as much as I—''

He caught her by the arms. ''As you what, Carly?''

As I love you, she cried silently. She stared at him, her throat clogged with tears.

She freed herself with a jerk and took off toward the doors, running. Tears were streaming down her face, blinding her. She could hear Jess making his way through the crowd, hear him curse as he bumped into someone and then tripped over a trash can.

She took the slick stairs as quickly as her new pumps allowed, but halfway down, her feet flew out from under her, and she fell painfully on one knee.

Jess was beside her in an instant, as were half a dozen other people. He waved them away with a fierce word, going down on one knee beside her. He reached for her arms and ran his hands all the way down them.

''My God, Carly, are you hurt?'' His voice was shaking, and his eyes were wild. Gently he inspected the injured knee. Cupping her calf, he tested her shin and ankle. ''I can't believe this,'' he said in a tortured voice, sounding like a man possessed.

''Jess! Let me up.'' She pushed him away and tried to stand up, painfully aware of the curiosity on the faces of the onlookers.

''Do you feel faint or anything?'' Jess asked urgently.

''No, only embarrassed. Will you please let me up?'' she said through clenched teeth. ''Everybody's looking.''

Oblivious to the audience, Jess lifted her solicitously and would have swung her into his arms, but Carly held him off with a fierce look.

He stared into her eyes. ''In your condition, a fall is very dangerous, Carly. Think of the baby.''

Carly's mouth fell open as realization dawned. The reason for his paranoid behavior was suddenly clear. "What are you talking about?" she demanded softly, their audience forgotten.

"I know about the baby," he said quietly, holding her gaze. Moments passed while they simply looked at each other. Neither of them was aware of the ebb and flow of the crowd or the noise of rush hour traffic less than fifty yards away.

Carly shook her head slowly. "Oh, Jess."

"Now will you come with me?" he urged.

She let him take her arm, and they went down the steps together. "Leave your car," he told her. "I'll send Mike for it later."

Not another word was spoken until they had crossed the courthouse grounds and were standing beside Jess's Jaguar. He opened the door and waited for her to climb inside.

"My place or yours?" he said with a wry inflection in his tone.

"I don't care," she murmured, not looking at him.

"Yours, then," he said. "The best times of my life were spent there."

He drove directly to her house, taking her key when she fumbled slightly trying to fit it into the lock. "Let me," he murmured, pushing the door open and ushering her inside. He watched her sink onto the sofa, then he went to the bar.

"Do you mind?" At her go-ahead, he fixed a double Scotch for himself, tossed most of it back in one swallow, then walked to the sofa and sat down beside her.

"I'm not pregnant, Jess."

He stared at her. "What happened?"

She ignored that. "What made you think I was?"

"Penny overheard you and Rachel discussing it, then she told Mike, who told me." He set his drink down and turned so that he could see every nuance of expression on her face. "You should have heard him. He was gentle with me, but firm, as if I was the kid and he was the old man. He spelled out my responsibility in no uncertain terms and let me know that he was disappointed in me."

She stared at her linked hands. "I'm sorry."

He reached for her chin and turned her eyes up to his. "Don't be. I'll talk to him and explain everything." His mouth twisted in a wry smile. "We're big on communication now, Mike and me."

Looking at him, Carly's mouth twitched.

"Thanks to you, lady." Her lashes fell, screening her eyes. Gently, he asked, "So what happened to communication between you and me, hmm?"

"I did think I was pregnant, Jess. I think I told you my doctor prescribed birth control pills after my pregnancy. But when I missed my period and there were other symptoms..." He lifted his eyebrows inquiringly, and flushing, she explained. "My breasts were tender, and I was dizzy and nauseous occasionally."

He looked concerned. "Why, if you aren't pregnant?"

"I saw my doctor Tuesday. He found me slightly anemic, which would explain the dizziness and the fainting spell in my office. The birth control pills themselves could have caused my breasts to be tender—I just switched brands—and the intensive aerobics I've been into lately could have interrupted my cycle. Everything was purely circumstantial."

He leaned back, studying her with an enigmatic look. "You suspected you were pregnant when, exactly?"

"A week or so before Thanksgiving."

"When did you plan to tell me?"

She released a weary sigh. "I wasn't planning on waiting too long. Maybe you won't understand, but I was so thrilled and surprised, so...so happy at the thought of another baby that I simply wanted to enjoy it, keep it to myself and savor it for a little while."

"I can understand the thrilled and surprised and happy part," he said in a voice laced with feeling, "because that's exactly how I felt."

She glanced at him quickly and felt a swift rush of pleasure. "But then everything fell apart."

"How, sweetheart?" It was more a plea than a question.

"That Thanksgiving weekend at your place was an eye-opener for me, Jess. That's when I realized I'd been living in some kind of fantasy world, a fool's paradise." He started to say something, but she stopped him. "No, let me finish. I need to try to make you understand why I don't think it can ever work between us, Jess."

"Carly, if it's what I said about my marriage to Lianne and having Mike so early—"

"No, please. It's not that entirely. Although until that night, I never realized your distrust of women was so dark and deep-seated, Jess. After you told me about Lianne, I did think you'd be reminded of her treachery and would probably accuse me of the same thing. As I said, it's more than that. I know I can't survive another flawed relationship. I make strong emotional demands. I don't mean to, Jess. It's just my nature. I need love and commitment and true intimacy. Our relationship would be doomed from the start."

He shook his head. "No."

"Yes. You remember saying you made it a practice to be up-front about the rules so there'd be no broken hearts? Well, I'm just not tough enough, Jess. I survived a divorce, but I don't think I could survive an affair with you."

"I don't want an affair!" he burst out harshly, rising from the sofa in one swift motion. "I can't believe this." He raked his fingers through his hair.

"Jess—"

He headed for the Scotch and fixed himself another double.

Carly's gaze widened in alarm. "Jess, I don't think—"

He shot her a look that dared another word. "Look, if a man's going to be rejected by the woman he loves, what's the harm in dulling the pain? Cheers!" He saluted her with the glass and tossed half of it down, then wiped his mouth with the back of his hand.

"This is a hell of a note," he said with a short laugh. "Were you just going to have my child and keep it? Move off somewhere and never even tell me?"

"No!" Carly jumped up off the sofa and went to him. "I hadn't truly decided what to do, Jess. I would have told you—"

"Sooner or later," he put in bitterly.

"Can you blame me after the things you said that night?"

"I said a bunch of stupid things that night. I want you to forget them, forget everything." He pulled in a deep breath, trying to find the right words. "I guess I just had to let off some steam and you were there—as you are always for me, Carly. It was just my anxiety over Mike's future and...hell, it could have been the unaccustomed stress of having the responsibility of my son dumped on my shoulders all at once." He looked at her. "Don't get me wrong—I wanted the responsibility, but like you said, I overreacted."

He reached over with an unsteady hand and gently tucked a silky curl behind her ear. "You remember that case we had—the pregnant woman whose live-in boyfriend raped her?"

"Caroline Simpson," she said. "I remember."

"You believed her even though the evidence could have gone either way. You said that day you hoped there would never be a time when you needed me to believe in you. You remember saying that?''

''I also remember you saying her pregnancy might have been planned to force her lover into marriage,'' Carly said in a voice that trembled. '''Victimized by the oldest trick known to man,' I believe were your words, Jess.''

He winced. ''Don't remind me. Those words have been echoing in my head all week long. I knew you would remember them.'' He tilted her chin up so that he could look deep into her eyes. ''Carly, I didn't feel like a victim when I learned you were pregnant. My first thought wasn't that you'd lied. I knew you wouldn't. I knew it in my heart and in my head.'' His eyes on hers were dark and pain filled. ''I knew you were a woman to be trusted, Carly.''

''No—''

''Yes!'' He slammed the drink down on the bar and caught her in his arms, burying his face in her hair. ''Carly, how can you say a relationship between us is doomed? How can that be when I need you so much? How can that be when I haven't felt lonely or empty a single minute since you came into my life? I don't care anymore about the bitter things in my past. You freed me of all that. You gave me my son again. How can a relationship like that be doomed, Carly?''

She pushed back to look directly into his eyes. ''Jess, are you saying you love me?''

''Love you?'' His face was incredulous. ''Love you? Of course I love you. It's a unique experience for me, so maybe I haven't acted the way a man is supposed to. I've made some dumb mistakes, but I do love you, Carly. If I wasn't so crazy in love with you, I couldn't possibly have screwed everything up the way I have.''

Carly felt a rush of sheer joy. It was so intense that her skin flushed and her knees almost gave way. She shook her head wonderingly. ''I didn't know,'' she said simply.

He put a hand to her cheek, and she could feel it trembling. "How could you not know?" he asked softly, looking deep into her eyes, not caring that she, who was so perceptive, would be able to read everything he felt. He wanted her to see how completely he loved her.

Holding his gaze she rubbed her face against his palm. "You didn't believe there was such a thing."

He pulled her back into his arms. "I was a damn fool," he said softly, cradling her against him as though she were a precious and fragile gift. And so she was. Just how precious and fragile, he hadn't truly realized until he'd almost lost her.

"I've been miserable because you wouldn't see me. All these incredible changes were going on in my life—Mike and my work, hassling from Lianne—I honestly wondered if I could bear another minute. And then I found out you were pregnant. First I felt sheer delight and then overwhelming relief." He stroked a hand over her hair. "It meant you'd have to marry me."

Carly turned her face into his chest.

"Unfortunately, I couldn't get close enough to you to propose," he said ruefully.

"I'm sorry," she whispered, clutching his shirt.

"And so you should be," he said, nuzzling her temple. "In fact, I don't think I'll take any more chances." He leaned back and forced her chin up so that he could look her right in the eye. "Carly, will you marry me and be my love?"

She smiled softly. "Yes."

"When?"

"Whenever you like."

"Doesn't Padgett close down for the holidays in about a week?"

"Uh-huh."

"The grand jury also recesses about then."

"Uh-huh."

"That's not too soon?" He looked a little anxious.

Tears shone in her eyes. She shook her head. "No, Jess."

He cupped her face in his hands and sealed her mouth with a kiss. Carly clung to him fiercely, kissing him back with all the pent-up longing of the past weeks. She hadn't expected to be in his arms ever again, and it was sheer heaven.

"I missed you so much," she whispered against his mouth. She ran her hands over his back, down to his hips, holding him against her, melting into his hardness. He felt so good—he smelled so good. She loved him so much.

Jess stroked her hair in silence for a few moments. "The strange thing is that on some subconscious level, I think I recognized you right from the start as my mate, the other half of me. Until I met you, I didn't even believe in that kind of thing." His arms tightened around her convulsively. "Don't ever leave me again, Carly."

She shook her head, too full of love to speak.

"I want us to go to bed together every night and wake up together every morning. I want us to live at my place across the lake, make it a real home, a place for Mike and for the children we'll have together."

His hands on her were fiercely tender, possessive. "I've decided to resign from Crescent City. A practice across the lake will mean less violence, more time for Mike, for myself. For you. Will you share that with me, Carly?"

"It sounds wonderful." Emotion made her voice as husky as his. She nestled close in his arms, so happy, she was almost afraid to breathe.

He tipped up her face, taking in her flushed and happy look. *The look of a woman who knows she's loved,* he thought with a rush of gladness. "Did I tell you I think you're wonderful?'' he asked, setting her gently away from him.

She shook her head, smiling. She knew that look and what it meant. ''I think you're wonderful, too.''

''I'm not,'' he said, his hands working the buttons on the front of her dress. ''But I'm glad you think so.''

A delicious warmth started deep inside Carly and blossomed quickly. She ran her fingers through his thick dark hair, smiling as he nuzzled against every bit of her naked flesh as he uncovered it. She closed her eyes, awash with emotion. It had been so long, and she'd been so afraid she'd never know again the ecstasy she found with Jess.

''Carly, Carly, I've missed you so much.'' His mouth was everywhere—on her face and her throat, then the lush fullness of her breasts. ''I don't think I can take this slow.''

He pushed gently and she tumbled to the soft rug. He fell on top of her, covering her body with his hard ready warmth. There would be other times for slow languid loving. Now their need was too great. He quickly stripped away the rest of her clothes and his own. Then, without finesse, without thought, he entered her, catching the cry that came from her with his kiss. She took his hard maleness joyfully, pushing up wildly to meet his every thrust. The world turned white-hot; light exploded around them. He plunged faster, rushing toward the sweet dark fulfillment that beckoned.

''I love you,'' he rasped, feeling his climax coming.

Carly felt the words against her mouth and took them into her heart. ''I love you.''

And then together they hurtled off the edge of the universe.

IT WAS A LONG TIME before they stirred. Sleepy and satisfied, Jess nuzzled Carly's neck. One hand lazily traced the sweet curve of her breast, then wandered down the center of her body to her abdomen.

"Just think," he said, his breath caressing her ear. "We'll be able to look forward to this every day for the rest of our lives." He smiled against her skin. "Does that sound as good to you as it does to me?"

She drew in a rapturous breath. "It sounds like heaven—you and me together forever."

Suddenly he stopped his stroking. Carly pulled back to look at him. His dark eyes had a gleam in them that made her smile. "What is it?"

"When you thought you were pregnant, I'll bet you stopped taking the Pill."

A tremor of dismay went through her.

He lifted one black eyebrow. "Am I right?"

"Oh, Jess, I just wasn't thinking. I—"

"Hush, sweetheart." He stopped her with his mouth, kissing her with slow sweet passion. "I hope you forgot. I hope this time it's the real thing, no false alarm. I hope my seed went straight to your womb and that right this minute a tiny life has been created by the two of us and our love."

Her heart in her eyes, Carly searched his face. "Are you sure, Jess?"

"I've never been more certain of anything, except my love for you, Carly Sullivan."

Carly settled back against him with a contented sigh. Dreamily she stared beyond him. With a flash of insight, she saw the years stretching before them, Jess's loneliness and isolation at an end. Their love for each other would grow stronger, binding them together with golden chains. And all their tomorrows would be bright with love and promise.

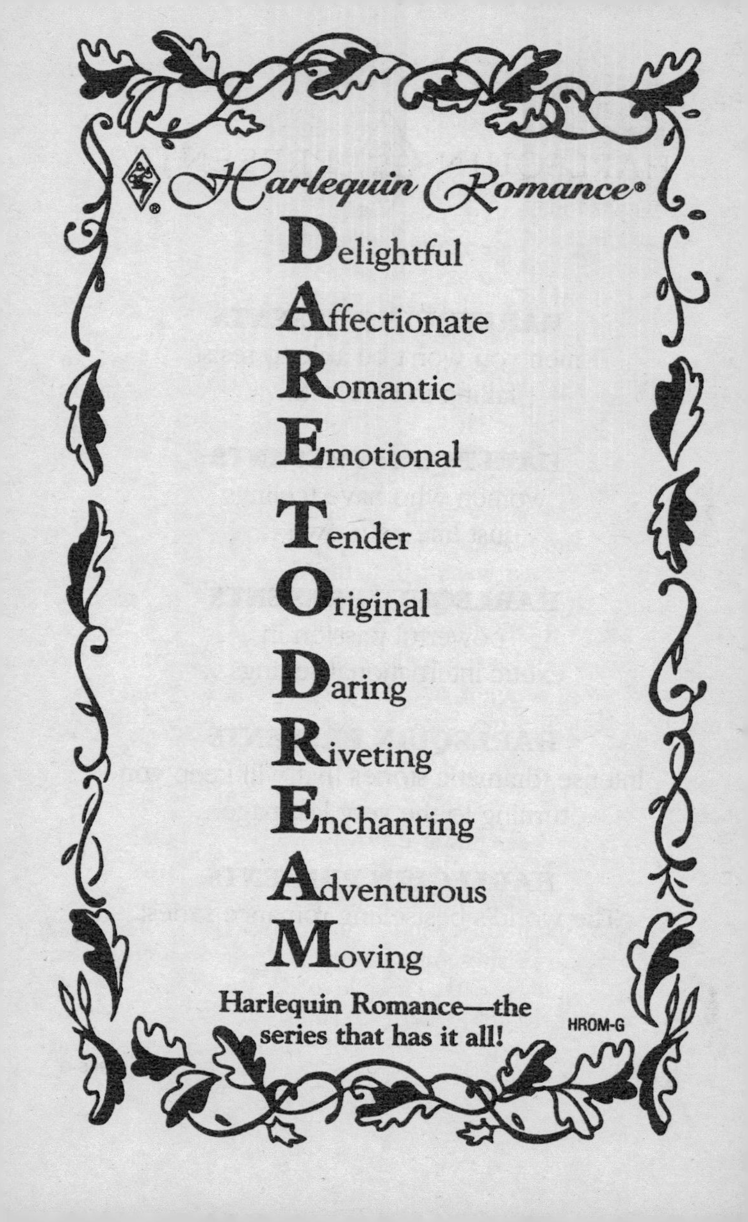

HARLEQUIN PRESENTS
men you won't be able to resist
falling in love with...

HARLEQUIN PRESENTS
women who have feelings
just like your own...

HARLEQUIN PRESENTS
powerful passion in
exotic international settings...

HARLEQUIN PRESENTS
intense, dramatic stories that will keep you
turning to the very last page...

HARLEQUIN PRESENTS
The world's bestselling romance series!

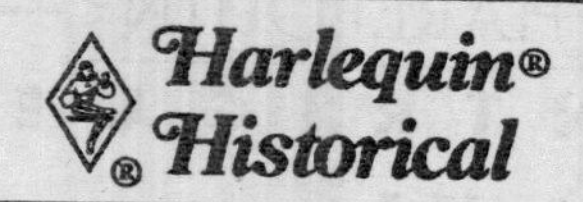

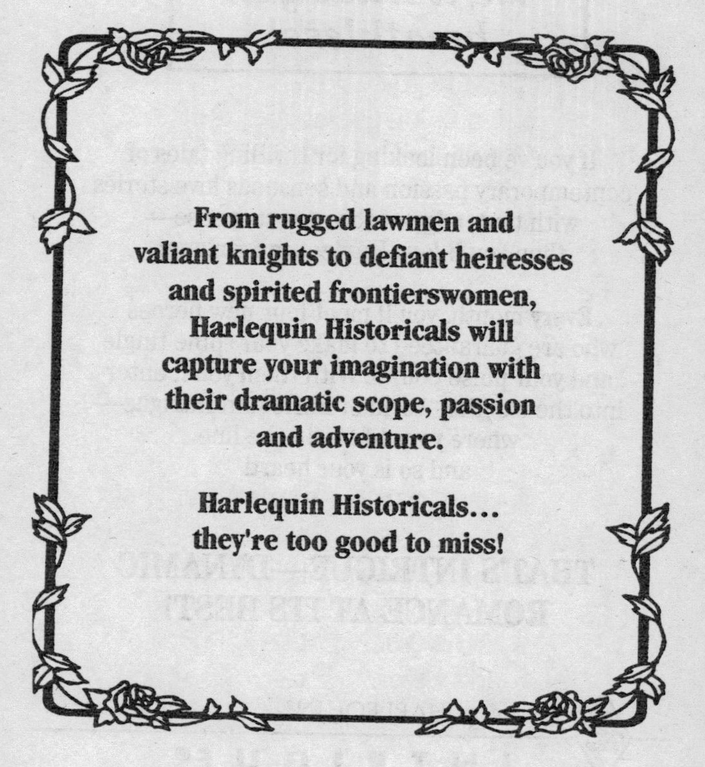

From rugged lawmen and valiant knights to defiant heiresses and spirited frontierswomen, Harlequin Historicals will capture your imagination with their dramatic scope, passion and adventure.

Harlequin Historicals... they're too good to miss!

HHGENR

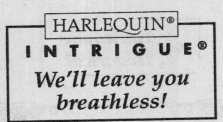

LOOK FOR OUR FOUR FABULOUS MEN!

Each month some of today's bestselling authors bring four new fabulous men to Harlequin American Romance. Whether they're rebel ranchers, millionaire power brokers or sexy single dads, they're all gallant princes—and they're all ready to sweep you into lighthearted fantasies and contemporary fairy tales where anything is possible and where all your dreams come true!

You don't even have to make a wish...
Harlequin American Romance will grant your every desire!

Look for Harlequin American Romance
wherever Harlequin books are sold!

HAR-GEN